Worlds A

Book one in the 'Worlds' trilogy

by V. E. Bolton

Contents

Acknowledgements

One thing that every new author should know is that you will, if you are even a little bit like me, be wracked by a self-doubt bordering on embarrassment on a regular basis. You will, many a time, feel the need to leave writing to the professionals and turn on the television. So many people are responsible for helping me get to the end of the writing process by hushing these daemons, for this book anyway. *Worlds Away* would not exist without these people. Most likely, it would be a cast aside draft in my spare room for years to come. For a long time, it was destined to be something I might have discussed, reluctantly, over a drink, in my dotage.

I am lucky to be blessed with many friends, all of whom need to know that every smile, every reassurance, every indulgence, has played its part. I cannot thank you all by name, but I thank you wholeheartedly anyway. Forgive me if you are not named here.

Special thanks must go to my loyal proofreading crew. I am forever indebted to Kevin Colton, who endured many a long run, listening to theories of relativity and improbable plot twists. You epitomize kindness and loyalty. Thanks also to Adam Best, Mary Ormandy, Paul Stanton, Anna Caig and Maria Scott for their kind words and very gentle criticism. You are priceless, all of you.

I would also like to thank the very talented Emma Marshall for her stunning cover photography. It sums up the book perfectly and, Emma, I hope you agree when you read it. Thanks also to my siblings for their advice and guidance in publishing this book digitally.

My family deserves an entire novel of their own to be thanked, and of course there isn't room here. Thanks to

Julie Bolton and my father, David Wolverson, for your unbending support in being some of the precious few to read the earlier drafts, known as the 'Dodgy Ones.'

A special thank you to James and our two boys, because, obviously.

And a final thank you to whoever is reading this. You have helped me to fulfil my dream of being a published writer, with a reader or two. This book has been an absolute labour of love, and my only wish now is that it speaks to you in some way.

Part One: The Cause

Prologue

Neon lights beamed on the waxed pine table as the Panel assembled. Eight men and five women, greying and obese, gathered to discuss the future of the planet. Enormous, rectangular windows reflected the Panel members, making them ghosts. Had they been interested enough to glance at the glass, they would have seen themselves suspended fifteen floors above the ground, treading on the balconies of the flats opposite. The dark blue carpets and bespoke suits turned grey in the reflection.

A particularly portly woman, artificially blonde hair bleached further in the fluorescent light, tapped a long red nail on the table. Her gold bracelets jangled above the hum of the air conditioning. "So, as you can see, if we do nothing, Earth's resources will be depleted in this decade. We are living too long and consuming too much. We simply must do something about this monstrous Expansion." She shuddered on her final word.

Several sagacious nods. Nobody in the aged audience felt the irony of the issue. Of course they had all spent sleepless nights on the issue of the Expansion. Too many people meant too many mouths to feed, too many clothes to produce, too many homes to build. For at least a decade, cars had clogged the roads, the poor had been house-sharing, and food had been scarce. Overseas, there was no more land to cultivate or settle on: it was becoming clear that there was no more anything.

"We propose that the Earth's resources go to those fully deserving - the intelligent – those who can contribute some form of a solution." Nods of approval. "We further propose that all available resources go to Science, to help in this noble Cause."

A balding gentleman, notably thinner than the others, raised a reluctant hand. "And what exactly is this noble Cause? Nobody seems to have said."

The blonde woman snorted, highlighting her porcine features. "Well, this Earth, of course. We need to reduce our population enormously. Talk of *streamlining* has been vehemently dismissed. Here, in England, at least." A glare at the thin man before she continued. "So this is the next best solution. If there are too many of us for Earth, we need to colonise elsewhere. This has been a focus of research for several years anyway now – it is not new. But resources have been limited. Until now. Of course, Panel members will still enjoy their privileges as outlined in Clause 22. Cuts will be made elsewhere. Should we hurry progress along, we will need more land for our expanding race."

The conference continued with several images and masses of data – talk of how the Earth's population was due to "explode" from ten billion to thirteen in the next thirty years. Frightening graphs and maps covered in red dots caused the elite audience to shuffle their chairs in discomfort; the idea that they would soon be sharing their seat was simply too much.

On the floor below, a Panel representative, facing five hundred filled seats, informed the crowd of a decision already made. The Panel were committed to transparency, after all. Hawk-faced reporters scribbled until their fingers were black, dancing on the curled pages of their notebooks.

7

And so it was decided. The status quo had to be preserved, they said. Numbers must be managed, they said. It was the way to save the Earth.

The date was the 12th August 1997. After this, everything changed.

Earth

November 2014

"We are all in the gutter, but some of us are looking at the stars." Oscar Wilde.

Leanne

The stars broke the darkness, but only just. Leanne Kent could not see them, anyway. As she stalked her way, head down, eyes down, through Kolwick's back streets, Token Day wore heavily on her mind. Today had been bad enough, but tomorrow would be terrible, and she needed to prepare herself in the fresh air. She liked to walk in the darkness of Kolwick's Black City, despite the stench and danger. Every terraced house she passed seemed to watch her, its broken face of masonry cracked and tired. Tired like the Earth. The tiny front lawns that the Panel had deemed unworthy of claiming were overgrown and the occasional one sported a small tent. It had long been decided that one should ignore such things; if people were brave enough to camp out on someone else's front lawn, who was Leanne Kent to stop them? They would be found soon enough, and at least they had nobody to blame but themselves.

She would sleep in the shop tonight. God knows when they would be clamouring at the door, asking her what was available, and it would be better that she was there. She remembered last month: the man with the breath that smelled of sulphur grabbing her arm, strongly enough to bruise, when she told him that there was no beef to be claimed. The animals were not big enough yet and the customers could only wait, Sir. So sorry, Sir. Can I interest you in a chicken thigh or two? You can get four in exchange for a beef steak token. He had jerked his hand away from her then, as if he had suddenly remembered what he was touching. Perhaps it was her use of the word, "Sir." He had

11

left soon after that, but not before shattering a window with his fleshy fist.

That afternoon, when they had all left, she collected the glass shards for recycling and reflected on how this space, in the Before Years, had been what was known as a charity shop. Apparently, people would give away their unwanted clothes and they would be sold, cut price, to others. All those things were gone now, of course, and all that was left behind was a threadbare carpet that she imagined had once been red but had now been trodden into a tired black, and a fitted table in the corner of the room where she would stand. The idea of giving anything away now was unthinkable. Leanne Kent owned one black duffel coat, three jumpers, two pairs of jeans and a modest underwear collection of which she was really rather proud. She owned the one pair of brown boots that had belonged to her sister, only one size too large, and repeatedly repaired the soles with sellotape or whatever adhesive she could find. As a Supplementary, of course, she didn't get tokens. If she ever felt daring, she would imagine holding a set of tokens, reserved for Betters, in her dry hands. She imagined the thin paper, usually pastel-coloured with serrated edges. She would hold the tickets up to the sun, the backside facing her, and see the thick black numbers wink through at her, offering a world of luxuries she would never know.

But she knew things that the Betters didn't. They didn't really know what it was like to be hungry, or to have a house with no heating and water, or to be forced to share a room with three strangers. What was really annoying was that they thought they did. Just because everyone had a little bit less nowadays, they thought that they were suffering. They were idiots. She had realised that since meeting the Captain.

It was in the Black City that she had met the Captain, just over a month ago now. She had been walking in the darkness and silence and he had beckoned her over. She remembered it so clearly – her parents would have never believed her capable of remembering something so accurately – but he had beckoned her over with a smile and offered her a cigarette. He was standing with his door open, light streaming outwards, as if electricity was something to be using whenever one liked. She could feel the heat emanating from his house and shivered to think that he had central heating.

She had never seen a cigarette before, except in pictures, and its rosy glow drew her in long before the man holding it did. Its smell, thick and sweet and heady, made her feel powerful and adult. He was the first man who spoke to her like she was not stupid, like she was not a Supplementary. He was Supplementary too, of course, but the black-market luxuries he paraded for the world made him fireproof, somehow. Had she considered it in enough detail, Leanne Kent would have realised that what she liked most about this man was a cockiness in the face of adversity like she had never seen. Surely, anybody *that* confident must know something, some way of making the world better.

In the Before Years, she had heard her parents speaking about her in hushed voices, wondering how she would ever be seen as 'normal' and whether or not she would ever make friends. The Expansion had ended their concerns. Intelligence testing had been introduced and she didn't even sit the exam – an automatic Supplementary. After that, the hushed conversations became more frantic, her parents' faces even more drawn than before, but before anyone knew what was happening the Panel came for her.

But the Captain never mentioned any of that. He just welcomed her into his home and treated her like she was any other girl. He never even mentioned what she had heard her parents mention, years before, as her 'syndrome.' He didn't make comments, like almost anyone else did, about the shape of her face, her small eyes, her square body; he just let her speak, and listened, and gave her cigarettes. He told her of his wife, who the Panel had taken when the Cause was declared, but even to her, his eyes were cold and black when he spoke of her. People may have thought that she was stupid, but she knew he didn't much care what had happened to Mrs. Captain – she knew *that* at least.

The Captain's house was a mystery; a cursory glance into the hallway revealed filth and yellowing walls, but he never allowed her in to see further, preferring instead for the two of them to sit at his open front door, regarding the sky. She only ever visited at night, when nobody at the home would notice her absence, and a reassuring coat of blackness held them both each night. It was when they were looking at the sky that the Captain mentioned the Cause, and how doomed it was. When he had first said this, Leanne had ignored it, hoping that she had misheard, but he came back to it – again and again – the Cause is doomed. About a fortnight after they first met, she replied, as best she could, "You shouldn't say that. It's bad."

The Captain cackled then, loudly, rasping on his cigarette smoke. His teeth were yellowing stumps in a cavernous

14

mouth. Leanne felt genuinely hurt. So he would laugh at her like the others did.

As quickly as the laughing started, he seemed to notice her hurt expression and stopped, "I'm sorry, darlin', but it's them that's bad, not us." He looked at her for a long time, long enough to make her shuffle in her deck chair and look at the floor, then continued, "All those messages on the telly, all those lies. They're going to abandon us here. You know *that*?"

She felt like he was telling her something she already knew, something that everybody already knew, but that nobody really ever said. She wasn't sure she wanted to hear it; she liked coming here, speaking to him. He was her friend; why complicate things? Despite her silent pleas, he continued, "There." He pointed an arthritic finger to the sky - that great gulf of nothingness above their heads, "They are finally going *there*." The drama suddenly went from his voice and he drew on his cigarette again, "Or at least that's what they say."

She stared at the blackness above her. Could that blackness up there be better than the blackness down here? She was terrified to think it. Just under where the Captain had pointed, glittering and white, the enormous rectangle of Dawns' Laboratories loomed over the Black City. It wasn't news that they had been working on ways to visit another world for a long time now – as long as she could remember – and she remembered, fleetingly, the Supplementaries she had known to walk through the doors of that majestic building to never walk out. The Americans had tried and failed, the Russians too – lots of people – Supplementaries mostly – had died in the efforts, but she had never really believed that they would do it. And so close to home.

As she thought, the Captain continued, and a listener more perceptive than Leanne Kent would have known that he wasn't really talking to her anymore, "Of course they won't take the likes of us. The telly says they're taking Sups, though, hundreds of 'em. Can you imagine that?" She turned to shrug in response but he was not looking at her; he was looking at the great dark dome above their heads, and he simply continued, "But there is another way for us: an escape. Have you heard of the Underground Movement?"

****

The queue on Token Day was the longest she had ever seen, and Leanne registered with a rising alarm the fact that there was not enough food. Not nearly enough. The Panel had sent less than half their usual rations. *Feeding on it themselves, the pigs*, she muttered. She almost laughed aloud at the blasphemy of what she had just said. Such freedom to think such things, and for nobody to know! Fumbling with the half empty cardboard boxes, she regarded the supplies before her: out of date soup sachets; tinned beans; tinned fruit (as well as a few tins with no labels) and some chocolate bars. Nothing else. No meat. No fresh food. She felt sick as she went to open the door, regarding the hateful faces of the Betters clutching their tokens. They weren't Superior Betters, but she knew that they still expected more than the scanty offerings she had been lumbered with.

The first Better to enter was a blonde lady in her forties, shoving a double buggy in through the narrow doorway. The

16

mewling toddlers chewed on hard plastic toys and dribbled profusely; Leanne couldn't help her resentment of them. If only there were fewer... The woman's eyes widened as she saw the array of supplies on the desk, "Is that all you have?" Her voice was angry but her face desperate. Leanne nodded. A deep intake of breath. She took more than her fair share and Leanne let her: they'd run out soon anyway. Besides, the woman sported a stitched red apple on her lapel; anyone who worked for Dawns' Laboratories deserved to take more. Leanne had been told that a while ago. She took the crumpled tokens and shoved them into the black envelope they had provided her with; they would count every single one back in, she knew.

By the time the tenth person entered there was nothing left. Leanne regarded the sea of faces hating her, blaming her. She heard the mutters, "She was the first one here. Bet she ate it herself. Not too skinny for a Sup, is she? Don't know why they let them dish out vital supplies. Asking for trouble. Total scum." The crowd surged forwards, and she knew at that moment that they meant to hurt her. This was not new: she just hoped the damage would not last.

It was only when she moved back behind the counter that she saw the Captain, leaning on the glass window, smiling. The grey drizzle of Kolwick seemed to hardly touch him, and for that moment, she saw only his kind face. His eyes told her that it did not matter what those people said, what those people did: they were wrong and everyone knew it. At the end of the day, they would starve just as she would, because there just wasn't *enough*, no matter who you were. She took a deep breath, declaring, "I haven't eaten a thing, but I wish I had. I will next time! There are people you don't know about, hidden under the floor, people who will beat you one day!"

Hidden under the floor. That wasn't quite right, but she couldn't fully remember what the Captain had said. It filled her with hope, though, all the same. Some people in the crowd looked angry. A handful started to laugh.

When the blows came, she tried not to scream. It was not long before she was on the floor, feeling a fist here, a boot there. A man she recognised from before – she thought – was it the man who had broken the window? – came at her with a stick and she brought her forearms upwards and closed her eyes in readiness.

The stick never touched her. Instead, she saw the Captain's bony arm catch the stick instead. It would have been heroic, except she heard his fingers break.

The man continued to hit as if there had been no interruption, and the crowd did not stop. They only stopped when the screams did – man and girl both, motionless on the floor. They left then, one man holding a stick and a black envelope.

The Captain was right – they were idiots. Leanne thought this but did not move, as his limp and lifeless body concealed her living one. She would find them. She would find these people under the floor – *Underground* – that was it. The old man had not died in vain. He was heavy, though, and bleeding. She felt his blood leak onto her face and cried aloud, but there was nobody to listen anyway. She had seen lots of dead bodies before – everyone had – but she had never touched one, and it made her want to vomit.

Slowly, she wriggled under the Captain's heavy corpse, looking into his grey eyes that were greyer in death. Doing so, she looked up into the faces of two new men at the door, suited and smart, and she immediately recognised them as Panel Representatives. One man carried a clipboard, the other merely clasped his clean hands in front of him, as though in prayer. They smiled at her but she knew that their smiles didn't mean what other people's smiles did.

"Supplementary 568944, I believe? We have heard reports of insubordination. Do you know what that means?"

Leanne shook her head. Everything, she realised, was trembling, her voice, her body, her lip, "They killed my friend. They beat us both."

For a moment, both men looked alarmed. They surveyed the man on the floor carefully, and then smiled. The first man, the praying one, spoke, "Oh! That Supplementary. For a moment there, you had me worried! Nathan – I think sector 5 at Dawns' needs more fuel – send him there."

The second man wrote something on his clipboard but did not move. "Will do." He rolled the body over, in the same way one might roll over a barrel or sack of potatoes, and paused. Slowly removing the cigarette packet from the Captain's pocket, the man regarded her coolly. "Been having a bit of a dabble with things we shouldn't, have we? I bet you've been stealing supplies too. No wonder those poor people outside are going hungry." The man placed the box in his back pocket.

She turned again to the first man, already knowing, despite her low IQ, what he was going to say, "She's a sly one, isn't she? Best not send her for processing yet." His teeth glittered – how were they so clean? "She can come with us. I'd like to know more about this place *under the floor* that she spoke of."

Charlotte

Steam consumed the windows of Dawns' Laboratories so badly that they resembled a waterfall. The workers there, accustomed to the icy conditions, laboured on regardless. A careful observer would notice the relics from the building's past: long tables that once served as packing lines; a wall of superfluous plug sockets; pale rectangles on the floor where plastic moulding machines once stood; out of date yellow markings where neat little mechanisms once trundled, collecting the plastic frivolities that Mankind used to make and put into boxes. Now, each person wore the regulation factory black, lifted only by the single red apple on their chests. They worked in groups, generally, huddled around whiteboards or microscopes, muttering complex equations and bold hypotheses to one another in hushed tones.

Charlotte Dobson, several floors above this, downed coffee number seven, suppressing the shaking of her fingers as she manipulated the Speedlight capsule for the sixth hour on end. Not for the first time, she felt like her fingers would lose their grip on the cold handles of the titanium box before her. The set-up was simple: Charlotte worked on one box and an identical box, containing a small weight, lay dormant at the other side of the room. The two were connected by a thin tube, which arched over her head. Every so often, a pimple of green or amber would flicker on the corner of the box and she would start, freezing for a moment before continuing. Fleetingly, she wondered what the excess caffeine and potential radiation would do to her growing foetus, before remembering that she would never allow the pregnancy to reach term, anyway. Cursing this job's capacity to give her thinking time, she noted that she had not yet booked the procedure. She did not note how she continued to trivialise what she planned to do. Nor how she was letting time slip through her fingers.

"Ms. Dobson, your work space does not meet our regulations. Kindly follow the cleansing procedure correctly before you continue your work."

Perhaps it was his sanctimonious air, the way he emphasized "correctly," or just the fact that he could not refrain from staring at her body rather than her face, despite her manifold qualifications, but Charlotte flinched at Thomas's presence yet again. She was accustomed to working with Supplementary Humans; despite their proven lack of scientific ability, many of them had been chosen by the great Richard Dawns to help further the Cause by assisting at the laboratories – the hub of the action. Even so, being a daily presence made them no less disquieting, no less of an awkward addition to the work environment. And for one of them to actually tell *her* how to act – the Associate Scientist working next to Daniel Dawns on the development of Speedlight and antimatter technologies – outrageous was not the word. Staring at her work more intently was the best response she could muster.

Charlotte made an effort to steady her breathing. Of course she shouldn't allow a mere Sup to rile her, but Thomas was one of the worst. She hated herself for thinking it, but how *dare* he speak to her like that? His job was to maintain a healthy work environment and support when requested, and requests from Charlotte were rare. Casting a cursory glance around the room, Charlotte noted derisively how he wasn't much good at his first job, either. Ever since the Expansion, to say that resources were scarce was a horrendous understatement, but even so, she believed that they could do better. Old books, no longer relevant to their mission, operated as makeshift tables and paperweights, the windows, drowning in condensation, were grimy and rotten and her beloved kettle, her only contraband item, was plundered by lime scale. Even in the regulation dark light, she felt the filth crawl on her skin.

Perhaps the poor working environment was a deliberate ploy to enthuse the workers. Feel too cosy on a planet and why would you be so keen to find a manner of leaving it? Doctor Richard Dawns wasn't known for his carrot tactics: stick was far more his style. But there, on the filthy magnolia walls, it was plastered: Oscar 70 - or the paid artist's impression of it, at least- the poster that all workers at Dawns' Laboratories were encouraged to display. The carrot.

Charlotte did not need encouragement. To her, Oscar 70 was the most beautiful thing she had ever seen. Like her, like everyone, it floated alone, isolated and vulnerable in the darkness. A perfect sphere, 30% larger than Earth, Oscar 70's perfect curves beckoned like a lover. The interstellar probes indicated that this planet had less water than Earth, but more land, something that everyone, certainly Charlotte, craved. Earth that beautiful things can live on. Earth that bears fruit and food. Earth that would feel warmer under an alien and youthful Red Dwarf sun. She saw mountains and valleys the colour of her beloved coffee, milky and rich, spill forth from the virgin landscape, whilst the surrounding seas remained supine and silver, calm despite the tumultuous life above. If she wasn't careful, Charlotte could stare at this image for hours on end, feeling her feet touch that strange ground, feeling the heat of the sun on her face. It was everything to her.

So, to return to work. A small reminder of why she surrounded herself with Thomases and grime and freezing cold conditions was all it took to get her back to her desk. Antimatter's relationship with Speedlight was relatively new, and every time she returned to the box, Charlotte cared less about its massive potential to kill if placed in the wrong hands, but more the potential it held to reach her beloved other world. For that, she would die ten times over.

 Her breath caught in her mouth.

She had done it: the weights had moved from the box in the corner to this one seamlessly before her unblinking eyes. She checked the numbers. The particles had moved a fraction more slowly than light. They had moved so quickly, in fact, that return travel to Oscar 70 would be possible. Easy, in fact. If her calculations were correct, the Speedlight they had would facilitate interstellar travel on an enormous scale.

For a second, Charlotte felt that anything – breathing, responding, thinking – would be forever impossible for her. She just wanted to live in this moment of possibility and hope. If she was wrong, it was back to the grime, the cold and the loneliness. If she was right, her perfect Oscar 70 would belong to other people. She'd be forced to share it with Sups and Betters alike, and the thought made her shudder. But, time was of the essence; Earth was suffocating under the weight of people. She must report her findings to Doctor Dawns.

She clutched her growing tummy. For the first time in her life, she feared progress.

Martin

"Come in." Doctor Richard Dawns barely looked up from his work as Sup Martin entered the room. Martin took in the vast opulence of the office and felt a shudder of revulsion that he no longer had to think to suppress. Doctor Dawns rested on a vast leather armchair surrounded by expensive bronze statues and potted plants – almost certainly stolen. Martin glanced at the pile of pre-packed dried food in the corner – out of date but valuable nevertheless, and felt a familiar pang of hunger. He was sure that Doctor Dawns kept that food there to torment the Supplementaries that he called into his lair, to remind them of his power and his full stomach.

"Ah, so it's you they have sent me." The word "you" was accompanied with a little spit, barely noticeable but certainly there. "Martin…Huthwater is it?"

"Martin Huthwaite, Sir, Supplementary Species 81873, at your service."

"Oh, of course. You're the one whose family…" Richard Dawns offered a cursory wave of his hand as he organised several stacks of paper in front of him.

"All gone. Yes, Sir."

"Very good. Well, we thought you an ideal choice for our next endeavour, Sup Martin." Doctor Dawns finally placed his papers on the desk and looked at the man across from him. His thick black-rimmed glasses seemed wedged to his thin head, and matched the colour of his jet-black hair. Martin noted that the doctor's hair had been styled with gel, and wondered where on earth he could have gotten that. He noted also that, in classic terms, Richard Dawns might be described as handsome, sporting high cheek bones and dark mahogany eyes, which he wore quite well on his sixty-five-year-old face. His black suit was classic and tailored, and, Martin noticed with a start, seemed *new*. That said, he seemed so *artificial*, and Martin imagined how, under the hair gel and the streamlined clothes, he would be flabby and wrinkled. The thought gave him a rush akin to a blasphemous thought in church.

"You see, Sup Martin, we are finally in a position to travel somewhere else. Not a great deal is known about it yet, and I shan't bore you with the details, as you wouldn't understand anyway, of course." A snort of derision to which Martin didn't react. "But the fact of the matter is, you're going. Congratulations. The sterilisation procedure will be reversed and you will help settle on a new planet."

Despite the lurching in his stomach, Martin's well-rehearsed composure remained. "Thank you, Sir."

"Damn and blast, man! Is that all you can say? I'd have thought you'd be a little more *grateful*."

Martin did his best to ignore the large painted copy of Oscar 70, proudly displayed behind Richard Dawns' desk. Whoever had painted it had added a glowing red star in the corner, which served to illuminate the planet in what Martin thought was an overly flattering way. The efforts did not serve to improve an impression of what he felt was really quite a barren and dull landscape, overwhelmed with brown and grey. He had very little desire to go there – he assumed that this was the "somewhere else" the doctor had referred to – but he didn't really care to stay here either. "I'm sorry, Sir. I truly am grateful, of course."

"Yes, yes. Honestly, I'll never understand how you Sups process emotions, really. But hey," Richard Dawns leaned closer, as if sharing a joke with an old friend, "As soon as you're on a new planet I won't have to worry about you lot anymore, will I? Gosh! We really are so generous." In his excitement, Doctor Dawns rose to his feet. "Many other countries have simply executed their Supplementaries but we," Richard Dawns' chest increased in size, a predatory bird displaying his plume, "we get you an entire *planet!*" He concluded with a quick slap on the poster behind him.

How like a Better to think that what he was offering was a gift, Martin reflected. Of course, the fact of the matter was that the Betters wanted to populate Earth *and* what Doctor Dawns had just referred to as "somewhere else," but the Sups were guinea pigs, servants, accessories. Interestingly, Sups were allowed to breed "somewhere else" it would seem, and Martin thought, not for the first time, that he really wasn't the stupid one in the room. It might take thousands of years, but this problem would return. People, whoever they are, consume and take, and breed. Another planet wouldn't solve that – it would only delay the inevitable.

Martin rose to his feet. The queue behind him was a long one. Richard Dawns had a lot of good tidings to deliver today, it seemed.

Charlotte

"Do you need me?" Martin hovered at Charlotte's door. Charlotte was glad that Doctor Dawns had sent Martin. Of all the Sups in the Labs, she liked him best. It wasn't so much that he knew his place (she hoped she was better than *that*) but he respected the mission for what it was – an escape route from an otherwise worthless existence. She had often reflected that Sups must feel this worthlessness even more keenly than Betters, being earmarked early for interplanetary travel and receiving, due to standard regulations, so fewer privileges than she ever would. But something about Martin made him special, for a Sup. He carried himself with an undeniable dignity, whilst nevertheless retaining that open and helpful air that was so necessary to his status.

"Close the door, please, Sup Martin," Charlotte responded, barely looking up from her work. "I have some very exciting news."

Her manner of telling him had been no less composed than when she had told Doctor Dawns. It felt important to be a neutral and composed scientist at this point. Interplanetary travel was possible, she thought. The antimatter particles she had been gradually combining with Speedlight could fuel a ship large enough for a little over two hundred people initially, give or take the amount of funding given to create antimatter fuel. They could go to Oscar 70 to see how habitable it was and then a selected team of Betters would return. It would be a seven-year round trip, give or take, when 1G acceleration and deceleration, a year on the planet, and the return journey were taken into account. In their absence, her team of scientists could continue working on Speedlight technology, to enable bigger ships and more people to travel to Oscar 70, if their initial trip was a success. *It will be a success*, her mind echoed. She would never return to Earth either way, of course.

Martin had sat very still throughout her speaking, hands folded, and remained as such when she had finished. Charlotte would love to know his thoughts, as the first Sup she had delivered this news to, but she was sure that to ask him his feelings would be an intrusion too far.

"Anyway, of course it is up to you. At the moment you still have a choice," Charlotte inwardly winced at the inherent threat in her statement, "but we would very much like you to be one of the first Sups to settle on Oscar 70. There won't be enough of you to call this a colonisation, but that will follow. You would come with us for the initial trip, but for you it would be a single journey. Doctor Dawns would like us to take roughly one hundred Supplementaries initially. The Betters who choose to return will drop you there and remain in constant contact when they leave. You see, we need to monitor the new planet for its habitable features."

"All right," Martin managed a smile, "I suppose it's quite exciting, isn't it, Miss Dobson?"

Charlotte was staggered that he had no follow-on questions. Had she been sitting in his seat, she would have had all kinds of questions. Would it be safe? What can I take with me? Will I be able to choose loved ones to accompany me? But

Martin just sat and smiled, his ginger beard rising with his obedient smile and his ice-blue eyes twinkling in anticipation.

The saddest thing at that moment was that she knew Martin did not *really* share her enthusiasm. That was no surprise, but his absolute and unbending compliance was heartbreaking. It was not enough that Supplementary humans had restricted access to everything one might hold dear - health care, education, food, housing – but to be deported to an unknown and frightening world, at great personal and emotional risk, she would have felt that may be a step too far, but there was this man before her, being given his life sentence having had committed no crime, and he sat there and *smiled*. He said he was excited, and his body language, limited and obvious as it was, supported his words. Charlotte reflected that no amount of acting classes could perfect his stance, had she been him, and limited in intelligence as he was, she felt a glimmer of respect for Martin at that moment, and she was glad that he was going.

She managed a smile. "You must be wondering how it works. Let me show you."

Martin

Saying goodbye to the cat was the hardest thing, which perhaps explained why he didn't care that he was leaving. As Martin bundled Hubble into her carrier, it occurred to him that this dust-covered residence would not register fondly in her feline memory, or his. Ever since pets were banned, she had long since been hidden away inside, mewing at the walls and pacing each corner. Now she would be simply moved to another cage, another owner. Wryly, Martin reflected that her situation really was not so different from his. Saturday morning light sliced through the blinds and played havoc with floating dust particles - pieces of him that would linger here long after his departure.

"Project Eden, Dawns' greatest achievement to date, means that near light speed travel may be possible within our lifetimes..." warbled the voice on the television. The red-haired reporter waved her hands frantically on the word "lifetimes" and beamed an artificially white smile next to scarlet lips. Martin flinched. It had always interested him that people on television seem to insist on garish colours and noise, perhaps because so many television sets were becoming paler and quieter as they sang their swansongs. There would be no more after these. As seemed to be the standard response, substance was replaced by meaningless noise and animation. Martin wished desperately for an empty planet, somewhere he could call his own, somewhere he would be welcome, and not a Supplementary species. For somebody deemed unintelligent at birth, he certainly thought a great deal.

Charlotte's manner in the antimatter room had fascinated him. She had led him down the steps as if he were a child entering a haunted house. Like everything at Dawns' Laboratories, the room was uncomfortably cold, abrasively white and yet filthy. The concrete floors slept under a layer of dust that scraped under their regulation work boots as they walked. The first thing Martin noticed as being markedly different was how bright this room was; electricity was a rapidly dwindling luxury to all but the super-rich, but this room glowed ultraviolet and intense.

The brightness was coming from a series of enormous boxes – thirty feet high each – filling the back wall of the capacious cellar. Each box was a dull rectangular silver, like a gigantic safe, but there were no locks or security codes. They didn't even have doors. The only markings visible were three small apples, one engraved in each. Richard Dawns certainly liked his branding. Martin had been unable to hear anything, save a gentle hum almost like a refrigerator, and it would seem to a casual observer that the boxes were empty. But Martin knew what was in the boxes, and he grew even colder. He found himself whispering, a child before a ghost, "That's the antimatter."

Another Better may have made a sarcastic quip akin to, "Well, we are in the antimatter room," but Charlotte simply nodded. Clearly, her respect for this material equalled his, at least. "Of course we can't open the boxes. Each one contains *half a tonne* of antimatter, held in stasis in a powerful vacuum. If anything causes it to touch the sides of the box, well..." She offered a nervous laugh, "There'd be no point running, anyway. I've been working with tiny amounts of this material to see if it can be used as fuel to propel an interstellar rocket and, well, it can." He heard a smile in her voice but it did not appear on her face. Not for the first time, he considered how attractive she was. Her elfin features glowed with an intense energy and, despite being petite, she seemed very formidable in a world that needed such strength. He imagined her running a marathon without breaking sweat, or boxing a champion and not ever falling. Her complexion was very much like Snow White's – an inversion of his own – jet black hair and white skin interspersed with a healthy red flush, but looking at her, Martin knew that she would never, never eat a poisoned apple. The huntsman could have never taken her heart. Notwithstanding this, she was also so vulnerable, like a little girl. She seemed to seek approval from anyone and everyone, even him, and Martin wondered why. She glanced at him to see if he was listening, and then the excitement regarding the mission seemed to pour out of her. "Of course our main concern was how we could *store* such huge amounts of fuel on a ship travelling at such high speeds. We need a tonne of magnetic material to store one gram of traditional antimatter, so moving all of this, particularly if we want to *get* somewhere, becomes a nonsense. You've probably noticed that half a tonne of this stuff is so *compact.*" As she paused, Martin noted that he had never seen her so happy, so excited. This mission was her lifeblood; her neck and face flushed red as she spoke even quicker, "It was Doctor Dawns Junior who had the idea of depositing antimatter in space for us to *pick up* on the way, but that didn't work. We wouldn't have been able to get far enough out to deposit the fuel, without using more antimatter than we had. It was a catch-22. Besides, there were accidents in the initial trials."

Martin knew instinctively that these "accidents" would certainly have involved the deaths of many Sups, but he stayed respectfully silent on the matter. "So what did you do?"

Charlotte was unable to suppress a beam of pride. "We created Speedlight, a condensed form of antimatter that is easily suspended in a simple vacuum and can therefore be transported safely. We can then use Speedlight at intermittent points in the journey to give us the required thrust to reach Oscar 70 in a little over three years."

"Three *years?*" Martin attempted to do the calculations in his head but failed.

"Yes. We'd be travelling at around 99.3% the speed of light. I won't lie to you, Sup Martin: the implications of this are not yet known. And I'm sure you're also aware that if one speck of our fuel is handled in the wrong way, we will not only destroy ourselves, but surrounding planetary bodies. Earth included."

Everyone knew *that*, Martin reflected. It was the one reason that, despite Mankind's growing desperation to leave the planet, nobody had used antimatter to date, to his or the public's knowledge, anyway. He furthermore reflected that he had already asked her a lot of questions – something he was loathe doing. Martin made a point of not placing himself at the mercy of the Betters, even in small matters such as being seen to ask for information. But here he was speaking to one of the leading scientists in the world, somebody who had *handled* antimatter and calculated a possible pathway from Earth. He had to ask her one more question. He could have asked her how they could possibly remain in contact when he is left on the planet, or how the antimatter was transported; such issues were of a passing interest to him, but he knew that those answers would come in the fullness of time anyway. In this room, in this moment, he was one of the first people to be in the presence of this almost divine material. The potential and power of this room rushed over him. He breathed steadily, not taking his eyes off the coffin-like boxes gripping to the walls. "What does antimatter look like?"

Charlotte shrugged. Clearly, the question disappointed her. "It looks like whatever it is made to look like. You create a ball of antimatter and it looks like a ball. You could make it look like Doctor Dawns' face if you wanted to."

Unbelievably, Martin found himself laughing at her joke, and it was a full-throated laugh, warm and genuine. "It doesn't, does it?"

Charlotte smiled. "Oh, no. I created this antimatter. It's beautiful, Martin. Each antimatter unit is a perfect replica of Oscar 70."

Martin smiled at the memory. Only Charlotte Dobson, it seemed, could make the very fuel that propelled her a love letter to the destination. It had been three decades now that Earth-like planets in other solar systems had been catalogued and numbered using a combination of the traditional phonetic alphabet and numbers, the phonetics denoting the order in which they were discovered and the numbers rating a planet's Earth-like features. Martin had chosen Oscar 70, nestled in the welcoming and not-too-far away Star 4, for research himself, knowing that the authorities would likely prioritise its Earth-like features and relatively close distance as Earth became less like Earth daily. Not that distance was a bad thing, anyway. With the Expansion ever worsening, leaving was the only option. All he knew was that his life on Earth was over, if one could call it a *life*.

The bedsit he was leaving would be taken by another Sup, and then another. It was only due to its small size that Martin had been able to have his own place, and for this he was thankful. Like anything else, it was trapped in the era when resources finally ran out, down to the ironically-preserved 2002 calendar on the wall. Importantly, Martin reflected, this made him no different to anybody else; even the beautiful Charlotte Dobson would never be able to buy a new television, new furniture or replace the carpets in her house. The result was that Mankind was in a permanent state of decay – money was pummelled into Science and Science and Science, leaving nothing for manufacturing of any kind. Everyone on Earth had what they had, and when it was gone, that was it. Theft was the ultimate crime, and it had occurred to everyone living that things became a lot more important than people a long time ago. To Martin, lack of resources was the great leveller. It was the reason he could look Doctor Richard Dawns in the face every day.

Of course, his choice to go had not really been a choice at all, and not only in the sense that Charlotte had implied. Of course they could force him – Betters could force Sups to do anything – but they could never make him *want* to go. He had decided that he wanted to go anyway. Who could say no to a one-way mission to a new world? To possibly meet other life forms? At worst, to see new landscapes and to breathe fresh air? The idea of dying in a space explosion didn't bother him: at least he'd be remembered in some small way. The wide world had dealt him nothing, so he relished the opportunity to offer it the final fuck you: to leave what was never designed to be left. He exited and left the door unlocked.

Charlotte

A determined and icy drizzle clung to Charlotte's exposed face as she navigated her way through the grey streets. Even before the streetlights stopped working, this would have been a dark area of town, but now, on the 5th November, the sky began to turn purple as early as 3.30pm. Such an evening as this, she reflected, would, less than a decade ago, be full of delicious anticipation, with scarved children attacking toffee apples and purchasing overpriced glow sticks, enveloped by the scent of frying onions and too much sugar. The Expansion had put an end to such frivolities. Now, the streets were teeming with people but only due to the stringent traffic restrictions in place; Charlotte did not know anybody extravagant enough to drive to work. Most people had either moved closer to work, or gained a job closer to home, and now, at 5.05pm, the grey of the streets was met with the grey of people making their way to a brief evening free from the humdrum of work work work.

She kept her eyes cast downwards as she manoeuvred the tide of people. Had she looked up, all that would have met her gaze would have been hundreds of downcast faces, their eyes not meeting hers. It was not for the first time that she considered how empty Oscar 70 may be at that moment: all that space and freedom. Here, it was difficult to see the floor for trudging feet in black boots.

Despite the late hour, the town's Intelligence Testing Centre still boasted a snaking queue leaking from its doors. Charlotte awarded a passing look to the subjects awaiting testing – ashen faced children and even more angst-ridden parents clutching onto one another as if they were about to tumble down a precipice. The building was the only thing properly lit within sight, its glass windows gleaming in the autumn night. Through the glass, hundreds of computer booths were visible, each one occupied by a ten year-old child as a parent or guardian looked anxiously on. The testing would go on throughout the night.

Like everybody else, Charlotte remembered her testing day. In the same manner as these subjects, she waited outside, (but, unlike them, in the cold sunshine of her January birthday) aware at the tender age of ten what the implications were of failing the Intelligence Test. To be a Supplementary Human would be to sacrifice your right to populate the planet and to receive hugely decreased numbers of food, heating and goods tokens. Worse than that, though, far worse, would be to carry the Supplementary label until your dying day. Proven to be of a lower intelligence than the Betters, she would have been doomed to a life of servitude, compromise and humiliation.

The test itself was gruelling, which in many ways was a good thing. The Panel had designed the test to "stretch" every subject by dint of the questions beginning simply and increasing in difficulty. A ten-year old Charlotte had seen the merit in this: the longer you are tested the better you are doing. For her, the questions began with, "Compete the pattern: 2,4,6,8..." and continued with, "Joe has three times as many as Tom, and Tom has four times as many as April. Altogether they have 153. Make three true statements, using numbers, elaborating on this." The later questions involved some of the complex Astrophysics that Charlotte was to pursue as an adult. It was a strange experience; it was almost like the test *knew* her. In the years following it, she had questioned, as many others who passed the test did, how anybody could *possibly* fail such a simple test. All one had to do was learn the manner of the questions. It really was that simple. Like many lucky people, she was blind to her own smug arrogance.

Her test had taken three and a half hours, one of the longest on record. Her parents had gushed with pride. Not only was Charlotte a Better, but she was bordering on a genius IQ at ten years old. The pink-nailed receptionist who awarded her the score quipped, "Not that being a genius makes a difference. You only needed to get 60 right." Charlotte, stung by the scant congratulations received, reflected with derision how this woman probably only scraped through the test herself. Adult testing had been notoriously quick, and Charlotte wondered, after only half an hour of enjoying her status as a Better, how much *easier* the test might have been ten or fifteen years ago, whenever they got round to testing this woman.

"You only needed to get 60 right," as if any knowledge beyond that were a waste of time. Since that day, the pursuit of knowledge had been Charlotte's oxygen. She would not settle for a life of scraping through, like the vast amount of people in the queue.

And yet...Standing outside her parents' house, scraping through would be good enough tonight. From this position of safety, it was easy to think how this was more gruelling than any Intelligence Test. How her parents would react to the news of her leaving was anyone's guess. Of course, they had been aware of her research since the beginning, but it had always been a theoretical hope, until today. Charlotte

41

had excelled throughout school, and had been met with pride and indifference in more or less equal measure. She loved her parents dearly, but the message they sent on a daily basis had left her with a complex idea of what they wanted from her. They seemed to say, "Well done on being such a fantastic scientist, darling, but we'd really rather you didn't bother. We'd far rather you count test tubes for a living and be *happy*."

The matt plastic of the door was replaced with a rush of warmth and her father's imposing shadow. "Darling!" he gushed, and pulled her tiny frame into his hefty embrace. Charlotte allowed herself a moment luxuriating in the familiar smell of their home. Despite resource cuts, seeing her mother and father was still synonymous with the clean scent of soap and food cooked in real butter. She was more than aware that the mission could not begin for several months yet, but she nevertheless took in every element of the room in the manner of one dying. She regarded the mahogany floors and stained glass windows with fresh appreciation, and every tick of the pristine grandmother clock in the corner registered in her anxious mind. One thing that Charlotte loved about her parents' home was how it seemed largely unaffected by the Expansion; when it became a certainty that the manufacturing of luxury items was to cease altogether, her father had commented that anything worth making had already been made anyway, and the world could do with slowing down a little.

And now Charlotte was to speed up their world in a manner that even she found shocking. Her mother, looking thinner and paler than ever, took Charlotte's arm in one icy hand and led her to the kitchen, where she continued to dust.

Charlotte imagined her like this all day, dusting and cleaning and polishing, a distraction from the relative madness of retirement in a world that has itself retired.

"So what's new with you, darling?" Charlotte's mother chirped, a jollity masking the terror of Charlotte realising that the curtain poles had not been dusted that day.

"Oh, God, please don't let me have to tell mother first," groaned the voice within. Luckily, her mother didn't wait for an answer, as she was wont to do, moving on to wider issues such as "how crowded the streets seem nowadays" and "I wish this job of yours didn't take up so much time that you can't find a proper boyfriend" or "it's near impossible to get contraband cleaning products, now Paul doesn't come round anymore. Soon, I shall have to be using some of the vinegar from our food tokens."

When she finally escaped into the living room, Charlotte found her father in his usual pose, on the left corner of the settee, newspaper in hand. He didn't comment on the leading story – something about a failed interstellar launch in California that she was of course already familiar with – but instead smiled and waited expectantly for Charlotte to speak.

She didn't, but instead sunk into the red leather armchair that had been hers when she lived there. She felt like a teenager about to confess a pregnancy. With a start, she remembered that she *was* pregnant, finding some humour in the fact that this secret was a trivial concern compared to her impending mission. She fell into the familiar habit of sitting in silence as her father read, glancing every so often at his concentrated expression as he pondered the latest scare story or tragedy. Many an evening had been spent like this, and her heart ached as she remembered that these evenings were numbered; she had lost sleep about her parents dying, as most children had, but now she was opting to leave and never see them again. She attempted to remember every detail of his face, from the double chin to thin, golden glasses poised on a reddened and large nose. She was about to accelerate away from him in an irreversible way, altering not only distance but the very fabric of time that was currently so securely wrapped around them both.

She coughed. "Daddy, you know what I do for a living, don't you?"

Her father turned the page of the paper and coughed. "But of course, Charley. I think you are aware of how much your mother and I are proud of you." He barely looked up, which made her thankful.

Charlotte attempted a smile, but felt too weak. "Well, the thing is, I think we've succeeded. I think we can finally travel to the planet we've been researching." She did her best to sound casual but her voice shook.

"Oscar 70?"

Charlotte felt a pang of embarrassment, as if he'd mentioned a lover of hers inappropriately. "Yes, Oscar 70. Our calculations indicate that we will be able to travel at something like 99.3% the speed of light."

"Really? But the Americans have only managed 80%, and the newspapers have been saying that isn't sufficient but there's no other way..."

"Well, we found one."

"I see." A pause. "Congratulations, my love. I suppose you will be on this mission?" He folded the paper and set it beside him, possibly to denote the momentous nature of her declaration.

Charlotte took a moment to look at her lovely father. It was obvious that his heart was breaking at the thought of losing his only child to a dangerous and uncertain mission, but none of this showed on his face. Since being a child, he had reminded her of a cuddly teddy bear, and she wondered if she were indeed too old and sophisticated to wrap up on his sizeable knee for one last time. She regretted that she probably was, although his warm smile and open expression suggested otherwise.

"The mission should take around seven years, in all. Although travel at the speed we calculated will take *far* less, we need to accelerate at a speed of no more than 1G to keep the inhabitants of the ship safe, so a return journey will obviously take a while. Plus we plan to stay there a year to carry out crucial research."

"All that way and you only stay there a year. I've had longer holidays." It sounded like a joke but he did not laugh. He turned to face her, "Is it very dangerous?"

Charlotte sighed. He knew it was dangerous. Every second of the mission was more likely to fail than succeed. "It's all I've ever wanted."

He nodded slowly. "I'll explain it to your mother. She won't understand."

"Dad, do you remember how I explained time dilation to you?"

A deep intake of breath. "I'm afraid I do, yes. You see, in this world, it is funny to think of intelligence as a curse but, well...I think I'd love nothing more than to wave you off in the sure and certain hope that I would see you again." He stopped, perhaps registering the pained expression she imagined she wore. "It's not your fault, of course. You are a true servant of the Cause, and we are ever so proud of you. Your journey will be seven years, you say?"

"Yes."

"How long will we wait for you?"

"It depends on the gravitational pull when we reach Oscar 70, but around 50."

She took in the sight of the grandmother clock, ticking, reliable and lovely, in the corner of her childhood living room. She could not imagine it ever changing, ever being different to her time, for who can imagine such a thing? Although she had hoped otherwise, she had always expected to live out her minutes, hours and days on Earth, living beyond her parents as she nurtured them in their dotage, but she knew that this journey would change everything.

Her father nodded, and mouthed the word, "ah," although no sound accompanied. The grandmother clock ticked as they shared a silence. Charlotte started to wonder whether or not she should speak again, not that she could say anything meaningful, or comforting. "I love you, Charlotte, and you were always so determined. I'll do you the favour of not insulting you by asking you to stay. Honestly," he glanced at the paper, "I don't want you to anyway. This is who you *are.*" He looked her up and down but with an air of protection rather than judgement. "And besides, what kind of a world would this be to bring up a child?"

****

"What kind of a world would this be to bring up a child?" Her father's words rattled around Charlotte's thoughts. With a sinking feeling, she knew that he knew her too well and had looked her too squarely in the face for it to be a throwaway generalization. He wasn't talking about her as their child, but *her* child. But did he know who the father was? That, she doubted. Had she not known better, she would not believe it either. With a shudder, she imagined the shame of her father learning the truth about how she gained her prestigious position at Dawns' Laboratories. What was worse was that, should she abort the child, her father would both know and not know: she was not in the habit of keeping things from him.

Leaving the comfort of her parents' semi-detached home, Charlotte took in the relative quiet of the street. Most people were home now, it being a little after eight, and the black pavements, potholed and uneven as they were, gleamed silver in the moonlight. Charlotte enjoyed this time of night. It was easy to imagine that these were the Before years, her clinging to her father's hand as he took her for an evening walk to look at the stars. Her breath would emanate from her in tiny gusts of steam as the cold air made her face feel fresh and full of life, despite the cloying stench of the nearby chemical plants. Now, the stars were brighter than ever, mainly due to the lack of streetlights, and it didn't take long for her to locate Star 4, the Red Dwarf giving light and life to Oscar 70. Of course, being a Red Dwarf, it was invisible to the naked eye, but its position was etched like a tattoo on her mind.   As a child, she had gazed at those stars and imagined traversing the great distance between her and them, but never did she think that it would be possible. It was difficult to imagine where she would be now, were it not for the Expansion.

The town of Kolwick had thrived on its plastic production, which had been one of the first industries to be "scaled down" by the Panel.   The result of this was that the teeming factories of Charlotte's sleepy, northern home town became makeshift laboratories, producing and researching anything which might find Mankind an escape route from Earth. Looking back, Charlotte could never decide if her enthusiasm for Science had really arrived before, or after this. She would never allow anyone to hear her say so, but the Expansion served her very well indeed. Her excellent IQ was fostered by a world which wanted her to succeed, and there was never a question of her losing the support of everyone around her. Her father had kept his job lecturing at the university and her mother was able to live as she always did – cleaning and worrying, although perhaps now her worries were more real.

So why had she allowed herself to be used in such a way by a man three years younger than her father? Worse still, an avaricious, selfish and heartless man? She could blame ambition, but she had been almost certain that the job was hers anyway. And yet she had allowed him to run his fleshy hands all over her virgin body, to bite her neck and thrust himself into her. Thinking about it now, she was sure that a small part of her had been certain that she would *like* it, that a scientist of her status could handle such adult encounters and who more adult than the head of Dawns' Laboratories? She had been drunk with the knowledge of her own status, and this monstrous tryst had seemed markedly appropriate.

Afterwards, she was violently sick and sobbed like a child. No matter what scientific boundaries she broke in her life, she could never remove the utter shame and revulsion she felt at this memory, and it could never never be undone. And now Richard Dawns' child was growing in her belly. Worse yet, she was certain her father knew, and she hated herself for it.

With a shock, Charlotte realised that the abortion was no longer a certainty in her mind. Despite her revulsion of the baby's father, the fact that she would soon be settling on a different planet made her giddy with the possibilities. If she did keep the child, it could be the youngest living thing on the entire planet. If she left the child here, she would be gone for most of the child's natural life. It would be like an abortion anyway. Whatsmore, Richard Dawns would remain on Earth to head the mission; she would never see him again. The tangled web of filial politics she would have been ensnared in would vanish. The baby would be hers, and hers to enjoy in a brand new world.

But abortion did make the most sense; she was set to be the woman who saved Earth from hopeless Expansion and barren lands – her name would go into history books. Her burgeoning career left little room for motherhood. And yet. She clutched her stomach again – a habit she was developing at an alarming rate – and imagined aborting this child. At the age of 22, Charlotte Dobson could not have really known that many other women had experienced the exact same internal debate. Everything pointed towards the fact that she should rid herself of this mess, and yet. And yet...

The sight of a group of homeless Sups interrupted her reverie. Foolishly, she had been so absorbed in her own thoughts that she hadn't noticed her legs go into an autopilot trip to Dawns' Labs, rather than home. She was less than a street away, in a neglected area full of piled up car skeletons and makeshift fires, laid by the rebellious homeless. She could hardly remember a time when most streets were not piled high with debris from the Before years – relics of the wasteful and greedy lifestyle that Mankind was now paying for. In fact, yet another reason that she loved her parents' home so much was that the outskirts of Kolwick were still largely rubbish-free. She suspected that the wealthy in the suburbs had a deal with farmers who would take their waste for free, but she had always strived to maintain a blissful ignorance.

The cars had naturally been stripped of all that was useful, but their frames, piled high in scores, seemed to serve as perfect living spaces. Head down, she passed the group. She was confident in the fact that they would not speak to her or, worse, ask her for anything - to do so was punishable by death – but she nevertheless felt a slight frisson as she walked. It was like being relaxed in bed and suddenly seeing a spider scurry across your blankets. A cursory glance revealed a party larger than what she was used to seeing on the streets; there must have been at least fifty of them, all told, cramming themselves into spaces with almost impressive dexterity, but the ones nearest to her were clearly a family. A gaunt and serious toddler stared at her with huge eyes, rubbing thin arms against his frayed jumper. In another life the boy would be beautiful – blonde with enormous hazel eyes, but in his current condition he looked barely human. Behind him, a skeletal woman and man – possibly a similar age to her - were trying to calm a screaming baby. It squirmed and stiffened in their arms, yelping and screaming like a siren. The screams were punctuated now and then by a violent and rasping cough. They didn't speak, but stroked and soothed the child as best they could, the woman planting repetitive soft kisses, as light as a ghost, on the wet cheek.

Looking at the haggard group, Charlotte knew that they wouldn't survive the winter. The toddler was clearly starving, and the infant was obviously suffering from some illness that would take too many resources to treat. Charlotte shook her head; she really had no idea why any Sup would reject the care offered to them by the Panel. Yes, Sup Units were small and the residents were naturally expected to work for the upkeep of them, but to run away and live in squalor seemed *petulant*. It was difficult to have sympathy for a couple foolish enough to sacrifice their own children, just to serve a self-interested and stubborn pride.

She pulled her coat closer around her torso, and kept walking. She remembered that she had Sunday lunch with Daniel and Karen at the weekend, and wondered whether or not she should take a dessert.

Martin

The next two days at Dawns' Laboratories had been a flurry of note-taking, calculation checks and planning. Everyone had seemed at once serious and excited, as their ashen faces bent downwards to their work, focusing on the future – possible escape at last.

For Martin, the days had been spent mostly with Charlotte; she has been so focused on her calculations and plans for transporting the Speedlight, she needed Martin to do more or less anything else. The Sup who had served her recently, a man Martin had never spoken to, had been moved somewhere else and Martin had not seen him. Naturally, he did not give that a second thought. It was not customary for a Better to have an 'assigned' Sup, but Charlotte, it seemed, could do whatever she liked. Martin had therefore spent the majority of his time cleaning her workspace, checking her inventory, monitoring the Speedlight for hours on end to check for anomalies, and making her lunch. This last job was by a long way the hardest. He would hand Charlotte freshly made sandwiches, salads and cooked meats, feeling the hunger knive his insides. Despite himself, he didn't really mind. He had often considered how he would behave if he were a Better, and had started to think, or like to think, that he wouldn't behave considerably differently to the way she did. It would be nice to claim that he wouldn't, in her shoes, carry a certain air of privilege or, worse, entitlement, but he was sure that in reality he would. Everybody who has been unbelievably lucky in life believes that they deserve it, and Charlotte was no different. Although she never treated him *badly*, as many Betters had, there was always the clear divide between them. But what Martin liked about her was the passion she had for the Cause. To say she worked tirelessly was an understatement, and as she worked, Martin noticed that she moved with an almost dreamlike quality, as if she had transported herself to Oscar 70 already and was simply waiting for the rest of them. He would see her staring through the grubby windows at the unfriendly grey sky, but seeing beyond the dust and the filth – seeing something beautiful. He saw her operating the Speedlight capsule with the steely determination of a driver in a race, her delicate hands gripping the metallic controls like a vice. He saw her chewing her pencil down to the lead and tapping it on a page idly, her mind 25 light years away from home. Despite himself, he had started to admire her quest for something better, and not to simply save herself, but to save everyone.

In fact, he had failed to notice just how preoccupied with her his mind had become. Perhaps this was why, when he was returning some files to the store cupboard at the back of Doctor Dawns' office and he saw her sitting at the imposing desk that he sadly knew so well, he thought nothing of taking a moment to watch her.

She was sitting in the chair opposite the lush leather one belonging to Doctor Dawns – the one Martin had sat in just two days before. Here, she didn't have the usual distracted air that he had observed recently. She was sharp and nervous, as if about to undergo an interrogation. Her loose limbs and relaxed pose had been replaced with a straight back and tightly clasped hands. Martin saw the pale skin around her knuckles stretch as she tightened her fists.

Martin had been so focused on her that when he heard Richard Dawns speak, he was in danger of gasping and revealing his position as voyeur. "Well, Charley, you are to be congratulated. You and my son have between you created the perfect formula for interstellar travel; your combination of Speedlight and high powered storage units really is inspired."

Martin had not really considered how Charlotte might behave around Doctor Dawns. It was hard for him to reconcile his admiration for her and contempt of their boss, but he had always assumed that their relationship was a good one. After all, she was his top researcher and her enthusiasm for the mission acted in many ways as a love letter to him and his plans. Perhaps this was why Martin was so surprised to see her respond, in a manner which was unquestionably disrespectful, "I prefer Charlotte, thank you. Only my friends call me Charley." The familiar red rush spread across her neck and face. "And I think the work between your son and I was more 30, 70 than 50, 50."

Almost the entire frame of Doctor Dawns was hidden from his view, but Martin heard the chair creak and assumed he was leaning forwards, in the manner of a confidante. His husky chuckle filled the space between them. "Now, now, *Charlotte*. There really is no need for this formality or hostility. We are on the same side. And besides, we know each other *very* well, might I remind you."

And all at once he saw it. He saw her stricken face, devoid of colour and emotion, so different to the smile she had worn almost continuously for the past two days. After living for years with an abused mother, he knew the face of the exploited, and it made his blood run cold.

The lovely, confident Charlotte suddenly became a harassed schoolgirl, shuffling in her seat, uncomfortable under his glare. "Could we please get to why I'm here? I'm making excellent progress with the project; current estimations are that we will be able to board Eve One in three months-"

Doctor Dawns scoffed, "The Sups can keep me informed of timelines." Another creak of the chair. Martin imagined the doctor moving his face closer to hers, and felt, yet again, an urge to protect her. "I wanted to speak to you regarding a matter far more urgent. Something that will come to the fore in less than seven months. I trust you have considered my proposal carefully." Martin saw Charlotte's face drain yet again. Had he been closer, he would have held out his arms in fear of her falling into them. But Doctor Dawns simply continued his verbal assault, "In this overpopulated planet, another baby is a curse, not a blessing, but on Oscar 70, my dear, a baby, the *first* baby, especially ours, could be *King!*" Martin saw the same cursory wave that he suffered yesterday. "Or some similar title."

Charlotte's silence said it all. Her face took on a sort of relief, as if she was clear of the worst part of this conversation. It seemed a little like jumping into a cold swimming pool: once you are in, the water around you does not feel so hostile, and you can start to swim to combat the cold. She sat herself further upright. "I'm sorry, but I shan't be taking this child·to Oscar 70: this pregnancy ends now." Martin saw the red flush hit her pale skin again, but clearly this time it was from nerves rather than excitement. She blundered on, her words again running together in a hurried speech, "Of course I come to you because abortions are so *expensive*, and I know they are not strictly allowed, but I thought you might have some resources that might help…"

No movement from the chair. Martin would have loved to see Richard Dawns' face upon this news. Although he was far from the image of a loving father, Martin was sure that, to him, Charlotte and her child were mere chess pieces. Doubtless, the man was already shifting them in his mind. Martin wondered if she knew that.

After a long pause: "Charlotte, you and I both know that this cannot happen. We are talking about a child of *mine.* You will raise this child on Oscar 70, with my name. My child will be the youngest human, the first child to be born and raised, on an alien planet." Already, it seemed, he imagined his name living past him; he had marked this child down as yet another commodity. He rose to his feet and Martin saw nothing now but his square back. "I really am disappointed that you have not considered my proposal more carefully, young woman. You see – I have been a widower for a while now, and it does not aid one's image. A *family* man, one who is willing to send his wife and child to Oscar 70, will prove my faith in the mission. *That*, my dear, is an image to covet!" The square form sank to the chair again with a satisfied thump.

"But why do you want to marry me? You are well aware that the mission will take over fifty Earth years. You'll be long dead when I return."

"I know, dear girl. So I will forever have a wife and never have to see her. It really is perfect. You carry on my name, I enjoy bachelorhood, your bastard child gets a name to be proud of. Everyone's happy. Apart from you, really, but you'll not see me for the rest of your life, at least, so it could be worse." Richard Dawns' throaty chuckle ended his speech.

Poor Charlotte was lost, Martin knew. With a mixture of horror and sympathy, he observed how her *real* baby was Oscar 70, and that this human baby inside of her was pestilence. It was a part of Richard Dawns that was inside of her, and that was to be abhorred. Worse, she was to become his wife, and she couldn't do anything about it because of her love for the mission. He wasn't sure why, but the clear look of disgust on her face brought him relief.

As Charlotte opened her mouth to protest, Richard Dawns delivered his parting shot. "Without this child, and without being my wife, you do not go to Oscar 70 with my funding. Daniel will be the poster boy of this project, and him alone. Go to Oscar 70 as my wife and the propriety of Project Eden remains intact. We will be a family set to colonise the stars like royalty."

Charlotte recoiled as if he had hit her. How sad, Martin thought, that it was her determination and intelligence that had got them to this stage, and her determination that also undoes her. Yet she was answerable to this man, this representative from the Panel. Under his control, she was powerless.

She did not answer either way. Martin was looking at the floor when he heard the door slam. He wondered why he felt so disappointed.

Charlotte

The cracked biro trembled in Charlotte's slender fingers as she struggled to write the first word. She had left her parents' home feeling so dissatisfied with how the conversation ended, but, faced with the chance to tell her father more, she was unable to summon the right words. She knew that she had to tell him of her pregnancy and impending marriage, and she was a coward for not visiting them again to deliver the news in person, but she knew all too well that to burst into her childhood home with news of future marital bliss between her and Richard Dawns was impossible. Her father would have gotten the truth out of her in a second. With a sudden pang, she realized that for this to work, she may have to never see them again.

Dear Father,

I have good news. I think, perhaps, you already know, but you are to be a grandfather. I cannot go into the reasons behind this sudden gift, but I've decided that it is a gift.

She stopped writing. How treacherous to tell her loving parents in a letter and then abandon them forever. She scribbled over the phrase *you are to be a grandfather* until it was covered in a shiny black oval and replaced it with *I am having a child.* It was the first time she had seen it written, and, despite the impossible situation it placed her in, for the first time the pregnancy made her smile. She realized that, despite Richard Dawns' futile attempts at dominating Oscar 70, he would never be there, but she and her child would. The child would be hers, and hers alone, and they would enjoy their time together on a new and fertile world. Her mind was saturated with images from the interstellar probes of the greenery and life on the surface of Oscar 70; she would show it to her child and they would settle there together. Nothing else mattered.

She tried again.

Dear Father,

I am going to have a child. I am sure that this news does not come as a surprise to you, for I have never been able to hide anything from you and Mother - from you in particular. I am delighted that I will not be going to Oscar 70 alone, and that I will soon have a family of my own, although I shall of course miss you and Mother.

She tore the paper to shreds, tears suddenly heating her face with incontrollable rage. It was so monstrously unfair. She had never lied to anyone in her life, and to lie to the people she loved the most about her private emotions seemed unnecessary and callous. The third version was her last one.

Dear Father,

I am being bribed, and I cannot do anything about it. Because I was foolish enough to indulge in one night of teenage rebellion I am now forever tarnished with Doctor Dawns' child. I think I will love the child, but I shall never love him, despite having to become his wife. I have to marry him because going to Oscar 70 is my dream and he can take it away. Help me, please. Tell me what to do.

Calming, she read the letter back to herself. Of course she could never send this. She screwed it into a ragged sphere and threw it in the corner of the room. It joined an ever-increasing pile of rejected papers, consisting of attempted letters, journey plans and antimatter storage calculations – a mixture of the scientific and emotional that she would have felt reflected her very well at present, had she considered it. Just like her work space at Dawns', her home had the appearance of being unloved and haphazard, displaying no care over matters such as fine furnishings and colour schemes, but in fact everything that mattered was just where she wanted it. Another reason that Charlotte had coped so well after the Expansion was that possessions mattered little to her, so being unable to get more hardly caused a concern. If her flat was neglected it was because the things in it didn't serve any purpose for the Cause; the dust, grime and clothes on the floor were testaments to her commitment. Those belongings that she cared for, she knew exactly where they were. Her Astrophysics tomes and essays on Quantum Mechanics were well-worn and grubby with grease from the kitchen, due to many an evening rushing dinner and working, but they were stored with an intricate attention to detail on her work desk, chronologically according to date of publication. Her photographs, precious moments of her life, forever frozen, were pristine and dustless next to long-ignored trinkets; a passing glance would display the faces of her parents and Daniel and Karen, as well as scenes from her graduation.

Charlotte often enjoyed staring at those images, moments in her life that were like possessions to collect and display as trophies. Now, more than ever, she saw how time was rushing by, and she was becoming ever distant from the girl in those pictures. The glass on the frames, shining and thin, encased her past in an array of decorative gaols. She placed her fingers on the cold glass barriers, knowing that there would be no way of ever climbing back into those moments captured so long ago. Absently, she picked up a faded golden frame from her desk. A fourteen year-old Charlotte beamed back at her, embraced on either side by smiling parents. Taking and printing photographs for pleasure had been deemed a waste of resources soon after this, so this was one of the last photographs she owned, which seemed apt, given how it captured a bridging moment in her life. She had been accepted by the Cause at a young age, owing to her genius IQ, and had therefore graduated from school early. She remembered her graduation day as one where she was overcome by relief, relief that she was no longer being held back and relief that her life had been given such a clear purpose.

Looking at that girl now, Charlotte wondered how she would react to her future self. There would certainly be shock at the current situation, but in many ways, she thought, she could justify herself to her past quite comfortably. She had been the first scientist in history to utilise Speedlight as a viable fuel option, and she was to be the first woman to step on an alien planet. She reflected on how successful she had actually become. What was one secret in the face of that? Her parents were so proud of her, every person on the planet was so proud of her. Doctor Dawns thought her worthy to marry. She would speak to her parents and she would do it with pride. She didn't have to justify herself. With a lifting heart, she started to realise that in her position, she didn't have to follow the rules: she made the rules.

Martin

The aged beams of Kolwick Library yawned with each gust of wind outside as Martin, its sole visitor, pored over volumes of useless and irrelevant fiction. Anything deemed helpful to the Cause was apprehended years ago, and Martin's heart ached a little to see volumes of Shakespeare, Milton and Harper Lee gathering dust on the shelves, rejected and left to wither, until the time would come to use them for fuel.

The other Supplementaries in his Unit had mocked his love of reading. Most Sups, on failing the test, gave up such pointless enterprises, but Martin had been determined to redeem himself in the eyes of his mother and stepfather. Both successful teachers, they had been shocked when he had achieved a painfully close to the pass-rate score of 58. He felt cold as he remembered their faces when he told them in the waiting room. He had expected a hug, a smile, some form of reassurance, but instead they looked at him as though he was a puzzle to solve – a jigsaw that they had been working on for years only to find, just before completion, that a piece was missing.

Because of course he had presented them with a real problem. Anyone over the age of forty had been excused from testing just after the Expansion (an older Martin thought wryly that this was of course *nothing* to do with the fact that the youngest member of the Panel was forty-one) so his parents had been exempt. For this he was glad. Despite their clear love of learning and knowledge, they had no Scientific understanding whatsoever, and their particular field of expertise was moribund in a world hell-bent on progress. His elder brother and sister had passed, and had achieved the status of Betters. For failing to tick the final box at the age of eleven, he was eternally sorry. His main memory of that day was not knowing what to do with his hands as he stood before them all, delivering the news that he had failed them and he really wasn't sure why, or what it meant. His mother had wept, his stepfather couldn't look him in the eye, and Dinah and Joseph had been sent to stay with their grandparents. Martin's sole comfort was that his father was safely locked away and never to be heard from again, so at least he wouldn't be beaten for this.

The year had been 1997 and Martin had been a part of the first wave of children to be declared Supplementary. The guidance from the panel was very clear: anyone scoring below 60 was no use to the Cause and was therefore living on borrowed time on this planet. All Sup children must report to their nearest Supplementary Unit for further assessments and reassignment.

Martin paused on his page of Genesis 22: *And they came to the place which God had told him of; and Abraham built an altar there, and laid the wood in order, and bound Isaac his son, and laid him on the altar upon the wood. And Abraham stretched forth his hand, and took the knife to slay his son.* Surely the Panel had never thought that it would be so easy. To tell thousands of parents that their children were worthless because of a seemingly arbitrary test was incredulous. Except it *had* worked, largely. There had been tears, protestations, demands for retests (which were always, without exception, refused, of course) but in the end, parents had largely seen the bigger picture that the Cause presented and waved their children off, telling themselves that these Units would care for them well, until the time came to release them again. Yes, they would never bring them grandchildren, but that was the price they had to pay as good citizens. And with the world so overcrowded, and with resources so scarce, they could see the point the Panel had made. So children had been waved off in their thousands, sent to Supplementary Units for a life of hard labour and abuse. But Martin's parents had been different. Both of them were academics with lofty ideals, and they had, after a painful day or two debating the issue, refused to give up their son. They had refused because they loved him, and it was the worst crime they could have committed.

...And the angel of the LORD called unto Abraham out of heaven the second time, And said, By myself have I sworn, saith the LORD, for because thou hast done this thing, and hast not withheld thy son, thine only son: That in blessing I will bless thee, and in multiplying I will multiply thy seed as the stars of the heaven ...

His memories of the following months were hazy. He remembered a lot of hiding, and being terribly hungry, the latter of these things being something he was now unfortunately used to. He also remembered the elation of being rescued from his fate, the feeling of being loved so much that his mother and father would risk everything without a second thought. They travelled from hotel to hotel, and later on from one abandoned house to another, using up every penny they owned in ill-advised bribes, yet some of Martin's loveliest experiences were sitting on his mother's lap in a decrepit twin hotel room, reading her much loved and tattered Bible, searching for meaning in a world rapidly becoming devoid of it. He remembered her long red hair flowing like a mermaid's down her shoulders as he nuzzled close to her. He remembered the sweet scent of her mid-price perfume. He remembered feeling safe, and loved, and warm in her arms. His stepfather, who had previously been happy to settle with a volume of Chekhov, had more recently taken to scouring the newspapers for updates regarding current policies regarding the treatments of Sups.

Martin had never been a particularly happy child, and a constant source of guilt to him as an adult was the fact that his runaway months had actually been the happiest of his life. His parents had told him everything would be fine, so they would be. More importantly than that, Martin was now the centre of their universe. Dinah and Joseph were enjoying a life as Betters, back at his grandparents' home, so he savoured the experience of his parents' undivided love. They could not do what Abraham had done because they loved him so much, despite their unbending Christian faith, and that had made his heart swell. The Cause was not, after all, *God*, they had said to him, with a smile. Their love had made him feel safe. He was almost invincible under their reassurance and protection.

Martin was far too young when he discovered that your parents can't protect you from everything. The Panel Representatives had found them early in the morning, in a quiet seaside hotel. Holidaying had been a redundant pastime for many months at this stage, and the couple who owned the hotel had seemed very happy to gain custom from a lovely family "passing through." It was too late to learn that they had turned in many families during that first year, and had actually received recognition from the Panel for their services to the Cause.

The most dominant memory from that dark morning was his mother's screams in the next room. He never actually saw what happened, as he was bundled into the back of a battered blue minibus. His mind raced with hideous possibilities and it raced still, as he sat in this cold and abandoned house of knowledge. He did see his stepfather run out in pursuit of the vehicle, though, and he saw the explosion of blood as the guns stopped him going any further.

Martin closed the book with a snap. The silky thin pages slid together, to remain in this position for many weeks before his return. Enough indulgence in past thoughts. He turned to his real purpose: a stolen paper from Dawns' Laboratories, written by the young Daniel Dawns: *The Truth About Time Dilation and Interstellar Travel*. Martin had known for a long time that he wasn't really stupid – the test was worthless and recent discussions in the Panel had even hinted at such an admission – but even so, this went over his head. He had spent hours poring over images of moving beams of light, clocks passing each other at different speeds and ticking at different rates, and he had gotten no further to understanding how the mission would alter his life. He did know, though, from cautious glances at Charlotte's notes, that they were set to travel 25 light years at 99.92% the speed of light. The return trip would take about seven years in total, but fifty two years would pass on Earth. This didn't bother him per se – he had nothing to stay for. What he did find puzzling, though, is how this mission was meant to save

Earth, and yet in fifty years time, it was very likely that there would be no Earth to save.

He found that he had a rather remarkable level of faith in the project, and in Charlotte's capabilities in particular, but sitting here, surrounded by centuries of genius cast aside like trash, the feeling that they were rats leaving a sinking ship was impossible to shake off.

Charlotte

Sitting in the relative peace of Daniel Dawns' small back yard, Charlotte remembered her love of Sunday afternoons. Unlike those who dreaded the return to Monday's Rat Race, Charlotte savoured the languorous hours between waking and sleeping, the lack of direction, the time to reflect on the week to come. The November chill clung to her fingers as they gripped yet another of Karen's long hoarded wines (in the shock of being told her husband was leaving, Karen had opened one of their only remaining bottles of red wine – a 1994 Merlot) but Charlotte was determined to remain outside, breathing the fresh air and watching her living breath float through the mist. She reminded herself to compliment the garden soon, and imagined Karen Dawns digging, sowing and trimming all the living things around her: waging the gentlest of wars against a falling universe. Ever since the Expansion, garden space came at a premium, but Karen had forsaken other luxuries to afford their four square metres of space, currently filled with Japanese maples and greenhouse orchids - anything of a startling fragility that Karen could nurture in lieu of children. In a moment Charlotte saw the frailty of it all: the project, the future, the entire planet. Why sow seeds in a world that cares not for beauty? But most of all she saw the frailty of Daniel Dawns' striking wife. Her weather-beaten arms, freckled as so many red headed women's were, remained clamped to her torso, crossed in a stubborn sulk that Charlotte knew wouldn't last. "You can't possibly agree with him, Charlotte. His hypocrisy is unbelievable."

Charlotte knew this was the case. She had known that Daniel was going to forbid Karen from travelling to Oscar 70 with them. She had also known that Karen simply would not understand. But Charlotte did. She felt that she knew, more than anyone, the importance of leaving something beautiful behind, the importance of having something to *save*. Seeing Karen's anger had made her realise how reasonable her own parents had been about her going on the mission. She had removed herself from their lives forever, for they would both be long dead when she returned, but being aware of this had had a strange effect; she found comfort in the fact that they would never see her die, or fail - she viewed these two disasters in equal measure. But this way, a mission that would last a few years of her lifetime and yet all of theirs, suspended her in a state of permanent success, and life, from their perspective. Like Schrodinger's cat, she would be forever alive and dead to them, simultaneously successful and striving for success. To explain such a concept to Daniel's loving wife, however, was an exercise in impossibility. Karen was being abandoned and she knew it. She didn't idolise her husband in the way Charlotte's parents idolised her. She simply loved him, and wanted him to be with her. He wasn't an ideal or a trophy: he was a person made of flesh and bone. Charlotte found such affection humbling, but also found it impossible to tell her so without appearing condescending.

"Do you know, Charlotte, he actually said that there wasn't *room* for me? How ironic! Racing away from Earth to find more space and yet there isn't room for me to go!" At her final word, Karen drained her glass and immediately poured more. Both women listened to the luxurious glug of the merlot.

Charlotte sighed, "To be fair, Karen, there really isn't. The resources on board Eve One will only sustain so many passengers."

Karen's lack of eye contact concerned Charlotte; she was usually so *warm* and loving. Since being a child, Charlotte had always adored how Karen treated everybody she met like they were the most important person in the world. As a terrible listener herself, she had marvelled at how Karen would sit in silence and take in all that she was told. She would take it in and your thoughts would become hers. Karen *knew* you, and she cared. Karen thought. Karen would know you better than you knew yourself. She was the empathetic and thoughtful mother that Charlotte never had. That nobody ever had. Today, though, all that Charlotte deserved was a sideways glance. "How many Sups are going?"

Suddenly flustered, Charlotte was unsure how much vagueness she could get away with. "Oh, a hundred or so, I should think. But most of the people going are highly experienced doctors, architects, scientists and so forth. They are all people who will make a big contribution to the creation of a settlement before the other ships arrive. In many ways the Sups are test subjects — they will test the planet's habitable nature before we send too many Betters. Daniel told me he's planning to send you on the Eve Two, when we've found that Oscar 70 is safe. You can join us then and will only be a year behind us."

Again, Karen pouted. "Fantastic. Karen Dawns: the lady who went on the other ship. Hundreds of Sups! If there is room for them, why not me? My husband *invented* Speedlight! The whole mission is his."

Charlotte flinched. Daniel discovered Speedlight, yes, but he could only use it because of her. Probably best to pursue personal pride at another time, though. "Every civilisation needs a class of workers. We have to take them in order to -"

"I can work too. In case you didn't notice, I can cultivate any patch of land. Surely this is a desirable skill?" She gulped at her third glass hungrily. "Imagine all that land! I could plant food, grow herbs for medicines..." Her voice began to crack. "He should let me build *something.*"

"But it's so dangerous." "You're like my own flesh, Charlotte, and you're going. The love of my life is going. Don't give me that."

Charlotte took a deep breath. She had promised herself that she would tell Karen today. She was going to build up to Daniel, and the rest of the world. In reality, it was fairly easy – the words flew out:

"Karen, I'm pregnant. I'm carrying your father-in-law's child."

She had expected shock, of course, perhaps a hug, an exaggerated gasp. Instead, she received a scowl and uncomfortable pause. After what seemed like far too long, Karen said, "Oh, Charlotte. Do you really want to be a part of our family so much?"

After having nothing but approval from Karen and Daniel her entire life, this was a bitter pill to swallow. "It wasn't like that! It just...We spent a lot of time working and researching and...I don't know a lot of people my own age."

"Darling, that's pathetic. Oh, Charlotte." For the second time that week, Charlotte felt like a teenager who had let a parent down. Karen didn't say anything for a moment, but Charlotte could almost touch the disappointment between them. "Does this mean you won't be going on the mission?"

She expected scolding, rebuke, even anger, but not this. "Of *course* I'm going on the mission! Doctor Dawns – Richard - was insistent on this. In fact, he considers it a testament to his faith in the mission that he is going to send his child and wife-"

"Wife!"

"Yes. And for your information, we are very happy about it." The story felt as thin as water to Charlotte as she delivered it, but it was all she had. She decided to push further, "and of course we know that we will never see one another again, but by sending me Richard is making a sacrifice to the Cause, and using our love to unite the two planets." She felt sick. How could she lie so easily to a dear friend? Karen knew that Charlotte was a complete believer in the Cause, and would never distract herself with nonsensical notions like love.

The silence can't have lasted more than a moment or two, but Charlotte knew she would not be the one to break it. Another lie passing her lips could very well make her a different person. Who was she, anyway?

Karen's rough hands enveloped Charlotte's and she kissed them. Their faces were inches apart, and Karen's eyes refused to leave hers. "Answer me this. I'm sorry. I have to ask. You slept with my father-in-law?"

A nod.

"And you *wanted* to?"

How to answer that? In a way, Charlotte knew that she *had* wanted to, because he had everything that she ever wanted. Had she used him as a gateway to reach her goals? She shook the thought aside. No. She was good at what she did. She didn't need him. She did it because she was drunk and he had – a euphemism her parents might use – *taken advantage.* The lunch she had just eaten rested heavily on her stomach.

She fixed herself into a confident pose and smiled her sweetest smile, "I wanted to."

Finally, Karen smiled also. "The first child on Oscar 70! And it's a Dawns!"

Perhaps the idea had occurred to Charlotte subconsciously before she had even admitted it to herself. Here was Karen – to many intents and purposes an ideal mother – and here she was: ungrateful, cursed, ready to unburden herself. "I think I might know of a way you could come with us. I'll have so much to do during the trip," Charlotte stopped and smiled her warmest smile, "I'll need someone to care for this child, since I can't. Who better than the child's half sister?"

Any further disagreement was drowned out by tears of joy. One thing remained to be said, as Karen snatched the merlot from Charlotte's weak grasp, "And no more of this stuff, Mummy!" She placed a hand on Charlotte's stomach.

Perhaps leaving Earth as a different woman would not be so terrible.

Martin

Ever since the Expansion, weddings had been simple affairs, and the union of Charlotte and Richard Dawns, monumental as it was, had been no different. The bride, five months with child, wore her mother's antique ivory dress, and a registrar had dealt with the proceedings in a matter of minutes. Despite his enhanced years, Richard Dawns cut an impressive figure in his black suit, the same one that Martin had recognised as new four months ago. In fact, with both of them sporting jet black hair, ivory skin and slim bodies, they were every bit the celebrity pair. The public adored them. Charlotte was dazzling and, to add to her appeal, she seemed unaware of that fact.

Charlotte's parents had attended but Martin noticed how they seemed sullen throughout, preferring to, it seemed, stare at their shoes or the ceiling rather than the man their daughter was marrying. He wondered how much or how little they knew of this engagement. Perhaps they were simply worried, or sad that their daughter was leaving, particularly when she was so heavily pregnant. He found it difficult to imagine saying goodbye to someone he loved to go on that mission, and yet for Charlotte, so lucky and so loved, it had seemed easy. That worry had been taken from him long ago.

Martin, one of the few Sup employees to be given the honour of attending, albeit in a working capacity, found that his ability to recognise awkwardness surrounding this marriage was heightened. He noticed every wistful glance, every nervous cough, every seeming tear of joy. He wished he hadn't heard the conversation in the office; he would much rather, as the masses did, believe that this was a fairytale romance being sealed off in a fantastic and final farewell. The newspapers had loved the idea of this final expression of love between the honoured head of Dawns' Laboratories and the genius scientist who made the mission possible. And their child was to go with her. What nobility! What sacrifice! It was perfect, it seemed. Had he not known of Charlotte's suffering, he would have despised her, of course, but at least the fallacy of a happy union would have said something for the new world they were about to discover. The course was untravelled and already they were to carry lies and schemes with them. Martin applauded with the others at the chaste kiss to seal the alliance.

After the ceremony, the celebrations were combined with the farewell party for the brave explorers set to board Eve One the following morning. Again, the papers had lauded the frugality of this combined party. How *like* the great and selfless Richard Dawns to offer to share his nuptial celebrations with something so focused on the Cause. Everybody had believed, without question, that he was making the ultimate sacrifice, sending his son, wife and future child to another planet, laying down all that he treasured for a mission that he believed could not fail. Martin felt differently. He saw the charade for what it was – a marketing ploy. Unfortunately, the marriage was real, the child swelling Charlotte's belly was certainly real, and Doctor Dawns' reputation was untouchable. He could enjoy a future on Earth surrounded by wealth and privilege, relative as it was, thanks to this final noble act of his.

The party was held, again in the name of frugality, on the top floor of Dawns' Laboratories, a little used storage room that had been cleared for the occasion. Fittingly, the ceiling was a glass observatory, and the partygoers were drunk with the notion of celebrating under the stars that these intrepid voyagers were set to visit. The black February night sucked in the brightness of those stars and the windows were again steamed, but this time the condensation was on the inside due to how many bodies were cramped into such a small space. Perhaps it was simply the steam on the glass, or the blackness of the night, but the stars seemed especially small that evening – mere punctures in a vast sheet of nothingness. The thought of sailing into that made Martin feel nauseated. That was the difference between him and Charlotte, he considered: she ran towards the light whereas he ran from the darkness.

Everyone key to the mission was there. Martin saw several significant figures who he knew were going on the mission: the famous technicians Roman Smith; Amy Terekhov and Guy Roberts were within whispering distance, not that they would have whispered to him. The only signs of recognition he did get were barked orders for more drinks and snacks from Roman, who snatched them from Martin with a ferocious alacrity. Martin had heard Charlotte mention once how Roman had been forced to give up smoking when supplies were depleted, so now he bit his nails down to childlike stubs, an appearance that provided a contrast to his middle-aged, weather-beaten face. Martin saw little of Amy and Guy, who seemed to spend much of the evening avoiding Roman's attempts at conversation. Looking around, Martin had little idea who would be on the mission tomorrow and who would not: he had not been treated to such information. Of course, Daniel Dawns enjoyed significant attention at this event, being, despite his father's implications to Charlotte in private, very much the poster boy for the mission as far as Martin could see. It was Daniel Dawns who rose to speak.

"It is with a full heart that I celebrate the marriage of these two wonderful people: my father and my friend. Karen and I have known Charlotte since she was a child herself, and now she carries one. It certainly makes a fellow feel old!" Martin inwardly cringed at the inappropriateness of this light-hearted anecdote; everyone in the room was attempting to ignore the vast age gap between bride and groom that was set to widen, starting tomorrow, but Daniel seemed oblivious to his folly in highlighting this. His speech continued with several amusing stories of Charlotte as a child, Charlotte as a teenager, Charlotte as a successful scientist. References to pride in his father were less prominent, and Martin wondered if it was only him that thought how this felt like a father of the bride speech, rather than the best man speaking. For him, it only served to indicate yet more strongly how the marriage was far from a union of souls, but cold and calculated exploitation.

The evening passed pleasantly enough, and Martin found, towards the end of the evening, that many of the guests were actually being kind to him. When they realised that he was going on the mission, he seemed immediately elevated in status. Guy Roberts actually called him "Martin" rather than "Sup Martin" and Amy Terekhov had offered him some of her wine. He had declined, of course. Had anyone objected, Martin felt certain that he would be punished for the transgression, rather than her.

By ten o'clock, he was nevertheless walking a little taller, which was perhaps why he felt so bold when he saw Charlotte in the kitchens. He was halfway through cleaning the glasses and putting them away – most of the guests had left for an early start in the morning – and he was trying to get a head start so he could leave early also. It had been six weeks since Martin had viewed the conversation in the office, and his first instinct was to assume that she was seeking refuge from the limelight. She seemed flustered and eager to gather her thoughts in private. The ivory dress seemed to dig into her slightly swollen stomach, and her skin flushed that angry red that Martin had seen before. He saw her take several deep breaths and close her eyes.

If he could have hidden himself somewhere, to save her the embarrassment of being caught in such a private moment, he would have. As it was, he had no option but to stand by the sink holding a wet towel and a glass in the centre of the room, utterly exposed. Before he could think, he blurted out, "I'm sorry."

She jumped. Of course she did. She was pregnant and confused and had believed she was alone. She placed a hand to her breast, "Oh! Sup Martin! No, no. I'm sorry. I had no idea anyone was in here. I was just...thinking about tomorrow."

Martin nodded. Plenty of excuses for nerves tonight. "We all are, Mrs. Dawns, if you'll permit me to say so."

Charlotte seemed suddenly garrulous. He had seen this in her before, where her emotions seem to reach a brim and then they spill out in words. There was so much she could say, he wondered where she would stop. "Oh, yes! Of course.

The mission means so much to you people too, I suppose. It's what I've dreamed of my entire life, but now there are so many loved ones to say goodbye to."

Martin couldn't help himself. "Like your new husband, I expect."

For a second, her eyes were hot, defiant. It occurred to her, Martin thought, that he was mocking her, but she seemed to decide that he would never do such a thing, so acquiesced. "Yes, indeed." Her voice took on a casual tone, as if they were discussing a holiday abroad, like Martin remembered doing when he was very young. "And what about you? Do you have anyone to say goodbye to?"

As soon as she said it, the air between them thickened. She knew about his family, he assumed, but it seemed she had forgotten. How she dealt with it next was critical to his opinion of her. As it was, her eyes widened, and Karen Dawns burst through the door. She was wearing a red sequined dress, clearly from the Before years, and seemed to have treated herself to a face covered in contraband make-up. "There you are, Charley! You are needed to dance. Your new husband awaits!" Her excited squeal made Martin wonder how well Karen really knew her younger friend. All of a sudden, she recognised Martin's presence, and spat, "Sup 81873! I know that you go on the mission tomorrow and your Sup status will then change, but tonight is tonight, and harassing the new Mrs. Dawns is simply not allowed! I could have you flogged for this!"

Charlotte's horrified face was too little too late. She mouthed, "I'm sorry" before being dragged away by her new relative like a rag-doll. Martin would have loved to know exactly why she was apologising: had it been her thoughtless questioning or Karen's treatment of him? The latter he was used to, and he would really have preferred it to be the first one. He wanted her to be sorry for his suffering – not the fact that she had asked. But he couldn't ask her, so he finished cleaning the glasses instead.

Part Two: The Dark

Prologue

After so much celebration and anticipation, Eve One's construction took very little time at all. In many ways, her creation was a testament to the Panel's efficiency; clearly, they had focused their resources well to create such a complex construction in so little time. She orbited Earth in a perfect and graceful sphere: a city in the sky. Composed of one large central cylinder which held together a series of five circles, everything about the ship was rounded and smooth. Its blackness dwarfed the blue dome below it. The inhabitants of Earth were told that she could set sail three months ahead of schedule. The world rejoiced in its own tired and deflated way.

Eve One appeared on every television screen the world over, and the crowds stared at the metallic creation with religious awe. The onlookers had seen many a tragedy over the years, many an explosion and many a failed engine. Some ships had simply left in a blaze of glory and disappeared. Although none would like to admit it, this was far less satisfactory to the human race's need for blood and drama. Everyone loves a good tragedy. Something to lament with hushed voices and overly sombre faces. But time was running out. The viewing faces were sombre yet again, but the feeling of hope that this mission was different electrified the air. A dozen tiny spheres, white and perfect eggs, glided towards their mother and attached themselves onto her. The masses closed their eyes in a brief prayer. Let the crew return safely. Let them find somewhere good to go to.

That is the thing about hope. We almost always want the wrong thing.

Martin

Stepping onto the luxurious platform of Eve One, you'd be forgiven for forgetting that the Expansion ever happened. Unlike her black metal exterior, inside the ship it was all plush furniture and whispering doors. The gaping entrance beckoned the travellers like a womb, poised to offer new birth, new life. The Sups, arriving on the ship, had never seen such opulence, and their silence added to the fear that they would never hear real noise again. Their faces, illuminated by the blue lights, were as wide-eyed and silent as evacuee children. It was difficult to hear the pad of their feet as they followed Doctor Daniel Dawns to their new life. He led them, a pied piper, through the tubular hallways and into the Central Meeting Area. 125 pairs of uncomprehending eyes took in the soft ivory walls, matt against the seven feet high curved windows; the deep brown carpets; the sofas and the tables and the baskets of fruit. Fruit! The overwhelming cleanness of the place mixed the scent of sweet pears and oranges with bleach and other artificial odours that Martin had not smelt since the Before years. How could *this* be a space ship? Thousands of people starved in Kolwick and yet they built this, but it would be celebrated, he knew, as a tribute to the noble services paid by those aboard. He imagined what the headlines would look like next to images of this palace in the sky.

The Sups were given clean living quarters, running hot water and three square meals a day, as well as the biological ability to have children. Moreover, they were told that they were no longer the inferior species: they were to settle on Oscar 70 as equals with the Betters and a democratic and equal civilization would prevail. That this civilisation would be headed by Daniel and Karen Dawns, with their elite scientists acting as deputies, was common sense. The Leaders would care for their people. All would be well.

Martin was markedly less impressed by the richness of their new existence than the others. Perhaps it is difficult to love anything when the freedom of choosing it is removed. 215 people in all had been chosen for the mission, 125 of them being Sups. The breeding group was diverse in terms of ethnicity and physical features but they were all rather young. Martin guessed they were all early to mid-twenties; he was likely to be the oldest. Every female Sup on board was currently pregnant, but none of them were at a stage to be visibly so. This entire notion was lost on him: of course a planet needed people, but to impregnate the majority of a ship's crew before a dangerous and three-year-long mission was ridiculous. Like many things, he chalked it up to Richard Dawns' hubris. Doubtless, he would be glorying in this splendid idea back on Earth. Like the Sups on board, the sperm donors had been from a variety of ethnic backgrounds and very carefully chosen: a further effort, he thought, to keep the potential gene pool wide. Amongst the diverse gathering, his eyes were drawn to a glamorous blonde with heavy make-up, who smiled archly as she caught his glance. Her left eyebrow raised and her hazel eyes sparkled as they met his. He looked away quickly. Everyone, Sup or Better, wore the regulation Eve One white suit, tailored and streamlined on such young and beautiful bodies. This was a marked change from the black worn at Dawns', but each fitted jumper sported the same crimson apple on the chest, marking the heart of every individual on board. The young

Doctor Dawns wore the uniform rather less well, as the trousers dug into his protruding waistline and cleared his ankles by a good one inch. His wiry black hair and eyebrows emphasised the whiteness of his outfit, though, and his smile, in the manner of one squinting at a bright light, made his dark eyes almost impossible to see from the back of the crowd. He spread his arms, much like his father had done for Martin only months before, and declared, "Welcome to Eve One, travellers! Here, today, we will propel ourselves to a new world and we happy few will..." Standing in front of the crowd so confidently, arms spread, Martin wondered if the image of a crucified man struck anyone else. "This honour will be passed to your children and your grandchildren. It is a privilege that will outlive us all..." Martin felt an elbow dig into his waist and he turned to see the attractive blonde. Her look alone seemed to weigh up everything about him and he felt like he was being interrogated without words. As Daniel Dawns spoke, she offered Martin a meaningful sneer and continued to tut at every positive word spoken. Martin appreciated the sentiment but not the intrusion, and he decided rather quickly that he resented this girl and her abrasive confidence. And so the speech went on. Martin's hands joined the applause, but his heart and his eyes did not.

Charlotte

True to form, the Better Section of Eve One spared no expense. Not only did the ship's anti-gravity drive and environmental regulator imitate Earth's climate exactly, but it was clear that those on the mission were being rewarded for their sacrifice. Magnanimously, the Panel had decreed that the scientists who had brought the magic of Speedlight to the world deserved every luxury. Charlotte's living quarters included games systems, a deep king sized bed, a bath that she could disappear in, and fill with hot water no less, and a plethora of artworks and useless artefacts from Earth that spelt luxury and affluence. When one considered the cost of propelling such artefacts through space at 99.3% light speed, the compliment to the travellers on board was staggering. Or foolhardy. What Charlotte loved most about her bedroom, though, was the window.

Filling the entire exterior wall of her corner of Eve One, the convex window bent against the air outside, kissing alien skies. Charlotte had worried that she would be bored on this long journey, especially since Eve One had been designed with the ease and comfort of the traveller in mind, but she discovered quickly that hours could pass her by as she pressed herself against the window and felt herself floating through space. Unhappily, the sight of the Earth had disappeared quite quickly, given the rate at which they were accelerating, but Charlotte felt that she would always remember that feeling of utter weightlessness, that sight that few people had yet seen. If she really clung to the glass and looked downwards, it was like flying alone in the universe. After living in a world marred by Overpopulation, it was exhilarating.

And yet it was lonely. It was at these times, conversing with the universe, that she remembered her father – the tears that he would never cry in front of her – his nobility in her exit. She remembered him nodding thoughtfully when she finally told him of her pregnancy, providing an almost perfect impression of happiness when her engagement was revealed. The worst thing was that her dear father, who was now long lost to her, had known her suffering just as she had known his. He had known that she did not love Richard, and yet he never interfered. Her father's remote awe of her had failed them both in the end, for here, elevated and tiny in the vastness, she felt like the least awesome thing imaginable.

Charlotte was in this position, pressed hard against the pane, her swollen stomach blending perfectly with the curve of the window, when Martin entered the room. She supposed that he had attempted to alert her to his presence via the bell outside her room, but clearly she hadn't heard. A polite cough shook her from her temporary hypnosis. Martin stood awaiting his orders, looking striking in his white uniform. With his strawberry hair and piercing blue eyes, there was very little on him that was dark.

"Good afternoon, Sup Martin." Charlotte offered a small cough in answer to his. "I was wondering if you'd be kind enough to accompany me; I need to perform some safety checks and could do with somebody to count and write for me."

That she had never needed such assistance before did not seem to register on his face. Perhaps Sup stupidity really did know no bounds. Or perhaps, just perhaps, he was as lonely as she. "Of course, Mrs. Dawns."

Too late, Charlotte remembered that she shouldn't address him as "Sup Martin" anymore. Technically, his status as a Supplementary had disappeared as soon as they left Earth. On Oscar 70, he would simply be part of the settlement, able to breed and share resources like anyone else. What was impossible now was knowing exactly how to treat the Supplementaries. She wished they had briefed her on *that*, rather than how to cope with a tropical climate and recycle water supplies. A cursory glance at her living quarters would make any sensible person conclude that she was clearly still regarded as a more deserving person than the man before her, but Oscar 70 may not have *any* life there whatsoever, and that changed things. It meant there was possibly more room, more resources and more respect for everyone. Added to this, the Sups outnumbered the Betters significantly now, particularly given the forced pregnancies of many of the Sups. Had any of this occurred to Martin? Of course she didn't know. To him, she was just Mrs. Dawns.

The storage of Speedlight on Earth had been challenging, but on Eve One, where it was to be used, it was a fine art. The fuel, stored at different points around the ship, was contained in compacted vacuums, just as it had been on Earth, but it was necessary to trigger these points at different stages of the journey. Only Charlotte and Daniel Dawns knew how to do this. As a result, Charlotte and Martin were compelled to navigate the cylindrical corridors of Eve One, stopping occasionally to scrutinise key figures. Charlotte would read a plethora of codes to Martin, who would write them down scrupulously. Not for the first time, she reflected on how glad she was that he was on the mission. Not only was he clearly capable, he was also respectful and fairly good company; the long walks didn't seem awkward in his presence. As the days turned into weeks, and Martin arrived regularly at her quarters at the assigned times without a summons, she found herself conversing about her childhood, life at school, her ambitions working at Dawns'. He had listened with a serious concentration that reminded her of her father; it was as if her words really mattered to him.

Fuel Point One was due to be triggered in three hours, so they spent quite a while at this one. The checks took around thirty minutes in all, and Charlotte felt her head aching after concentrating so intensely on her work, albeit for a relatively short amount of time. Her legs felt close to buckling under the solid weight in her middle, and she did her best to suppress the shaking of her fragile frame. She felt the need to talk about something as they walked. "How are you finding your quarters?" She made an effort to keep her voice light-hearted, carefree.

Martin didn't seem surprised by the question, but it would have been an aberration from his regular behaviour if he had been. "They are excellent, thank you, Miss."

"I expect you find the company different to what you were used to back on Earth. Of course your rooms are shared, and mixed sex. Is Olivia in your quarters?"

Why had she asked *that*? She had noticed Olivia occasionally, and had noted, as no doubt everyone had, her ostentatious beauty and flirtatious manner. She hadn't realised that it bothered her until that moment. Martin simply shook his head, and for several metres of slow walking she fought a rising panic that she had gone too far and, with a shock, she realised her greatest fear was not punishment, but a cessation of these walks.

 The silence ended with his statement, "I don't like her one bit, actually. We have nothing in common."

Odd for a Sup to be discerning in terms of sexual partners; she had never really considered such a thing before. Naturally, he would be aware of his role in the mission: to populate. It would not be long until this was being actively encouraged. "But you are both young and attractive and no longer sterile. Surely that makes her ideal for you?"

She detected it that time – the flinch, the look of disgust that momentarily flashed over his face. His formal response did little to dim the glow in his eyes, "Perhaps, Miss. I'm sure she will not be short of offers."

It was several weeks later when she dared raise the issue again. His comment about he and Olivia having "nothing in common" had jarred with her for some reason. Perhaps it was her own boredom, but she had started to genuinely wonder what a woman with something in common with Martin would be like. He was a mere Sup: surely his list of criteria was fairly short?

The day was like any other, and they had started to walk rather more slowly than usual. She was getting quite large now – Karen had insisted that she rest – and, indeed, many of her duties had been reduced, but she had managed to keep this one – the simple check of the Fuel Points. Her reasoning had seemed fair: she was one of the few people in the universe who knew the qualities and dangers of Speedlight – nobody could monitor it as well as her. A side-effect of this had been her daily communication with Martin. She had reasoned that questioning him on his plans to procreate was sensible, proper even, given his role on the mission, but how to start such a conversation? Just as she had done when raising the topic of Olivia, she kept her voice steady and nonchalant. She avoided eye contact. "What are your plans in terms of breeding when we reach Oscar 70?"

Martin continued to scrutinise the screen in front of him, "I have no plans. I didn't think it was compulsory."

She started to feel hot. It wasn't compulsory, strictly speaking, but procreation was one of the main reasons the Sups had been brought along; they were warm, reactive bodies to provide the young on Oscar 70. The population chambers were all well and good, but it had been decided long ago that *people* were needed on a new world, even if many of those people were Sups to begin with. He was no longer a Sup now, but she wasn't entirely sure that he could simply *decide* that he didn't want to either. Nervously, she stammered some form of non-committal agreement that for some reason seemed to make him smile.

"Anyway," he continued, "If I were to *breed* on Oscar 70," as you put it, "I'd quite like to fall in love first."

He should have been nervous of saying such a thing to her, such a frivolous and indecent thing. The archaic notion of love contradicted the Cause – everyone knew that. It was a reason for the Expansion in the first place. It certainly did nothing to solve the problem.

Charlotte knew she should quash this comment immediately, but she did not. Instead, for some reason she considered it. She was responsible for Martin, she had grown to like him, but it wasn't until this moment that she realised the unthinkable – she could learn from him. This man, this sad, fragile, damaged man, had known a world that she never would. It was only at this moment, at 23 years of age and on a ship floating in the middle of the dark, that she realised she was interested in this world. She whispered, every word vibrating on her lips, "There is no such thing as real love anymore. Real love is a myth. If we are to survive, the frivolity of love must be sidelined."

He nodded and continued to stare at the screen in the grey wall, "299.394.2."

It took her a moment to register. "Pardon?"

"299.394-3," he responded, "And rising."

"But that's too high; we don't need this Speedlight for another six months. Any kind of trigger now will be too much power at once!"

Again, impassive. How was he so impassive? "Yes, I know that."

The crisis called for the hands of many to intervene, and Charlotte's panic was lost amongst the panic of many. It seemed as if the entire crew of Eve One had something to contribute, with Daniel Dawns leaning against the offending screen, arm outstretched like a mechanic from the Before Years examining a car, barking orders at Sups and Betters alike.

Eventually, it was Charlotte who had managed to reduce the pressure to safe levels. It had been a simple matter, relatively at least, in the end, but it seemed that Fuel Point Three would need careful monitoring henceforth. With horror, Charlotte realised that this had been *her* error: Fuel Point Three had been neglected for the last 48 hours. Whether or not Daniel had realised, she did not know, but the sick feeling that rose when she considered how many souls aboard had been endangered by her lack of concentration, of that she was certainly aware.

After the crisis had passed, she and Martin remained: he was sitting at a ninety degree angle on a steel chair, perfectly poised and scrutinising the tattered notebook for what he had said was the final time. She had reassured him that the pressure had been a malfunction in the chamber itself and nothing to worry about now she had fixed it – a white lie necessary to retain his trust. Unusually, she saw him smiling. He continued to smile for several seconds before saying, as if it was the most natural thing in the world, "It was love that brought you here." He did not look up from the calculations scrawled in front of him, dead spiders on the paper.

She was too surprised to be angry. "I'm sorry?"

His voice was casual, as if they were discussing the weather back on Earth, "I mean that your passion for travel is what brought you here, your passion for the Cause, and your love of your husband."

That final statement stung. Was he aware of their sham marriage and mocking her? Or, worse still, did he really believe her as capable of loving such a man as Richard Dawns? She decided not to rise to the statement, either way. Back on Earth, he would never have said such a thing to her, but now, wherever they were, it seemed almost acceptable. She sighed, "The first two things you mention are beneficial to the human race: travel and scientific advancement. My marriage is a celebration of the Cause and the first potential interstellar marriage of all time. That's more significant than the indulgence of love."

Martin's gaze had not moved away from the book in all this time, and it still did not then. Charlotte started to think that she should simply leave, and had in fact started to exit the room. As she walked away, she heard him mutter something like, "To love and have loved. Ask no further. There is no other pearl to be found in the dark folds of life."

She had no idea what that meant. Perhaps the Supplementaries spoke to one another in some strange code. She knew that she should walk away and not question him, but she sensed, through his words, that she was on the brink of discovering something more amazing than Oscar 70 itself. Remaining there, after he had said such a strange thing, asked a thousand questions and, fittingly, he finally turned to face her.

He closed the book. "You see, I think that everything that people do should be motivated by love. Anything not forged from love - *that* is a total waste of time. If you don't seek Oscar 70 out of love – as I believe you do – it's a *total waste of time*." He laughed an empty laugh. "It's even more of a waste of time when you consider that we have simply thrown away a generation on Earth by leaving it."

She was shocked. Surely she should report talk such as this? How could anyone post-Expansion speak of the Cause as "a waste of time?" He said nothing more, his face immobile and perfect, awaiting her reaction.   She attempted to smile, reassuringly but not patronisingly, as she left the room. "Good night, Martin. I won't tell anyone what you said, I really won't, but I also can't agree with you. You must be careful who you speak to about this. For your own safety, speak of the Cause and nothing else."

****

As usual, Charlotte prepared for bed and decided to treat herself to a spray of her mother's perfume: the last scent of home. Naturally, she loved her parents, but loving one's parents was different, she reasoned. Martin was undoubtedly silly to speak of romantic love. The world had moved on. She was confused to realise that the bottle was not there, but cursed a busy mind. Surely, she would find it tomorrow.

Since leaving home, the thought that had dominated before sleep had been her mother. Before Eve One set off, the thought of leaving her father had caused her physical pain, and she had surprised herself with how close she came to not leaving because of the thought of never seeing him again. Perhaps she should mention *that* to Martin about what love is capable of doing: staying would have destroyed her dreams. But it was thoughts of her mother that kept her awake at night now. Her beautiful mother who she avoided fervently in order to avoid yet another awkward conversation. Her beautiful mother who nagged her relentlessly, only to have her pleas met with apathy, derision, or both. Her beautiful mother who suffered so, and didn't know how to say it. She should have been a better daughter. She should have recognised that her mother's faults were hers also. If she hadn't learned anything else in the past six weeks, Charlotte had learned that separation is a terrible thing, but irreconcilable guilt is worse.

But tonight something else dominated her thoughts. Every time she closed her eyes, she was met with another pair staring back at her, blue, soulful and telling the saddest of stories. He was four years older than she but he seemed fifty; most men she met seemed to wither next to her intellect but he, despite being a *Sup*...That should have been enough to shake her from her trance but it wasn't. If anything, the life he had lived and the suffering he had endured made him all the more fascinating to her, for he had a depth that she did not. Next to his, her knowledge was superficial and effortless; his knowledge had been forged through blood and anguish and he could offer her a profundity of experience like nobody else she had met. She knew why she had asked about Olivia – it was simple, childish jealousy and he would think her pathetic if he knew. Tonight, she was certain that she would not dream of her mother. She should be dreaming of Oscar 70, or her child, but she doubted that she would. She might not dream of anything – she seldom did – but on waking, the image that would meet her would be that lonely, lost boy and those sad, beautiful eyes.

Martin

Entering his quarters after visiting Charlotte's, Martin reflected that absolutely nothing had changed regarding his status. The stolen perfume, lodged deeply in his pocket, probably cost as much as his and Travis's room combined. Settling himself down for the evening, he took in the threadbare carpet, clearly recycled, the hard bunk beds and the general plainness of the room compared to the one he had just visited. That this was still better than what most Sups on Earth experienced was irrelevant; the claim that they were *equal* now on the ship was insulting. He closed his eyes and recalled the lushness of Charlotte's room; he imagined himself sinking into the softness of her white bed and breathing the fresh scent of her deeply.

He had no idea why he had done it. Martin regarded the perfume bottle– a clear square bottle with the italicised word *Madame* written across the centre in gold- and considered whether or not it had been worth the risk. The sensible conclusion was of course it wasn't. Stealing on Earth had been a serious crime, worthy of execution, considering the scarcity of resources, and this was surely one rule that was still exactly the same. If anything, stealing from your crewmates was *worse*, Martin reflected. They were hurtling through space and this ship and its contents were all they had. Although Charlotte clearly had a lot of possessions, certainly compared to him, this half full bottle of amber liquid was possibly the only perfume she owned. However, the people on board were the only people they had. He was one of 215 people to populate a new planet. Without him it would be 214. With a lifting heart, he realised that he was a large portion of Eve One's population.

His main concern, though, wasn't the risk, but his motives for taking it. He didn't need to sell it, and he didn't think he wanted it. As he held it to his nose, he took in the fresh and sweet fragrance of her and attempted to convince himself that he had stolen it simply because it was a pleasant smell. Why had he spoken to her of such things? Was he really so foolish as to ever think she would respect his views, yet alone allow him to discuss such matters openly with her? He had overstepped a mark – no question about that – but what alarmed him more than anything was how good it had felt.

"Are you OK, Mart?" Martin shook himself to see Travis Sanderson peering down at him.

Martin sighed as he placed the bottle under his bed. Perhaps it was the lack of privacy, something he had been lucky enough to enjoy on Earth, that was riling him. "Yes, thanks Travis. I was just thinking."

"Did it hurt?" Travis, guffawing at his own joke, clapped loudly and returned to his bunk.

Despite his bombastic manner, Martin could tolerate Travis quite happily. He had clearly been chosen to go to Oscar 70 because of his appearance; his cheekbones and ebony eyes were really quite striking. He was one of the few black men Martin had ever met to sport an afro, possibly because hair products were so hard to come by back on Earth, but Martin guessed that Travis's was effortless. What he liked the most about him, however, was that Travis's smile illuminated the room. Despite the awful quality of his jokes and his love of teasing anyone who would listen, he had a brightness about him that Martin found refreshing. He had not allowed his Supplementary status, or his presence on a compulsory mission to Lord-knows-where, to affect his spirits.

"You were seeing that pretty Better, weren't you?"

"We don't need to call them Betters anymore. And yes, I was. She had called for me to do some rudimentary checking of the Speedlight drive."

"Never heard it called that before." Travis flashed yet another gleaming white smile. "It's just interesting that she never asks anyone else."

Martin was suddenly angry. "And what the fuck do you mean by that?" he exploded.

Travis simply held up his hands. The knowledge that he had touched a nerve clearly pleased him. "I'm sorry, man. I don't mean anything by it." He was suddenly serious. "I was just thinking that it would be nice to see somebody in a happy relationship on this thing." He slapped the wall on the word "thing" to indicate that he meant the ship. "I've got somebody back home, you see, and I'm feeling sorry for myself."

"Oh. I didn't realise." Martin was reluctant to get too involved in such a conversation, but the question hung in the air before he even placed it there. "Why didn't you ask for her to come? They've reversed the sterilisation procedure for a reason, I expect. They might have listened to you."

That smile again. "Yeah. That'd be grand, if it was a woman." A pause, too long a pause. Travis's smile only got larger. "Didn't realise that I'm gay?"

"No. Sorry."

"Sorry that I'm gay or sorry for not realising?"

Martin couldn't help but smile, "Right now? Both."

Travis's smile this time took on a different quality – there was no room for meaningless teasing. "His name is Alex. He's a few years older than me but I'm still always the one to take care of him. Christ knows how he'll cope without me." His verbose confidence was threatened by a shaking voice. "He's blind."

Martin was embarrassed. He realised, suddenly, that the man he was sharing an interstellar mission with was a complete stranger to him. He had been so wrapped up in his resentful mood that he had forgotten who to resent. Martin imagined the handsome Travis caring for this man, who needed him desperately. One of his first thoughts was how Travis's good looks were somewhat wasted on a blind man, and he hated himself for his shallowness.

He decided to take the plunge and invest fully in the conversation. After all, this roommate could be his only friend on Oscar 70 – his only friend to ever have, in fact, "How did he take the news of you leaving?"

Travis didn't answer for a while. He turned his head to the wall and Martin found himself thinking that, were he in Charlotte's room, he would be looking into the vastness of space as they sped through it. As it was, the window was a thin strip above their heads so he was forced to look at the blank magnolia paint, already scuffed. "Ah, you know. He was hurt, of course. He kept asking if there was a way out."

101

An embarrassed laugh. "As if they'd ever offer *us* a way out – huh? But it's OK. He's going to wait for me."

Martin thought he hadn't heard him properly. "I'm sorry. *Wait* for you? How old is your partner?"

"Don't use that word. I hate it. Too businesslike. I love him – he's my boyfriend, not business partner or such nonsense. Don't water our love down just because he's a man...Sorry, oversensitive today. He's 43." The defiant smile started to return. "I like older men. I'm trying not to think about it too much. It's only six, seven years at the most. What's that against a lifetime of love? " A pause. "Oh – I see why you're confused. One way mission, right? Don't worry, man; I've got out of much worse. I'm sure I'll be able to charm my way onto the return trip. They'll have to take some Sups back, otherwise our pals on Earth will think they've slaughtered us all." A cheeky wink. Martin's stomach tightened. Something in Travis's head was very wrong if he thought that he could simply return to his boyfriend. "Hey – I might even work on that saucy Better you're so fond of. Just to show you how it's done. She doesn't know I'm gay, right?"

Martin quickly did the calculations in his head. Travis's boyfriend would be 95, or – more likely- long-dead, when he returned. Why didn't he know this? With a cold horror, Martin realised that Travis had no idea of the implications of the mission. And why would he? The Sups on the mission had not been told the intricacies of time dilation – Martin realised that he only knew because of his involvement in Dawns' Laboratories. No doubt, with it being a one-way mission, nobody had considered this essential information, particularly for the lowly Sups involved.

Unhappily, Martin reflected that he knew more than most Betters about time dilation. Despite his supposed stupidity (or perhaps because of it) he had made every effort to fully research everything he had been involved in at Dawns'. He could probably hold his own conversing with the marvellous Charlotte Dawns on the topic.

But the rub was that nobody really understood it because it had never really *happened*, not on a large scale anyway. He had heard all sorts of ideas, like how clocks move slower in a fast moving plane, or if you looked through the window of a ship travelling at close to light speed, the people in it would appear to be in slow motion. That was an interesting thought: he liked to imagine somebody flying past Eve One and seeing him inside, moving like an exaggerated stop-motion cartoon. All that he knew mattered, really, was that on this ship time was moving at a slower rate than back at Earth, even though to them it seemed normal. All Travis needed to know was that his boyfriend was probably already ten years older – or twenty by the time they set foot on Earth if they turned back right now, which they wouldn't. All he really needed to know – really – was that by the time the return mission landed, Travis's boyfriend would not be there.

All Martin could allow himself to say was, "Well, good luck with that." Before more conversation could continue, he quickly span to face the wall, arms crossed like a corpse. Luckily, this wasn't any different to his behaviour of the last six weeks, so Travis simply sighed and settled for the night himself.

As the night went on, Martin could not shake the sick feeling in his stomach. Correct, it was a one-way mission – Travis was completely misguided to think he'd be able to charm

103

himself back to Earth, no matter how much he flattered Charlotte, or anyone else. But what made him want to vomit was the insulting *secrecy* of it, like the Supplementaries had no right to know how the world would go on in their absence. It was not enough to be robbed of your freedoms, to be torn away from your life on a planet you shall never return to, but for the life you left behind to pass within a few years of yours and for you not to *know*. And for somebody to think that your ignorance of it doesn't *matter*! There was Travis, planning a life when he returned, and his lover was already at least a decade older. Martin felt the anger in him rise like heat. He was barely able to breathe when he imagined all the other Sups on Eve One right now, sleeping and dreaming of the life at home they left behind, perhaps the life that they believe they may see again, like Travis.

He'd been happy enough to join Project Eden because his life had been miserable and unlikely to ever change. In his selfishness, he hadn't considered that others like him were leaving behind lives that they possibly loved, lives that they didn't want changed. Had his family still been alive, he would have wanted to stay. Distance in miles would have been enough – a generation of time between them would have been unthinkable.

When the Sups find out, for find out they must, Martin knew that what would hurt people like Travis the most would be that, no matter what advancements are made, you can never, never, turn back time. You can never, never, retrieve years that have gone, and more years had gone than any of the others knew. Travis was right – a few trillion miles is easy to traverse – but time is another matter. He closed his eyes and tried, as he often did, to conjure up the faces of this parents and siblings. He tried to remember the fresh smell of water fights on the street, the sight of his mother's smile as she brushed her auburn hair, the sound of his stepfather's piano floating up the stairs on a Saturday morning. People say to make the most of precious moments, and you do, and you consider yourself wise, but when a moment is gone, it's gone, regardless of how strongly you felt it at the time.

Time is more terrible than distance. You can only go forwards. You can never go back. Martin shook as Travis slept soundly, as yet unaware of how close this terrible truth was to his dreams.

Charlotte

Back on Earth, it had never occurred to Charlotte how strongly she disliked the Betters she worked with. Her job had been a solitary one because she was the only person who knew how to do it, but now, on Eve One, she was forced to share her findings and plans with the likes of Guy Roberts and Amy Terekhov. Their self-interest and ignorance were astounding, and Charlotte liked to limit her conversations with them wherever possible. Today, though, it had been necessary to visit the data room to discuss work.

She was briefing Roman on the Speed light drives and Fuel Points. It had occurred to them that she may need to reduce her working hours soon, thanks to her ever-expanding waistline, so she needed a technician to cover her. Her opinion was that Martin was perfectly capable of informing anybody who would cover her, but she was certain that such a suggestion would be met with contempt. At least Roman was more bearable than the others; Charlotte could tolerate his New York honesty more than Guy and Amy's slick arrogance. Her and Roman's conversation was punctuated by their sarcastic comments as they tapped away on their computers. The data room was almost the opposite of her room – it was small, dark and metallic – and everything about it spelt functionality rather than opulence. Perhaps that was part of the problem: Amy, Guy and Roman expected to be taken so much more *seriously* than everyone else, even her, despite their nonchalant attitude to, well, everything.

It seemed odd that Charlotte was considering mentioning Martin's name when he burst through the door. She knew immediately that there was something wrong. His entire manner was different to his normal deference and his eyes seemed to sparkle with something unpleasant that she couldn't quite define. If the anger inside him could have leapt into her and attacked her, she was certain it would have. He stood, surrounded by black computer monitors and breathing heavily, waiting for permission to speak despite his unruly entry.

Charlotte spoke, since no one else did, "Are you all right, Sup Martin?" She checked herself. "Martin."

His rage did not subside. Every word was spat. "I am quite all right, thank you, Mrs. Dawns. Unfortunately, I am surrounded by 124 Supplementary people who are *not* all right."

She opened her mouth to speak again, but Guy clearly sensed some danger that was not there and leapt between them. His misplaced heroism was largely ignored, and Martin continued to shout above him. "They don't know! Nobody told them about time dilation!"

Guy tutted and rolled his eyes, and Charlotte found herself wondering if he had ever managed to placate anyone in his entire life. "Is that *all*? You're not going back anyway! In case you haven't noticed, you're going to a new *planet!* Don't you realise how lucky you all are that we brought you? Bloody fools!" Foolishly, he turned to Charlotte and laughed, before being pushed, roughly, out of the way by an even more incensed Martin.

His onslaught continued, "And that's just it, isn't it? 'Bloody fools!' We have been told we are now equals! It's a fucking joke! You're no brighter than I am, but you live in luxury and

107

we don't! Either you see it, and you're a hypocrite, or you don't and you're fucking idiots!" He pointed at them all in turn, including her, and she couldn't subdue a sharp intake of breath as he did so. Charlotte had never seen Martin like this; it seemed that there had been a porcelain seal around his emotions for the entirety of his adulthood, and the fragile surface had finally cracked. In that moment, she felt the overwhelming urge to apologise, to apologise for every disdainful thought she had ever had regarding him. She was also incredibly frightened, because if what he said was true – if he really *was* as intelligent as them – how could that be? Where would that leave them? What had they done?

Guy's red face seemed to grow hotter, even under the cold blue lights, and Charlotte was ready to move out of the way of any physical confrontation. She was pregnant, after all. As it happened, Roman was the next to speak, and his thick New York voice seemed to sooth everyone listening. "I agree, Martin. It's outrageous. It's unfair. Everybody should have been told, and they will be." He looked at Charlotte, clearly expecting support, his large workman's hands outspread, as if in surrender. "The time will have to come where we start treating everyone equally, won't it?"

Roman's calm exit left a tangible awkwardness behind, and for a few moments everyone just stood in silence. Martin was the first to speak, and Charlotte realised that he had not expected any kind of result at all – he hadn't thought that far ahead. He muttered something about that being all he wanted, and left the room far more quietly than he had entered it.

Roman

Back in the solitude of his quarters, Roman Smith couldn't stop shaking. The problem was, he supposed, that Betters and Sups had been actively encouraged to live separately, and now, they weren't. He had never believed, as had others, that Sups were a different *species*, but he knew that many others did. At least, he *supposed* other people thought that; it would have seemed out of place at best, treason at worst, to question the Cause, and none of his friends had really mentioned it anyway.

Besides, his status on the ship had served him very well. For the last six weeks, hoards of beautiful young Supplementaries, supple and firm, had frequented his sheets. He had watched them drink in the luxury of his life, absorbing the muted colours of his walls, the enormous bed, the copious rations. The bargain had been a simple one: you show me a good time and you shall have one in return. Of course he never said that explicitly. He wasn't a monster.

 The end to the party came when Lucy, a lovely little Sup with grass green eyes and jet black hair, had leaned over to him and whispered that she might love him. She had stroked his face and stared into his eyes, and he had wondered what she was waiting for. He just couldn't enjoy it after that. The bargain had suddenly become very unfair. It had become unfair because those girls didn't know he was incapable of loving them.

 He'd never be capable of loving anyone else. Squinting into the blurred stars, he wondered where she was, and what she was doing. He remembered her testing day. They had been seventeen when the testing had been introduced, and they should have been fine. Nicole was an absolute genius with a computer, better than he had ever been, but she had failed all the same. His last memory of her was a quick peck on the cheek before she left for testing. See you later; you'll be fine, he had said. It had been far from fine. He had waited for her for hours, in the same place as always, cramming himself between the makeshift tents that covered the surface of what was once Central Park. For some reason, the Panel authorities had so far left this area alone, possibly because it was so densely populated with Supplementary escapees that a simple sweep of the area would not have sufficed. The two of them had liked to see the Supplementaries who had gotten away: couples in love; skinny children; harassed families and worst of all, the loners. They never said so, but he and Nicole were thankful that they were not lost in the universe without someone to cling onto, and they looked at these loners as a warning for what could happen if they were not careful. For these people – so many of them old – their years had been said and sung and there was nobody left to care. These people would simply sit, for hours on end, providing a backdrop to the activity around them. Roman and Nicole had never thought that they would fall into the background. They were young, bold and talented and the world was theirs.

It was only when he never saw her again that he realised how disgusting their fascination with these people had been. The spectacle they had watched, aping sympathy, had been a sideshow reminder of their own luck. As the years went by, he started to think that there must have been something wrong with her, after all. He started to believe that her

110

limited intelligence had drawn her to these people, and he had just gone along with it. He remembered how she had clung onto his arm and whispered, "Roman, you and I are different." Perhaps she knew all along that she would end up there. If he tried hard enough, he could almost persuade himself that he hadn't enjoyed her company, that he hadn't loved her at all.

As soon as the Cause was declared in North America, it was deemed that the kindest and most efficient way to deal with the Supplementary Human issue was execution. The Panel had boasted that *they* did not use euphemisms as inhumane regimes in the past had done – *they* were honest and knew what was best for their people. So she was dead anyway, or so he thought. He erased the memory of her and convinced himself that he had been mistaken in ever loving her. The runaways in Central Park were caught and killed eventually, of course. He wasn't sure how, thinking about it years later, but at the time his heart had somehow suppressed the horror.

Years later, only a few months ago, in fact, he had been asked to help in selecting the Sups to assist the technicians on Eve One. The desk was scattered with hundreds of profiles, stating basic information as well as a mug shot. Hundreds of emaciated faces, trapped in small rectangles at the top of the page, stared at him, like distorted stamps. She was there, staring up at him in the midst of them, miserable and broken. Her chestnut hair was dank and greasy, and there were enormous bags under her brown eyes, but it was her. His heart had raced, and he had almost let an uncharacteristic gasp escape, but had managed to keep his voice casual. "What about her?" he had asked, pointing at the face he had once known so well. The woman filing the chosen documents sniffed. "Oh, no," she had said, "that one developed some kind of bone disease a couple of years ago. Very weak and brittle. Zero breeding potential. No good to us. Can't believe that one has been left on the pile, actually." She turned the face he knew so well upside down and the love of his life became a blank page.

And that had been that. Looking back, he wondered if he should have pushed the case further, argued her technological knowledge, but there was nothing he could have said. Gazing into the distance, he wondered if she was still alive, somewhere, and whether or not she ever thought of him. That she had escaped was impressive enough, but that she had gotten over to England, where Supplementary policies were less severe, was an absolute marvel. He had been wrong to think her not good enough. Perhaps he *was* a monster.

"A penny for them." Recognising that Amy had learned yet another British idiom, Roman smiled. At least there was her. During their training at Kolwick, she had made a habit of simply walking into his room and making herself at home, and he liked it. She wouldn't have called it sneaking, but her ability to travel anywhere like a ghost meant that was essentially what it was. The end result of her stealth was that Roman felt like Amy could appear at any given time, and that gave him a genuine sense of comfort, like she never really went away.

As his lovers had so recently, Amy threw herself onto his bed and sighed, but everything in her manner was different to those young girls. She was so polished and neat compared to them, like a particularly expensive racehorse. Her blonde hair was scraped against her scalp in a manner that Roman thought made her look too severe. He would have liked to loosen it and watch the golden locks tumble down her shoulders but he couldn't; he respected her too much for that.

He had watched all of this in his window, observing her greyed reflection. Next to hers, his image was squat and unattractive. Despite the sheen that the glass provided, his stubble and knotted hair were a dirty blonde against the gold of hers. She raised an expectant eyebrow. He hadn't yet given her his thoughts. "I can't stop thinking about what that Sup said earlier," he replied simply.

Her back stiffened. "Me, too. Do you think we ought to report him? I was frightened!"

He doubted that. To the best of his knowledge, Amy wasn't scared of anything. He wished he had a cigarette. She was clearly on a different page to him, perhaps reading a different book entirely. "That isn't what I mean. I think he might have had a point."

A half-smile flitted across her face and, had he not turned round to stare at her, he could have sworn that would have become a laugh. Roman sighed; he liked Amy for her cold practicality – perhaps he even needed her for that very reason – but that was not what he wanted to see from her on this occasion. She turned the smile into a shrug, "Perhaps, but there is nothing that can be done."

"They've been lied to, Amy, on every level. We could tell them the truth, for a start." He could see that what he was saying bothered her, and he didn't care.

Throughout his speech, Amy remained composed - in fact she hardly moved - but she furrowed her brow and seemed deep in thought. "Telling them the truth would just be dangerous, Roman. Nothing would change but over half of the ship would be angry. At us."

He sighed. "It would be dangerous, but not *just* dangerous. It would also be the right thing to do. We haven't done the right thing in so long."

This time she did laugh. "Speak for yourself. And anyway, it's not *right*, Roman, it's," she looked up as if the right word would find her there, "it's *silly*. They wouldn't understand anyway. It would be a waste of everyone's time and energy. Just leave it as it is."

He looked away again, and replied to her graceful reflection. "No. I'll be careful, but I think that they are far more like us than we know. They deserve to be told."

Amy flicked her hair, and he was reminded again of an elegant filly swishing her tail. "Oh, Roman. I do wish you wouldn't." She smiled, as if to indulge a childish request of his. "Cleanse your conscience, if you must. Just don't drag the rest of us down with you."

****

When Martin answered the door, Roman immediately took in the bare room that was his quarters. Nobody said a word, so Roman simply edged his way into the room and sat on the bed; there was nowhere else to sit. He ignored the neglect and apathy that had created this room, and tried to focus on the two human beings who lived in it.

114

The silence had been expected from Martin, but the handsome young man with the afro, who Roman did not know, clearly sensed an atmosphere. Roman felt a pang of guilt as he saw fear in this young man's eyes. Did he expect some kind of admonishment? For what? Simply existing?

He looked at Martin. "Time dilation?"

Martin's gaze was level. "I haven't said a word."

Roman leant forward, interlocking the fingers of one hand with another, forming a giant fist. "No. Quite right. I'll say it."

Charlotte

Some hours later, she was still struggling to process what had occurred. The silence and comfort of her room were welcome after the intense confrontation, but Charlotte was still attempting to decide why she was so upset. She had a great deal of respect for Martin, yes, possibly more than she should, and she had disliked Guy's treatment of him. She was also riled by seeing Martin so passionate, so angry: she wasn't aware he harboured such emotions. What confused her most of all, however, was that she had never fully considered the implications of this so-called equality amongst all the crew members on Eve One. Nobody had said so, but it was *clear* that the Sups were not equal to them, so why say it? Why ignore something that is staring you so strongly in the face? *"Either you see it, and you're a hypocrite, or you don't and you're fucking idiots,"* had been his exact words. Those words had been aimed at everyone in the room, her included, and that hurt her more than it should have done. She had spent the past two hours wondering which statement applied to her.

He had entered her room many times before, and he did so this time in exactly the same manner, in respectful silence. This visit was very different to his first one, though. He had always avoided her gaze but he did so now out of shame, it seemed, rather than respect. The aggressiveness of the afternoon had passed, and he seemed frightened. It appeared as if he wanted to take up as little space as possible, hunching his muscular shoulders into nothingness.

116

Usually the first to speak, Charlotte started to realise that something very significant was happening, and she was scared to start the conversation.

He took a deep breath and she saw him physically shake. "Mrs. Dawns, I hope that you will accept my sincere apologies for my behaviour this afternoon. Had I known you were in there, I wouldn't have entered like that. To be frank with you, it was the first Betters area I encountered. I wasn't thinking. I'm sorry."

Every sentence that she started in her head wouldn't come. He was apologising to *her* and nobody else, despite the fact that she had treated the Sups unfairly also. Eventually, she managed, "Thank you, Martin. I realise I haven't been entirely without fault also. I believe that, until recently, I have still used the Sup label with you, for example."

Apology over, she thought. They could return to work tomorrow with no awkwardness, but he still stood there, struggling with some internal debate that she couldn't even guess at. He continued, "What I wanted to say, really, is that I don't see you in the same way as I see all the others. You have always been kind even when you didn't need to be and I'm grateful for that. Whatever happens next, I want you to know that."

Her drive to reach Oscar 70 and make the mission a success had taken over everything in her life. Charlotte had known that for a long time, and it hadn't been an issue. What she now realised, though, was that the man in front of her was the closest person to her in the universe; he had shared her work and listened to her self-indulgent musings for hours on end. She had barely seen Karen recently, who had been preoccupied with preparations in Eve One's Birthing Lab, and Charlotte had noticed no loss, no void. Perhaps that had been because of Martin. This had never occurred to her, let alone the idea that she meant something to him also. Despite her renowned bravery, her reckless wish to hurl herself and others through the universe, she was terrified to know what that might actually mean.

She decided to be brave again, and ask something that she may regret later. "Can I ask you, Martin, what you really think of me? Can I ask that?" She looked away. "Of course I can't. I'm sorry."

Martin smiled. "But that's just it! We are supposed to be *equal!* You *should* be able to ask me." He threw his hands in the air, seemingly giving up on a conundrum that he just couldn't solve.

He was halfway through the door when she heard him say, "For what it's worth, I think you're wonderful."

Martin

Roman's declaration to the Sups spread like wildfire. Everywhere Martin turned, there was talk of mutiny. Although he had endeavoured, his entire life, to fight against the label of Sups being intellectually inferior, he was ashamed at the idiocy of some of their plans.

The day after the news broke, Olivia had been sitting with him in the eating area, picking at the dried offerings of the day, something that Martin believed was meant to resemble fish. They were surrounded by white plastic tables and white walls, gleaming and new, but what was clearly meant to produce an image of cleanliness and order in fact seemed to create mass stress and headaches amongst the Sups at their table. The food was actually better by far than anything he had eaten on Earth, and he had gained some weight, happily, in his month and a half on the ship. Olivia, however, seemed less impressed, and if anything her appearance had become gaunter of late. On that day, she simply moved her fork between the flakes of food, turning them into an even less recognisable mush; this displeased Martin greatly, and he was only stopped from asking her to give her food to him, if she was so intent on wasting it, by her speaking. "These Betters need to be taught a lesson. I say we kill them in their sleep — their doors don't have locks. We can then turn around and go home."

Her friends around the table had pointed out the several flaws in this plan: nobody else knew how to steer the ship, let alone land it, and that was if they were able to convince over 100 people to commit mass murder. So we should at least hold them to ransom, was her response. And so it went on. Aaron, a mild-mannered Sup who couldn't have been more than 17, advised caution. "After all," he concluded, "If we kill the people steering the ship, we'll die. No two ways about it. Travelling as fast as we are is complex shit. We need to respect that Dr. Dawns knows that better than anyone."

Olivia sneered, and her lip curled upward revealing pearly white teeth. She looked like a predatory tigress defending her catch. "Ask Martin. His woman knows how to drive it, I'll bet."

Martin did not rise to the bait. He and Charlotte had been a source of teasing for several days now, and he would have loved to roll his eyes and imply there was some truth in it, which of course there wasn't. Instead, he looked meaningfully at her bottle of strong beer. Eve One was packed to the rafters with luxury contraband items, the idea being, one supposed, to take as many items from Earth as possible to this brave new world, and many Sups had never even tasted alcohol before and were rapidly becoming accustomed to its pleasures. He couldn't help but criticise Olivia's relaxed sips, "Surely beer isn't the best idea for you? I thought the advice was that pregnant women shouldn't drink."

Olivia shook her head and released an ugly guffaw. "Not that I'd be fussed anyway, and thanks so much for your concern, but it's not an issue. I lost it." Martin had heard talk in the medical room that the reversal of the sterilisation procedure had not worked properly on many Sups; there was even a belief being casually bandied about that it was "unnatural" or "nature fighting back." Martin rather believed, however, that the pregnancies had been ended deliberately and this

120

certainly would not have surprised him in Olivia's case. She smiled and placed her hand firmly on his arm, shrugging carelessly when he inched further away.

A stark contrast to the previous fortnight, Travis seemed to shrink into the corner of the group. Even his vibrant black skin had reduced itself to a grey pallor, and his lips formed a thin line rather than his confident, white-toothed smile. He looked at Martin with an expression of blame, possibly even hatred, and his shoulders slumped so badly that he resembled an octogenarian. Martin said nothing, but offered Travis what he thought was a supportive and empathetic smile. Travis turned his entire body away and did not speak for the entire meal.

Eventually, they decided to challenge Doctor Dawns Junior about the lie at the weekly meeting. They would refuse to comply with their role in the voyage unless he agreed to their terms. What these terms were was beyond Martin, but he was certain it involved more freedoms and fewer controls than the Betters were willing to agree to. Olivia leading the revolt could only end badly.

In the days following this, Martin was to consider his lack of action in these events very carefully. He could have done more to prevent what was to come. As it was, Martin simply sat as far away from Olivia as he could possibly manage, and attempted unsuccessfully to make eye contact with Travis.

****

On the morning of the meeting, Martin was strangely nervous. He did not consider how much his capacity to care had increased in the last six weeks. Almost certainly, he did not want to pinpoint the reason. What he did admit to his frantic mind, though, was the fact that he did not want Charlotte to come to any harm. None of them had any idea how far this rebellion was going to go, and it seemed a very real possibility that violence could occur. He thought about her unborn child, nestled and ignorant in her stomach, a being that had also been denied freedom and choice. Why he should want to protect this child was beyond him, but he found himself trying to steady a racing heart.

It was 10.05am when Doctor Daniel Dawns approached the platform and declared the meeting open. He opened, as always, with a few brief business notices regarding crew duties, and then proceeded to plans regarding settling on Oscar 70. The strategy was to acclimatise Sups to "bite size chunks" of life on the planet, largely through the speeches of Daniel Dawns, in their weekly meetings. Martin was barely listening as Dr. Dawns instructed the audience to prepare themselves for tropical heat and asked them, yet again, to refer back to their specific duties. "As you are aware, Oscar 70 is a tidally locked planet which is in close orbit with Star Four. Many areas of the planet are totally uninhabitable, at present, but we are headed for the Paradise Strip, which has excellent conditions for humans. Charlotte Dawns chose this area carefully as our eventual destination. Many thanks for your hard work on this, Charlotte. The temperature will be a steady 25 degrees, although it will be cloudier than you are used to. One thing that you may struggle to adjust to is the constant daylight; of course this sun will never move in the sky like the one on Earth. Eve One's pods are well-prepared for that. They will land on the planet and form temporary living spaces, capable of creating an artificial night-time necessary for your physical and emotional well-being..."

Dr. Dawns' speech was eventually drowned out by a murmuring in the crowd, and Martin craned his neck to see Olivia wind her way through the chairs to the front. Why she had not claimed an aisle seat he had no idea, but a guess would be that she wanted to create as much fuss as possible in her walk to the centre of the room. Either that, or she had not really planned her speech as much as he had hoped.

To look at her, in the centre of two hundred chairs, looking up at Dr. Dawns' platform, you'd be forgiven for thinking that Olivia had lived her entire life for this moment. She spread her arms, claiming as much space as her small frame possibly could, and declared, "Dr. Dawns! This mission has been founded on lies! The Supplementary humans on this ship were told that we were all equal, and yet we are equal in nothing!" Martin was impressed by her opening eloquence, but quickly realised that these sentences had been rehearsed. What followed was a selfish rant. "The female Betters on this ship have all sorts of contraband make-up! And my room is simply *awful!* My one on Earth was better! And our toilets *stink!*" Her shrill sermon continued, but became impossible to hear above murmurs of either approval or dissent.

Things were unravelling quickly, and they were being made to look like fools. Aaron, who had so far seemed seriously invested in this speech, appeared to panic at her digression and interrupted. "Sir, what my associate is trying to say is that if we are really your equals, we should have been told about the implications of the mission, and we should be offered equal resources. We would like to discuss the

123

current living arrangements on board Eve One, as well as discussing the possibility of some kind of formal apology." Not for the first time, Martin noted how eloquently a Sup could speak if required. Unfortunately, nobody heard this eloquence, and Aaron's voice was drowned out by a cacophony of grumbles and exclamations.

Daniel Dawns seemed to be getting hotter and hotter under this scrutiny. He had clearly heard something of Aaron's speech, and his words became garbled. "Apologise? Surely, you don't mean it! I'm the creator of Speedlight, the reason you are on this mission. I am the hope of the entire human race! I don't apologise!"

There was a murmur from the side the Betters were standing. Somebody was moving away from the crowd, and Martin detected several mutters of disapproval.

A solitary voice declared, "You really should, Sir."

Silence. Martin span round to find the origin of the voice, and he had to suppress a smile. Charlotte was standing a good distance from her peers, staring fixedly at Dr. Dawns Junior. It occurred to him that, at this moment, she was every bit the opposite of how she had been in Richard Dawns' office. For the first time since he had known her, she was not afraid of confrontation with those she sought to impress, and she was fighting for the greater good.

She walked slowly towards him, as if approaching a man with a gun. "You should, you see, because these people thought they were sacrificing everything for our mission. Because we lied to them: they are actually sacrificing more." It was remarkable how gracefully she moved, given the sphere in her middle. Her slight frame seemed to click sideways with each step, but the passion in her voice put paid to any physical challenge. She continued to approach him carefully, and steadily, as if she had not fully decided yet why she was moving. She carried on, "They have been subservient and respectful, they have not argued until now. I think we should have told them about the intricacies of time dilation because they are a part of Project Eden and were therefore deserving of such respect. They are now our equals and it would be hypocrisy to keep them in the dark." The dark. Martin closed his eyes. He felt at that moment how strongly they were accelerating through the dark. All of them were.

He looked at her again. She was doing well, really. Her breathing was steady and her voice was barely shaking, but Daniel Dawns had the upper hand, because his behaviour was what everybody expected. Therefore, when he called for an end to the meeting, and for Charlotte and himself to meet in private, everyone else was forced to simply wait, and consider the implications of what had just happened.

What followed was around fifteen minutes of waiting and gossiping, which made Martin tired. He was certain that they would hear nothing more tonight, and he was also quite certain that they had failed. If he had gained anything from this embarrassing ordeal, however, it was the knowledge that there was a Better who had their interests at heart, so perhaps all was not lost on this alien world. That this advocate of theirs was Charlotte was all the better. Over the previous two days, Martin had developed the habit of spraying just a small amount of *Madame* onto his shirt sleeve, and smelling it at intervals throughout the day. He told himself that this was his one small indulgence – it was an appreciation of a luxury he would never have dreamed of on

Earth. Had he thought more deeply about it, he would have been forced to recognise that he simply wanted to carry the scent of her with him. Its freshness and depth made him feel alive.

He was one of the first to leave the meeting room and return to his quarters. He had not noticed Travis's absence in the meeting room, being preoccupied with nerves and embarrassment, but walking into his room now, he knew where Travis had been. Immediately, Martin tried not to blame himself. Of course he wouldn't have noticed his roommate's absence; Travis had been a shadow of his former self in recent days. But he should have known. He should have helped him. Seeing Travis swinging from the bunk, Eve One's regulation black leather belt cutting into the soft flesh of his neck, Martin knew he should have helped him. Travis's eyes were cold and accusatory. They seemed to say something to Martin, something he already knew: *On Eve One, the truth kills, and love kills. Avoid both.*

****

The day after, Daniel Dawns called for a second meeting. Daniel Dawns and Karen Dawns sat at the front facing their audience, and they both looked sombre yet purposeful.

As he had done the day before, the young doctor stood and faced his audience, and Martin was reminded of their first day on Eve One: his stance was less ostentatious than it had been on that day, but he was nevertheless confident and poised. The giddy enthusiasm had vanished, and what remained was more focused and serious.

Dr. Dawns glared at his audience, "Something very serious has happened, and it is up to the civilised amongst us to maintain order. I hope you see now that we had not shared the intricacies of our mission with you because we wanted to *save* you. Travis Sanderson was unable to cope, intellectually, with the demands placed on him by the complexities of time dilation, and he is now dead. I hope this tragedy will go some way to encouraging you to trust us. After careful thought, I have decided that the Supplementary label should remain, for your own protection." He ignored the grumblings from the crowd. "This is only, however, a temporary measure and future obedience may alter this. The time will come to discuss the possibility of expanding our team of Leaders to include a Supplementary Human, but that time is not now." Martin felt the familiar pang of anger, that heat in his stomach, but yet again he remained still. Daniel continued, "And we ask you to trust us yet again, in the name of the noble Cause for which we left Earth. I assure you now, we do have your best interests at heart, and, when we reach Oscar 70, there will be resources aplenty for us to share."

He paused, and regarded the audience with hawk-like eyes. "But for now there is not an abundance of resources to share, and we must be patient." A further pause and shuffling of papers. Daniel Dawns coughed, and it became clear that there was something more to come, something worse. "It has come to my attention, sadly, that somebody has not been keeping to their own resources, and has in fact been stealing from the Betters. To steal is to go against our most sacred belief systems. If you do not share resources, you are not a true believer in the Cause."

Martin felt like he had stopped breathing. The perfume. So Charlotte had reported it. That was why she wasn't there. Every neuron in his brain was alert and ready. He took a breath, ready to muster some excuse or reason, but before he could, Olivia was dragged into the middle of the room by some crew members he did not recognise. She was struggling and spitting like a captured fox and it took three grown men to keep her still.

Doctor Dawns continued, "Stealing will not be tolerated on this ship. Olivia Drake, you are charged with the theft of beauty products from the Betters' quarters. Luckily for you, every human life is precious on this ship, and the law on Oscar 70 will be formed to foster life, not expunge it. But your child is already lost, so I'm told, and you must be controlled before we land and decide on an appropriate course of action. You are therefore sentenced to a period of Suspended Sleep until we land on the planet."

The horror on Olivia's face made even Martin, who had little regard for her, feel sorry. Suspended Sleep had been the brain child of Doctor Richard Dawns, of course. It had been originally designed to enable crews to pass long interstellar missions in a safe state of unconsciousness, even restricting growth and ageing, but initial testing on Supplementary Humans proved its many dangers. It was therefore kept as a punitive measure and a deterrent, a way of keeping unruly crew members in line.

Everybody on board knew how dangerous Suspended Sleep was; an injection slows the heart rate and puts the body into a death-like coma, often to dangerous levels. Few tests had been carried out but it was common knowledge that Suspended Sleep could cut a human's potential life span in half, and that was if a waking heart attack did not kill you, which it often did. A hush fell amongst the crowd and Olivia's bold and spiteful face crumpled as she begged for her life. The tigress became a trapped kitten, and Martin was glad that she was being held by guards because her thin legs could surely not have held her upright. Daniel Dawns' voice continued, confident and levelled, "And I do not want any of you to think that this is due to the events at the recent meeting. This young lady's outburst was unfortunate, and does not help her case, but to steal is to not be part of a shared society, and that we cannot tolerate."

Martin couldn't look. Every fibre in him knew that he should say something, utter some defence or even confession, but he did nothing. Excuses in abundance flooded his mind: nobody would believe him; Charlotte needed his support; the mission needed him and Olivia had contributed little; theft was a cover story to control Olivia and his confession wouldn't stop that... The truth was, of course, that he was scared. Just as he had been when his parents had saved him, now this unlikeable but nonetheless honest girl was saving him by unknowingly taking the blame for his crime. He told himself that Olivia had already doomed herself and he couldn't stop events. As she was dragged away, he decided that the moment had passed. Even then, he knew it was unlikely that he would ever manage the guilt of what had just happened. Numbly, he supposed he had to find a way.

Charlotte

After her glorious rebellion, Charlotte allowed the terror to sink in. It was obvious to her that she had crossed a line that she was unaware even existed; she had defended a Supplementary, publically, before a Superior Better. Not only that, but this Superior Better happened to be responsible for the mission and therefore in control of *her* destiny. With a growing panic, she realised that Daniel Dawns had really no choice but to put her in Suspended Sleep; it was certainly what she would do, if she were in charge. What she expected he would do to the Sups made her blood run cold.

Leaning against her beloved curved window, she looked at the blurred landscape of nothingness passing them and breathed deeply. Her petite chest heaved angrily against the cold glass, and all she could smell was the fresh oxygen clinging to the edges of the room. Jealously, she imagined it escaping and scattering itself into the enormous vacuum beyond. Her stomach, once more curved against the window, suddenly felt so fragile under her small hand, and she imagined the baby with a consciousness, hating her, blaming her, for allowing it to be propelled through space to an unknown destination, for allowing them both to become felons in the eyes of their new civilisation.

She hated the animal growing in her stomach, and she knew that it would resent her for her foolishness. Why would you, when handed every privilege in the world, throw it away? And soon that animal would tear through her flesh, leaving her broken and sore, before it started to consume every resource she could offer.

But how would the labour happen if she was in Suspended Sleep? Would they wake her for the event or simply operate as she slept? Would she become a mother without knowing? Would mother and child both die in the process? Cursing her overactive mind, Charlotte continued to race through a thousand possibilities. Just as terribly, she had always fantasised about the views when the crew *see* Oscar 70 for the first time, the cries of excitement, the sense of accomplishment. Suspended Sleep would rob her of that, as well as the ability to say that she was a part of the mission through and through.

"My dear, dear girl!" Charlotte noted a flurry of ginger hair and musky perfume as Karen Dawns burst through the door, her face even more lined than it was a few hours before. In the absence of her father, Charlotte realised that Karen was exactly the person she wanted to see, and she ran to her, allowing muttered regrets and apologies to pile on top of each other like bricks. She crushed herself with each word. Karen's only response was to hold her close and shush her like the baby she always wanted.

Charlotte was unaware of how much time had passed, but she was jolted back to reality by the phrase "Suspended Sleep." She closed her eyes and asked Karen to repeat herself.

Karen sighed, and smiled indulgently. "Charlotte, my sweet girl, I was just explaining how angry Daniel is. He loves you dearly, as I do, but he feels that you have just undermined him in a very extreme way." A tender smile punctuated

Karen's version of admonishment. "But he does love you, as I do, and the mission must continue."

Charlotte hung her head. If only he hadn't sent Karen to deliver the news. The horror of those unconscious months started to creep into her heart.

"So he's putting that Sup girl in Suspended Sleep until we arrive. Of course we told them it was due to her stealing – we found so much expensive make-up in her room, some of it must be stolen - but I actually think it's the only way to prevent a mutiny. When we arrive on Oscar 70, the laws regarding Sup status will continue, to control worrying behaviours. No more nonsense about equality. They don't know this yet, though."

Charlotte thought a moment. She knew that she should try to defend the innocent Sups like Martin who deserved better, but the relief of being safe, along with her baby, flooded any good intentions she might have had. "I thought that he would put *me* in Suspended Sleep too."

Karen smiled that maternal smile yet again. "Of course not, my darling. You're far too valuable to the mission. We need you, and would *never* put your precious baby at risk. And anyway, to punish you when a mere Sup can take the blame is simply nonsensical."

Feeling the anger rise in her stomach, Charlotte had to remind herself that Karen wasn't to blame for thinking in this way. Of course it made more sense to put Olivia into Suspended Sleep, not her. So why was she so furious?

She tried to think of something to say, some way to stop the terrible order of events. All she could manage was a weak protestation regarding how Sups were now equals, how resources were no longer an issue.

Karen smiled indulgently, "It's our fault really, Charley. We raised their aspirations. We gave them lofty ideals that their limited intelligence couldn't cope with." She shrugged as if apologising for giving a spoiled child too many toys.

Charlotte's slow realisation that she was responsible for her life of luxury at the cost of others was becoming ever stronger. She took a deep breath. "No, Karen. We have enslaved a group of people and they are starting to realise it." Another deep breath. "I am starting to realise it."

Karen's laugh was the most irritating sound Charlotte could have heard, but what she said carried a weight that Charlotte could not have imagined Karen could carry, "I *have* realised this before, as you put it. Every Better has realised it. But ask yourself this: what harm have we done, really? The Sups on this ship were happy before they knew the truth! Is a person a slave if they don't know they're enslaved?"

Charlotte paused for a moment. "Yes, Karen, I rather believe they are."

Karen stared into the void beyond the window, and rolled her eyes. "You need to stop behaving like a child, Charlotte. You were always such a good girl – you never had your youthful rebellion. Now is not the time to begin. You need to stop being so self-indulgent and concentrate on the Cause. There is not *enough* for everyone. Rather them than us."

Charlotte was flabbergasted. "You think this was all a tantrum? You think I don't care about the Cause, after dedicating my life to it?"

"I don't know, Charlotte, but I do think you have been spending too much time with your Sup servant and not enough time with *me*. I forget how impressionable you are. But you need to wise up." She faced Charlotte now, her gaze unwinking, "All I do know is that our husbands have worked their entire lives to make this mission a success, and you have nearly destroyed that in less than five minutes! "

A pause. Charlotte did her best to sound like she was not sulking. "It's been my lifetime's work, too."

"Oh, please! You are too young to know what a lifetime is!"

Karen had never spoken to her like this. Charlotte sensed that, in these words, lay years of resentment. It could hardly be helped that she had been able to become pregnant, that she could equal Daniel's intellect, or that she had enjoyed a life of encouragement and support. The resentment in the air was tangible and, Charlotte believed, entirely unjust. With a sick feeling, Charlotte realised just how alone she was. No parents to support her, no Karen and Daniel, she had only Martin and the Sups to defend her, and they probably hated her most of all.

Her first instinct was to go and tell Martin the news. When she considered how he would never be viewed as an equal to her, her chest hurt.

Martin

The day after Travis died, Martin shaved off his beard. He couldn't have said why if anyone had asked him; perhaps it was simply to do *something* as a mark of respect. Or it could have been that Travis's death had changed everyone aboard Eve One, irreparably, and Martin needed some physical form of acknowledging that. Had he been brave enough, he would have created some form of tear or scar in his skin, something to convey damage done and never forgotten. As it was, he stared hard in the mirror at chiselled features and a youthful complexion. His blue eyes sparkled more with anger, and he cursed his own handsomeness. The fact of the matter was that he valued his appearance - he owed his position on the ship to this very thing. And yet he hated it. As Travis floated, helpless and lifeless in space, Martin enjoyed the comfort of Eve One and a perfect complexion. The desire to claw at his alabaster skin was equal to his need to be attractive to Charlotte. It was all he could offer.

He wished he could pinpoint the exact moment he had fallen in love with her. Really, he had always known it, ever since he had observed her pride and determination back on Earth, but more recently, he had found her need to help the Sups on board very brave. Charlotte had grown up, he reflected, without an enemy in the world, and it would be so simple for her to continue into a life of comfortable obedience and compromise. But she had stood up for something that didn't even affect her: she had lain herself on the line for a group of people who hated her. That was before he considered her understated beauty, her charm, her intelligence... He almost

135

laughed at his wandering mind. He had never, since the death of his parents, allowed himself to believe that he loved anyone, yet the first woman he fell for was so unattainable it was laughable. He closed his eyes and imagined ever telling her his feelings, putting his hands on her flesh, being on a par with her. Travis had been right - he was a fool to think the distinctions could ever have been blurred.

And yet any more *appropriate* pairings (and, given the lack of people on the ship, these were few and far between) he shied away from. A few weeks ago, Olivia had entered this room and attempted to seduce him. She had walked in without knocking and sat on his bed as if it was hers. Martin remembered her callous confidence and her absolute certainty that he would *want* her. Although she never touched him, there was something in her manner and conversation that was far too familiar. He didn't want her, and he had treated her very coldly. Her predatory nature and selfishness had irritated him: how ironic that it was his selfishness that had put her into Suspended Sleep.

Only hours ago, he had been performing safety checks on the Fuel Points and had walked past the Suspended Sleep room. Going in, he had seen the chambers laid out like digitised coffins, but only one was lit. Like all the lights on Eve One, it was a calm sky blue but nothing about it made Martin feel calm. Of course she was lying there. He could not have really expected that she wouldn't be. Entirely naked and without make-up, Olivia's artificial beauty had been stolen from her and Martin reflected that was far worse than the theft of any object she had supposedly taken. Her teeth, pearly white yesterday, were a matt magnolia like the walls, and her thin lips were partially open but no breath escaped. A stubborn

136

acne was visible on her chin and her closed eyes were covered with stubby orange lashes. Seeing her like this felt like a betrayal, and Martin considered how she looked like an emaciated Sleeping Beauty. Rather than clutching a rose, however, her fists were clenched at her sides, fighting still despite the fact that she had already lost.

His thoughts of Olivia were interrupted by Charlotte knocking at the door. He had known it would be her before he even answered.

She was nervous, he could tell, so he made it very easy for her. He simply smiled and gestured for her to come inside. She took in his surroundings, probably considering how they were so much less accommodating than hers. He had known that she would visit, and he was ready to apologise for overstepping the mark. Whether or not she would replace him as her assigned Sup he did not know, and he wasn't sure if he'd be relieved if she did. To go further in this friendship – alliance – whatever it was, was surely dangerous, but why stop? What could either of them really lose?

It could only have been a moment or two that she paced his small room, but Martin was starting to think that he should just apologise and put her out of the misery of trying to be polite. In her presence, silence was something to be physically felt. It pressed down on him, threatening suffocation, and he was too weak to fight though the thickness to reach her – to actually say something. Finally, she said, "You think I'm wonderful."

He hadn't expected *that*, and for a second he struggled to find a response that wasn't the apology he had been preparing for. "Well, I certainly do now. What you did in front of all those people was pretty wonderful."

"It didn't *feel* wonderful. It felt stupid. I've never done anything like that before. Everyone is going to be so *angry* at me. I'm probably going to lose my position, and it has helped nobody."

"So shines a good deed in a weary world."

Charlotte looked puzzled. He had forgotten that, despite her intelligence, she had probably never even heard of Shakespeare. Very few people had, after all. He shook his head. "Never mind. I suppose I'm trying to say that the *majority* of people on the ship are not angry with you, but I suppose they are not 'everyone,' are they?" His love of her really was impossible, he reflected, because *she* was impossible. How could the view of someone so bright be so – dim?

"But I've made it worse for you all. It's all going to be terrible now!"

"It was terrible before, so no harm done." He attempted to laugh, but that thick silence stopped him once more.

He hadn't ever considered how young she was until this moment; her idealism was clearly under threat and she didn't know how to cope with that. "But Oscar 70 is going to be different! It's going to be the perfect solution to an overpopulated world."

He was aching to disagree, to tell her how naïve she was.

As it was, she continued in what Martin thought was an attempt to convince herself, rather than him, "When we get there, it'll be different. Karen and Daniel are angry now because they feel vulnerable in this ship when so much is still uncertain, but when we are there, I can convince them to allow equality between Sups and Betters again. You'll see."

Martin spoke slowly, measuring each word, "Charlotte, you are here because, I think, you care about my opinion. If you'll permit me to say, I think you are very wrong about the Dawns. They are out to serve their own interests, not yours, and certainly not mine. I don't think we will ever be united enough in our interests to be successful in any kind of," he struggled for the right word, *"campaign."*

She clearly wanted to sit somewhere – anywhere – but her options were limited in such a small space. She eventually perched, awkward and round, on the edge of the lower bunk – Martin's bed. He suppressed an urge to sit next to her. She continued, "I know what you think of the Dawns, and I'm starting to agree with you in almost every way, apart from their past kindness to me. I was embraced as a member of their family for many years, and that is hard to turn away from."

"Even your husband?" Martin remembered Charlotte's look of horror as she faced Dr. Richard Dawns in his office.

She shook her head. "He was different. Work and nothing more." Martin couldn't help but notice how she stroked her stomach as she said this. Where was the line between life and work drawn for Charlotte? He felt like he would never know.

Her intelligent eyes had not left his, and he really wished that she would look away. It had been a long time since he had been this honest with anyone, let alone a Superior Better, and the danger of feeling like he *trusted her* was growing daily; it was an uncomfortable feeling to say the least. She continued to stare at him as she spoke. "Martin, you mention common interests, but I don't even know what your interests *are."* That silence again, closing in on them, as real as the air they breathed, "Like those words you said the other day. What were they?"

He shrugged, "They were just words, Charlotte. Written down by somebody lost in time."

He could tell that she was not satisfied. He felt his cheeks grow hot, and he started to wonder if someone as pale as him could ever outwardly blush: he doubted it but could not be sure. She continued, "But you remember those words. Why remember strange phrases written down by a dead person? Phrases that don't make any sense..."

"Because they are beautiful, Charlotte." He allowed himself a glance out of the small window above the top bunk, only to be greeted, as always, by blurred constellations, diamonds on black. "Just like you think Oscar 70 is beautiful; I think words can be beautiful, even if they were written down by somebody that I will never know."

She stood up and regarded the window also, and he immediately saw something light up inside of her; she knew what beauty was. He was certain that she knew what love was. Despite this certainty, or perhaps because of it, he felt awkward with her standing there, less than an inch from touching him. He still felt something akin to excitement when she finally asked him, "Will you tell me some of those words? I'd like to hear them and judge for myself."

And so he told her, and the hours rambled on without them. He told her of Tristan and Isolde, Heathcliffe and Cathy and even Romeo and Juliet. As he spoke she occasionally stood to look through the window, drinking in his words and the stars in equal measure, her fragile hands stroking her swollen stomach.

Finally, his throat was dry from talking, so he stopped. When his words ended, it took Charlotte a moment to move from her trance and when she did, it was slowly and painfully, as if waking from a deep sleep. When she spoke, her throat was also dry, "But those people all suffered, Martin. They suffered terribly."

Finally, something they could agree on. "I never said that they did not suffer, Charlotte. I told you that their love was beautiful."

She smiled, and he saw, in that simple curve of her lips, a youthfulness that he thought had died on her wedding day. "Yes. Yes, it was."

Aaron

The luxuries offered to the Supplementary travellers on Eve One surpassed any form of luxury that they had known on Earth. Rooms that were shared by only one or two other people were a real novelty for many, and the cleanliness of the ship and food available rendered many of them wide eyed and humbled for weeks. Aaron had seen the others taking in the ship as if visiting a museum, pacing the corridors in a dreamlike state; he had found it embarrassing, and would certainly not like any of the Betters to see him behave like that. His roommate, a boy two years his senior called Frankie, spent hours sleeping on the soft bed, breathing in the clean sheets and enjoying the softness. He much preferred to enjoy his luxuries alone.

To this end, Aaron spent a lot of time in the shower. Despite a vague knowledge of Eve One being encased in water, to shield the travellers from radiation, he had no idea how the water supply worked. He expected some kind of restriction to be imposed eventually, but nobody had ever said anything thus far so, for at least twenty minutes a day, he would stand under the hot stream of recycled water, allowing it, in all its opulence, to thunder onto his head, his back, his muscular shoulders. He would feel the grainy softness of the soap bubbles in his hands, finding it hard to get used to the chemical smell but being reassured by its overpowering cleanness all the same.

He couldn't recall the last time he had been so clean. Because the Expansion had happened so quickly, Supplementary Units, like the first one Aaron attended, had been intended as temporary residences. Any and every available building no longer deemed relevant to the Cause was used. It just so happened that Aaron, after failing the test, was moved to a hotel.

It must have been a luxurious venue in the Before Years. The room Aaron shared with three others had a comfortable double bed and even a bathroom, although the water only came on for one hour in the morning and was cold. Squares and rectangles of fresh paint indicated where there had once been a fridge here, a television there. Luxuries of a bygone age.

Aaron had been one when testing had been introduced, so he'd had nine years to prepare. He had always known that he would fail, though; his teacher, a friendly young brunette who was too softly spoken to wield any real authority, could not help her forty-five strong class. In any case, it wouldn't do to help any child too much; the Panel valued natural talent. Lessons were Science, seven hours a day, and he'd never understood a word. He tried, as had the others, for he had known what was at stake, but in the end he was lost. Parental support was a dead end for him also; he doubted that his most recent foster carer even knew his name.

Therefore, he had failed. Of course he had. He packed his bag before he even left for the Intelligence Testing Centre. He knew what they would say: we have decided what we need and it is not you. In some ways, he was looking forward to the honesty of it; nobody had ever needed him but they wouldn't just come out and say it.

He had thought he might have friends there, but friendship was too tiring. All Sups on the unit were required to

143

complete at least twelve hours Cause duties per day, so by the time they were packed into their beds, the only thing they had cared about was reaching oblivion: at least oblivion was better than life.

Mrs. Love, the Better who provided care for Aaron's unit, if 'care' was the correct word, had organised for them to work in the landfill sites for their Cause duties. He remembered her frosty voice, reminding them that the presence of the landfill sites was down to people like them: people who didn't work for the Cause and simply lived to produce waste and take good resources. She would sit on a chair a few feet away from where they were working, holding her worn copy of the Old Testament; he didn't think she ever read it. Their task had been simple; they were to sift through the waste that the Betters had produced and harvest resources. Once he had been beaten for throwing back a mouldy loaf of bread into the pile. "Good enough for you," she'd said. He had a vague memory of her forcing him to eat it, but he'd eaten so much rotten food in his life, he couldn't swear that this specific memory was true.

A month or so after that, he remembered returning to the foyer and being asked to line up in his underwear along with the others. At sixteen, he had felt awkward and skinny in his regulation white boxers, greying and thin. The other Sups in the line looked equally awkward, with many of the females holding their arms crosswise and tight over naked breasts. He remembered a middle-aged blonde woman, her suit a fluorescent pink, swaggering down the line and muttering yes or no to man scurrying behind her with a clipboard. Occasionally, she would poke a Supplementary with her jagged fingernail, testing the subtlety of their flesh, he supposed. She had stopped at Aaron and took in everything about him; he would always remember her weighing up his vulnerable and naked body with her eyes. She had chuckled, but the joke had been entirely lost on him. "Oh, yes. This one will do," she had said. Her fat legs continued their buckled path, and he heard her further down the line muttering similar comments to people who he did not know well enough to call friends.

So at least the ship was clean. In his first few days on Eve One, he had decided to simply enjoy that. It was only later, much later, when talk of rebellion was in the air, did he start to consider the desire for more than hot water and soap. Thoughts of desire led him to thoughts of Aru. Perhaps it was inevitable that so many beautiful Sups would be forced on the mission, but Aaron had been unprepared for the beauty of some of the Betters. Aru had quite simply taken his breath away. When he had been told he would be working for the ship's Senior Medic, he had expected a Richard Dawns type figure, humourless and aged.

Aru was different to anybody he had ever met. Her skin, silken chocolate, glowed under the blue lights of Eve One, an intense blue that matched her eyes. She had been kind to him, said please and thank you. He had only known her for two weeks, and yet he already knew that he would do anything for her.

A sharp rapping at his door cut his shower short, and as he exited the booth quickly, he could not suppress his resentment. Even if it was *her*, could she not wait until his shift started?

It wasn't her. Instead, almost as beautiful and certainly as accomplished, standing there, was none other than Charlotte Dawns.

Numbly, Aaron stepped aside to allow her in. She had never spoken to him before, and he was aware, painfully aware, of his total inability to start such an unlikely conversation. He was therefore resigned to wait for her to speak to him, awkward in his navy towel.

The room was full of steam, but if Charlotte noticed it, she did not say. Instead, she folded her arms and paced the small room. "Where is your roommate?"

Quickly adopting his formal tone, Aaron replied, "Out, Mrs. Dawns. He is four hours into his shift, I believe."

She continued to pace. He started to wonder if he was in some kind of trouble. Why else would she be here? She inhaled deeply several times before speaking again, "I am sorry to trouble you in your non-working hours, Sup Aaron." She stopped walking. "Aaron."

He nodded. She was very polite, but she looked so unhappy. An earlier version of himself would find that quite amusing: one of the most powerful people in the world being unhappy. Well, good, he'd have said. Not today. Today it made him uncomfortable, like he was part of her unhappiness.

Finally, she continued, "I am looking for some information regarding Martin Huthwaite."

Aaron felt a familiar sickness, "Is he in some kind of trouble?"

She reddened, "No. Nothing like that. I'm just trying to fill in some detailed character profiles of all the Supplementaries that are on the mission with us."

"Wasn't that done before we left?"

"Not to a good enough standard, in my opinion."

Aaron gestured to his bed, and, stiffly, she sat on it, her back a ninety-degree angle to her feet, flat on the floor. When he started speaking, he could see her drinking in his words, and he knew that she wasn't really filling in any kind of report.

"Not much to tell, really. He narrowly failed the test, or so he told me. His family are all dead, or so he told me. He's a closed book, I'm afraid. Are you sure there isn't more on his file already?"

She seemed suddenly embarrassed, "Do you know, I think I will check it one more time. So sorry to bother you."

As she rushed out of the door, Aaron smiled. Perhaps his fondness of Aru wasn't quite so out of the ordinary, after all.

Martin

Until his arrival on Eve One, Martin was hardly familiar with the concept of 'spare time,' but the reasonable working hours that the luxurious ship afforded gave him stretches of it, which he found rather hard to fill. After several weeks, he had accepted Aaron's invite to his quarters. If they ever reached Oscar 70, Martin supposed that there would be time in abundance to enjoy, so it might be worth getting some practice in early. He imagined aimless days and having a choice in how to fill them. It was hard to do. To this end, he and Aaron started to play cards once a week.

Martin was good at cards. He had played with his stepfather as a child, and he almost always won. He had some memories of playing five-handed bridge with his complete family, but those memories were like a blurry fiction to him now. There was something defensive and strategic about playing cards, something that chimed with his soul, but it seemed that Aaron had a natural skill too. He had never played with such a well-matched partner, and the hours would slip away as they battled out Blackjack, poker and gin rummy. The stakes were nothing more than pride, but that was a high enough prize. The cards were battered and bent at the corners, with famous Earth landmarks on the reverse side. Martin had memorised every single one, which helped, of course.

They happened to be free at the same time at the end of one night shift, close to four in the morning, and had arranged a quick card game before sleep, but when Martin arrived at

Aaron's quarters as planned, he had found Aaron in bed with that beautiful Indian girl.

Idly, Martin had just walked in – none of the doors on Eve One had locks – and he had frozen to see her. She had been in a sitting position under the white sheets, and she simply turned to him and smiled. She looked like a beautiful statue, untouchable and perfect, and he had resisted the urge to throw something at her. Had it been a Better that had walked in, it would not be her that was punished, but his friend. Her stunning looks did not cover that hypocrisy.

She had laughed, as if she had been caught making a childish error. Throwing Aaron's shirt over her gorgeous body, she kissed him lightly on the mouth, pardoned herself, and left.

Martin let her past, and remained motionless, his hand on the door. He simply stared at Aaron, awaiting an answer.

Aaron sat up in bed, his cheeks red. He ran his hand though his brown hair, spiked with sweat. "Don't blame her. It wasn't her. She resisted me for a while." He looked for some clothes as he muttered, avoiding eye-contact, "I love her."

 "She'll ruin you."

Aaron had found a dressing gown, and was busily tying the belt. On Martin's words, he laughed, "Ruin what, exactly? I have no free will, no options, no *life* to call my own. If what I feel when I'm with her ruins me," he turned to face Martin, finally, "so *fucking* be it. It's worth it. I've been ruined for a long time."

****

Martin had spent some time pacing the corridors of the ship, after that. He didn't know how long exactly he had walked – he wasn't timing himself. Like Aaron had said, he had no free will, no life of his own. What if he walked until he died? Nobody would really care that much.

He supposed he was angry at Aaron because he had looked so happy, lying on that bed with her. He had, quite literally, lain with the enemy. The thing that made Martin angriest of all, though, was how wonderful it had looked. As a couple, they were beautiful, and yet every authority on Earth would have them destroyed for what he had just witnessed.

Every authority on Earth. He needed to adjust his thinking. They were no longer on Earth. Like Aaron said, anyway, he had been behaving like he had something to lose. She was a Superior Better. She was married to *Richard Dawns*, for Christ's sake. But he had nothing to lose. Aaron and Aru had looked wonderful on that bed.

He watched his strong hand knock on Charlotte's door, and felt his lips smile when she answered it, but he was in another place entirely. The line between excitement and panic was invisible; he knew what he was going to do, but not how she would respond. She was wearing a white silk nightgown, like Victorian women wore, and she looked so pure, despite her swollen stomach. He wanted to touch that silk nightgown more than he had ever wanted anything. Her black hair, usually tied tightly behind her head, was loose and limp on her shoulders.

"Mrs. Dawns," he laughed, coughed and started again. What was he doing? Aaron was disgustingly handsome, perhaps he could get away with such behaviour, but not Martin…He was close to backing away, but his mere presence at her room, at this unholy hour, warranted an explanation, "Charlotte. I'm sorry to disturb you, especially at this time…"

His words died on his lips. How to explain feelings that he could not explain to himself? Everything in his body told him to back away, avoid the danger, but she was so beautiful, and not even angry to be woken by him at such an hour. She simply waited, smiling calmly, for him to speak. Looking at her then, her fragile hand on her large belly, her soft hair knotted and loose, her skin soft and pink, he knew he would never back away. He knew that having nothing to lose made no difference. She was worth losing things for.

"I've just seen something that would shock you. Can I come in?"

He didn't name anyone, but told her, quite calmly, that he had seen a Sup and a Better making love and what did she think about that? She listened without interruption, never taking her eyes off him, stroking her stomach all the while as she sat on her bed watching him pace the room. Eventually, smiling, she said, "You told me some beautiful stories the other day, stories about a magnificent love that made people suffer. Was this like one of those stories?"

His eyes did not leave hers, "I hope not. Truly, I do."

She patted the bed softly. He wasn't sure if she had invited him to do so, but she did not seem shocked when he sat a few inches away from her. Every cell in his body felt alive, with fear, with excitement, with desire. He did not know what would happen but Aaron was right – it was worth it.

151

She measured her words carefully, speaking gently, a mother before labour, "Everything is changing, Martin; we are on the cusp of a new world, in more ways than one. I would hope that Oscar 70 would never stamp out something beautiful, like love." She placed her hand on his, exhaling in a half laugh as she did so. "Is this all right?"

He was suddenly embarrassed, "Yes. That's all right."

She looked at their hands, interlocked, "I'm pregnant." He nodded, and she continued, "I'm married to the most powerful man on Earth."

He smiled, "Are you planning on going back to Earth anytime soon?"

Without warning, she grabbed both of his hands and kissed him stiffly on the lips. Had he dared to fantasise, it would not have been like this; her hands were clammy and cold and he was so taken aback at first that he stumbled backwards and she jarred against his chest. Soon, however, he found that his arms seemed to fit perfectly around her shoulders. He had not kissed a woman in a long time, and never a woman he cared for. On the contrary, when in the care of the Panel, if one could call it care, he had delighted in making women love him and then hurting them. It had been a hobby.

He didn't want to hurt Charlotte, though. He breathed in the scent of her hair and he thought at that moment that he had never smelled anything so beautiful. His kisses tore into her. As his excitement increased, so did his sense of wanting to undermine her purity. Yes, he wanted to feast on her beauty, and her social acceptability, but, by touching her, he knew that he was also destroying those very things, and he was certain that what was hidden underneath those things was better.

When the moment had passed, Charlotte still clung to his hands. Had she not, he may have considered the kiss churlish, a juvenile way to prove her point. As it was, she expressed regret but he knew she didn't feel it. She covered her mouth, "Martin, I'm sorry. That was totally unacceptable."

He said nothing, but smiled at her to indicate that unacceptable was far from what it was.

They sat like that for a while, looking at one another, judging what would be the correct next move. Suddenly, as if remembering something he had forgotten, Martin blurted out, "Charlotte! It was me who stole your perfume! I'm sorry – I don't know why I did it, really." He saw her staring at him blankly and continued, "So if you think I'm capable of being a hero, you're wrong. It wasn't Olivia who stole it, it was me. And I don't even know why. I didn't defend her and she's in Suspended Sleep because of me."

It was Charlotte's turn to be careful and weigh her words. "Do you think that Olivia was punished for stealing my perfume? Martin, I didn't even know anyone had taken it; I thought I'd lost it."

He should have felt relief, but the fact was that he had still been a coward, and considered himself unworthy of her. Despite that, he didn't turn away. After a lifetime of never getting anything he deserved, he felt some kind of justice in finally getting something he felt unworthy of. He smiled and kissed her again.

Charlotte

As the weeks turned into months on Eve One, Charlotte's relief that Martin had not been put into Suspended Sleep grew daily. They would wake together each morning, the gentle hum of the ship massaging them into waking. Lovemaking had been at once blissful and difficult; Martin was clearly more experienced than her, and he took control with a slow and gentle understanding. Approaching her thirty-ninth week of pregnancy, though, Charlotte was embarrassed by her lack of grace and swollen stomach. Martin never said a word about this, instead opting to plant gentle kisses all over her relaxed body. He had the air of a pilgrim finally reaching his destination, and she could not help but enjoy his adoration of her.

She had only ever been with two men, and Martin was so different to Dr. Dawns, who had fucked her with hands and teeth and nails. Martin was gentle and untroubled in his lovemaking, but something about his touch electrified her skin, and turned her desire to the point of pain. It wasn't enough to kiss him and stroke his skin; she needed to bite into his smooth flesh and taste him, whilst leaving no mark on his perfect complexion. Everything about him was magnified. The sight of his pale neck became synonymous with her need to plunge her hands inside his shirt; she wanted to sink her fingers into his hair and claw at the muscular bulge of his upper back. With a shock, she realised that she had never wanted anything quite so badly as to be in and share his physical presence. If she were asked to choose between him and Oscar 70, she would choose him.

Perhaps it was the freedom of not being bound to Earth, but they had told each other everything. Charlotte's heart had ached as Martin told her of his youth, being beaten by his father until his mother was brave enough to run away, and then of his own runaway story, which had ended in a devastating tragedy that she could barely imagine. She thought of her own parents, living their days on Earth in comfort and safety, and she wanted him to know how that felt – to know that somebody you love is safe and that they don't need to run from anything.

She had intimated as much to him one evening as they lay on her plush bed, the universe speeding past them outside. He had been thoughtful for a moment, before he turned to face her. "What I don't understand, Charlotte, is how you could ever leave them, if you love them so much."

She considered this, "I don't see how *staying with them* is the same thing as loving them. I've made them proud and they are happy. I'll never see them again but they know I'm going to be one of the first people to land on an alien planet. In fact, they know that I'm the Associate Scientist on the mission that may save Earth's expanding population. There aren't many people who can say that about their daughter."

"But it's not the same, is it? They'll miss you. They'll never know how the mission ended."

She looked out of the window, imagining how old her parents would be if she turned back right now. She didn't want to know the answer. "I imagine they'll miss me terribly. I miss them, but it's for a bigger cause."

"If you believe in the Cause."

She didn't want to enter into yet another argument about the Cause, so decided to say nothing and nuzzle closer into his chest. He clearly wasn't to be deterred, however, and gently moved her away. "I suppose my issue is how you could leave someone you love so easily. I haven't had anyone to care about for a very long time." His voice became jokey, but she wasn't convinced by it. "I just want to make sure you won't leave me so easily."

She did her best to not be offended. "It wasn't *easy*, Martin – it broke my heart."

"But there was never any question."

She considered this. "No. Never. Not really. They understood why I was leaving and that was enough. They didn't punish me so I don't see why you should."

Her anger started to subside, and in that moment she realised that she could never leave *him* – he had become, to coin a phrase, a part of her. She paused. "You see, I love my parents – loved them – love them. But in many ways the relationship between a parent and child is a dead one. Do you see that?"

"No."

"I suppose what I mean is you are always meant to say goodbye to your parents; they create you because you are the future and they know that it is the way of things to be left, eventually. I simply accelerated that-" Martin looked like he was about to interrupt so she continued quickly –"but with you, I'm not *ever* supposed to say goodbye to *you*. I know you don't trust my judgement but please try to trust this." She placed his hand on her heart. In doing so, she remembered black and white love films she had watched as a child and imagined that this was something a sultry heroine on such a film might do, but more naturally and confidently.

He sighed. "That's just it, Charlotte. I *don't* trust your judgement. I trust your integrity, yes, but not your judgement. It's just that, I'm trying to understand your relationships. You're wonderful – I've used that word to describe you many times, but you surround yourself with people who are, frankly, *hateful.* You're carrying Richard Dawns' child, for example. I'm just trying to make sense of that."

"I've tried to make sense of that a lot too." In the grand scheme of things, it wasn't so unusual anymore – most women on the ship were pregnant – but she was now so close to the end, she supposed, he had a right to question her about it. Unlike the other women, too, she had gotten pregnant the traditional way. "I think the best answer I can offer you is that it was a silly mistake. You know all about those, yes?" His silence gave her the confidence to continue. "I think I tried to surround myself with successful people to make myself more successful. You know, I knew even then that it was wrong. I left my parents and I know you consider that unwise but it just felt *right,* and I don't regret it now. I can't think, honestly, that I could have ever done anything but board this ship. I think-" she was suddenly embarrassed, but steeled herself and said it anyway, "I think I was born to be with you."

She wasn't looking at him when she said this. It was by a long way the most romantic thing she had ever said, so her stomach lurched when Martin went a step further, "Charlotte, I was born to love you too."

She smiled and laughed a tinkling, frail chuckle. "That's not exactly what I said, but it's the same thing."

Martin's face was suddenly solemn.   He wrapped his arms around her too tightly, like he was trying to erase any space between them. "No it isn't, Charlotte. It isn't the same thing at all."

Despite her feelings for him, there were many occasions when she did not understand Martin, and this was one of them. Had she asked him to clarify, she sensed that he would have ruined the moment with some ill-placed pessimism. She opted instead to close her eyes and enjoy this moment of measurable closeness in a cold and immeasurable universe.

Martin

Olivia had set the Sups back a long way. As Martin waited outside Aaron's room, he was aware of the need to tread carefully. Any more ill-advised tantrums or explosive outbursts would be the end of any campaign to receive equal treatment, which was why he had decided to approach Aaron. Despite his youth, Aaron had a solemnity in his manner that Martin found reassuring; there was something at once very appealing and serious about him. Whatsmore, he would want equality between the Sups and the Betters just as much as Martin, and for exactly the same reason.

"Oh, hi, Martin." Aaron, towel-clad, had clearly just been showering, and Martin took in his trim stomach and well-defined muscles. Clearly, the improved diet on offer on Eve One had been serving him well. He could see why Aaron had been selected for the mission. He was a fine specimen of a human being; his spiky chestnut hair positively shimmered with health, and his green eyes sparkled with a fierce tenacity. Unlike Olivia, the spirit inside him was purposeful and positive. Martin liked few people, but he had decided rather quickly that he liked Aaron. Aaron squinted a little as he waited for Martin to speak. "Can I help?"

Martin gave a deep breath. "Yes. Yes I think you can help. Can I come in?"

They spoke for over an hour, but after the hour, they felt ready. They were going to invite the Leaders to a meeting to discuss terms calmly, as equals. None of the full room chaos of before. They would ask for equal rights upon landing on

Oscar 70, and they would also like to have at least three representatives on the Leadership Panel. They would outline their terms calmly and without threat, but if their terms were not met, they would make it clear that it was a large planet, and they would seek to form a separate settlement once landed.

Aaron's optimism was striking. "Seems reasonable enough to me. After all, we aren't asking for anything more than we were originally promised. And if we don't get it, we aren't going to plunge into a full scale war. We'll just walk away, and take our freedom with it."

Martin was not so sure, but he didn't say so. He had several reservations about the Leaders' capacity to simply agree to the terms they had already decided were unreasonable. Equally, he didn't believe that the Sups would be allowed to leave without a fight. Earth law still applied, and they were the property of the Betters. At the same time, though, Charlotte was on the Leaders' Panel, secretly hating it every single day. At least they had one ally.

Aaron gathered up the papers they had been writing on. "Well, Martin, it's a big day for us tomorrow. I shall go and speak to Dr. Dawns in the morning and arrange a meeting."

"No. I'll go."

Aaron shrugged. "What do you think they will do? Flay me alive?"

"No. But we know what they can do." He suppressed a shudder as the memory of Olivia in the Suspended Sleep room rose to the surface, "I don't want to put you at risk when all this was my idea."

160

"Have you told Charlotte?"

Martin was silent. He hadn't been aware that Aaron knew about him and Charlotte. After so many years of carefully concealing his feelings, he had assumed that the only people who knew about his blossoming relationship were him and Charlotte. He dropped his eyes, "I shan't tell her, no. She has already put herself under unnecessary risk on our behalf. She has the worry of the birth to occupy her. This isn't her fight."

Aaron frowned, and Martin was again reminded of a man well beyond his years. "I don't know how far I agree with that. It's everyone's fight. There are so few of us in the world now, we should look after each other. Just look at Olivia and Travis."

But he didn't tell her, and the following morning when he knocked on Dr. Dawns' door, it was Karen Dawns who answered. When her eyes met his, they were impassive and cold, much like they were the evening before Eve One set sail. It seemed that she had been expecting him, or someone like him, and she simply stood, arms folded, waiting.

"I wondered if I could speak to your husband, Mrs. Dawns."

"No, Sup Martin 81873. My husband is otherwise engaged. Any information you have can be passed to him via me."

He had not anticipated this. Had he considered that Dr. Dawns may not be there, he and Aaron could have prepared a written agenda, formally outlining their terms, to pass on. He cursed his single-mindedness in considering this too late. However, Karen Dawns was on the Leaders' Panel; she would have to do.

He coughed. "You see, Mrs. Dawns, Aaron Moore and I have elected ourselves as-"

"Who?"

He decided not to rise to the bait. "Sorry, of course I mean Sup Aaron 726501."

She smiled, a smile Martin had seen so many times in his life: a school bully who has enjoyed a particularly good punch. He carried on, feeling a passion rise in his stomach that made his backbone that bit more rigid, "We have elected ourselves to speak on behalf of the Supplementary Humans on board Eve One."

That smile again. "Elected yourselves? How...democratic."

"We represent their interests, certainly, and we request an audience with the Leaders to discuss certain issues regarding our status."

Karen was immobile for a moment, retaining exactly the same pose as she had adopted when answering the door. "Could this sudden interest in preserving your status be anything to do with my sister-in-law?"

Martin felt cold. He and Charlotte had been so *careful*. He had entered her room late at night and left early in the morning. They never spoke in public outside of their professional commitments. How could she know? He had been interrogated many times in his life, so he had enough experience of it to know that lying was futile, but nevertheless the only thing to do. He hadn't felt like a trapped rodent in such a long time, he had almost forgotten the feeling. How much easier life is when you do not love anyone, when nobody can be threatened and taken from

162

you. His voice was significantly smaller than before, "I have no idea what you are talking about."

The smile for a third time. "Of course not. And of course we would be happy to discuss *terms* with you. As my husband has stated, we want to protect and save your people; you have nothing to fear. Come with me."

Charlotte

He was always on time, and today he wasn't. Today was going to be a bad day. At five past eight, five minutes past when he should have reported for duty, she was already frantic. She knew already, of course, so why had she done nothing? Her genius IQ had done nothing to teach her how to read people, and what they are capable of.

The Suspended Sleep room had two lit capsules. She knelt beside the second one and wept like a funeral widow. She stayed there for six hours, clutching the glass. For the next two and three quarter years, she visited him each day.

****

With Martin gone, Charlotte took to pacing the corridors of Eve One in the manner of a drunkard looking for home. She had been so organised before the mission, everything on the ship was set up beautifully and only needed to be monitored. Monitoring took only moments, and then the days were empty chasms. It was only then that Charlotte realised just how much the Cause had defined her; the terrible thing about achieving your dream is no longer having a dream to feed your heart. Her room was spotlessly clean, the antimatter drives were ticking away nicely and she was a madwoman scoring the walls.

Even the enormity of space was becoming uninspiring to her aching heart. She leaned against her window regarding the complexity of the universe that met her face on, but realised, where she hadn't before, that she could not control it. She could not control anything. She had ideas, yes, but they served a purpose that was not hers, they fuelled a ship that was not hers. She was forced to admit to herself that her ideas were propelling her and a group of strangers to a planet that would never be hers, either. The only thing that was even close to being hers was the child that was writhing within her and kicking her innards, anxious to break free of her also. Perhaps, once, she could have claimed Martin as hers, but he had been taken away as well.

Often, she would recognise the familiar heat and wetness burning her cheeks. She cried without knowing, and it had occurred to her that crying was now part of her existence, as natural as breathing. She cried soundlessly, knowing that no other human being in her world could help anyway. The only person who would understand her tears was Martin and he was lost to her.

When Aaron entered her quarters and saw that she was crying he didn't say a word about it. She was thankful for this, though perhaps less happy about it when she considered how his motives for being so disinterested were doubtless the blame he placed on her for Martin's current situation. Further tears threatened to surface, but she held them in. "Yes, Sup Aaron?"

"Are you not aware, Mrs. Dawns? I have been designated as your assigned Sup for the remainder of the journey." His cold professionalism was exactly what she needed.

Her voice was level: a poker voice. "Thank you, Sup Aaron. As a matter of fact, I'm rather glad you're here. I wonder if you could fetch a medic."

She had been in labour for several hours at this point. She had woken with a dull ache in her stomach which had progressed to what felt like a pair of fists clenching her abdominal muscles to the point of internal bleeding. She couldn't care less about this. She and Karen had barely spoken but she was sure that the Dawns would take the baby away from her, given recent events. She would feel intense pain, she was sure, but it would be over. It could not compete with the intense emptiness she constantly felt anyway.

A balloon seemed to be expanding in her petite stomach and there was no room for it to grow. Pain shot up her spine and across her middle in an unrelenting attack. The pain was so severe she was sure, for a moment, that she would die. All the better. She closed her eyes, and started to think that she would never open them again. Aru delivered the baby, as planned. Her sharp face hovered over Charlotte as she writhed in agony. At one point, she thought that she had her arms spread as if to catch a ball, but that could have been fantasy. All she could recall was the very real expectation that her body would fail her, nothing could hurt this much and be deliberate, and then all of a sudden, her pain was over.

Until the drugs wore off. What followed was days of soreness and exhaustion. Her breasts swelled to painful rocks which she ignored. To feed her child would be to enter into a camaraderie she wasn't ready for, and Karen was all too willing to hold the baby close and feed him with formula, closing her eyes and imagining the artificial teat the baby suckled on was hers. The Dawns named him Christian, and Charlotte had shrugged in assent. She regarded the child, a fragile mass of rose-coloured wrinkles, and she did feel an urge to hold him, to press him to her naked chest. She didn't dare, though, for fear of loving him too much before he was taken away from her. Easier to walk away, let the inevitable happen.

Too late, she realised that she had lusted for someone to share her discovery of Oscar 70 with, but this person was not her child. Every morning, she would open her eyes and remember how she was alone. It wasn't so much the blackness of the sky as the emptiness of her room that told her this. As it happened, she never saw Christian. Karen and Daniel were all too happy to remove her burden; she would occasionally see them in the communal areas and they would attempt to speak to her like distant relatives at a wedding, but their company was strange to her. Everything that was once familiar felt like white noise. As the boy grew from a babe in arms to a smiling and chubby toddler, they had started to keep their distance. Charlotte could hardly blame them. Even she could see that her cold indifference undoubtedly had an effect on the child. Happily, she was not the only disinterested mother on Eve One. Seven months after Christian's birth, fifty-three Sup women bore healthy babies, to then be impregnated again, an ordeal that the Better women were spared, happily. Nine months on, fifty-eight more babies followed. Scores of these children spent many an hour in the Birthing Lab, cared for in identical booths and soothed, changed and held by robotic arms, watched over as ever by a serene Karen Dawns. Christian simply received more attention than them: everything else was the same.

Charlotte didn't care. She didn't care about anything, really. The hours between waking and sleeping were vicious hurdles. Her fantasies, which had once involved discovery and celebration, had become fantasies of seclusion and reflection. Every day, she felt tired and bored. Every night, she felt relieved that oblivion would soon welcome her.

****

The day that they reached Star Four's system was a day like all the rest. When Sup Aaron entered Charlotte's quarters and brought the news, the news that she had of course been expecting, she didn't know what to say. Recent weeks had filled her with a new purposefulness; reaching Oscar 70 meant waking those who were in Suspended Sleep, and that filled her with dread and delight in equal measure. She felt like she herself was waking from a long sleep, and she did not know that she would like the person she had become when she was fully awake.

The ship had been slowing down for almost a year, but now, looking through her magnificent curved window, the mission finally felt real. 250 miles above the planet, she had expected to see its rich brown land and lush greenery, but the orange clouds covering the planet were thicker than expected. She had anticipated a new Eden – a more fantastic and younger version of Earth – but the stationary dust ball below made her feel empty.

Because this was just not how it was supposed to be. She had always imagined being at the centre of a celebratory crowd, champagne in hand, receiving loving applause, when they got this close to Oscar 70. She would look and see the brightness and opulence of the most beautiful planet in the universe.   As it happened, she clung to the edges of her precious ship and prepared for descent into the unknown. Alone.

Part Three: The Light

"The fault, dear Brutus, is not in our stars,
 But in ourselves, that we are underlings."
William Shakespeare, Julius Caesar

Prologue

Eve One floated above Oscar 70, much like she had done on Earth, but her view had altered. Locked close to its Red Dwarf sun as the moon is locked to the Earth, the habitable side of the planet would never see darkness, and few people noted the irony of how a group of intrepid stargazers would never look upon a night time sky again. The rust-coloured clouds prevented the landing travellers from seeing much, but as they descended, the clouds parted, a red sea, displaying a landscape very different to Earth. There were so many colours: red; gold; green; blue and white in blurred strips adorned the planet. The group were headed to the band of green and brown in Oscar 70's outer circle: The Paradise Strip. The crew members' minds raced with the possibilities of a world of constant tropical heat and perpetual day.

Eve One's twenty landing eggs floated downwards and connected to the planet's surface in a graceful whisper. They formed a cluster of white on the ground that rendered them, yet again, invisible in the universe.

After years of high-speed movement, the travellers were now still. A common purpose and shared enthusiasm would have led to a settlement and eventual colonisation.

As it was, Oscar 70 had been populated for one minute and it was already at war. Many of Eve One's crew did not know this, but their ignorance was not to last long.

Karen

They had spent thirty Artificial Days, or A-days, on the planet, but the term had hardly caught on. In that time, Karen had discovered over 1,000 different species of plant, and was well on her way to cultivating around fifty edible ones. The fruits that grew on Oscar 70 were voluptuous with liquid and they boasted a wider palette of colours than any she had seen on Earth. This had been a surprise. Initial research implied that the plants on Oscar 70 would be darker to store the optimum amount of Star Four's light, and they were darker, but the colours were richer also; it seemed that the plants took on a life of their own, almost as if they were sucking goodness from something other than the planet. They varied in taste greatly, but mostly they overwhelmed her with too much sweetness. To her, they seemed a condensed version of what they should be – never tasted or appreciated before. Several had been poisonous, and tester Sups had spent many hours fighting sickness in their assigned pods. No deaths yet, happily: people were few and far between nowadays.

And yet she was glad that she had put the boy into Suspended Sleep. Alone, he was merely a handsome face with a half decent intellect, given his Supplementary status. With Charlotte, though, he was positively dangerous. She had never seen Charlotte as blissful as she had been on the opening of the journey, and that displeased her greatly. To be in love with a Supplementary would lead to nothing but blurred boundaries and civil unrest. Especially *Charlotte.* She would never physically see her husband again but she had a responsibly to uphold the iconic Dawns image. Karen felt sick

173

as she considered the girl's ingratitude and immodesty. She had done the right thing to intervene. And besides, the Supplementary problem needed to be dealt with. As Karen sliced into the maroon earth, she felt Star Four beat on her back and reminded herself to reapply the UV protector. She was accustomed to the extra precautions by now, but it was still difficult to get used to the constant sun on the horizon, never moving, never setting. Because this cooler sun was so much closer to the planet than the one on Earth, it was over twice the size in the sky, and it seemed to stare at her constantly, a vermillion accusing eye.

The earth gave under her blade, sandy and hard despite the recent tropical downpours. They would be waking him around now. She smiled to remember how easy he had been to manipulate. He clearly had ideas beyond his station, imagining himself as some kind of hero, so when she had hinted that Charlotte might be in danger because of her association with him, he had positively begged for Suspended Sleep. About time, Karen thought as the blade dug into the earth again. The coward's parents had died for him, for no good reason: it was about time he stepped up to the mark. She had seen that in him, of course – that all-consuming guilt. All it had taken was the sentence, *"If this unhappy pairing becomes known, lord knows what could happen to her and the child."* A shame they needed to wake him, really, but to be seen as fair and just was critical now. She wasn't fool enough to ignore the danger of 123 angered Sups.

Still, it was likely that his body would be so weakened by the process that he wouldn't last long. Or at least his fighting spirit might be abated a little. Perhaps he wouldn't even wake up, she thought deliciously. That would be the ideal: to

174

be seen as magnanimous and yet still be rid of the burden of him. She dug harder and more ferociously than before, planning, always planning.

She heard Daniel's approaching footsteps but didn't look up. For several minutes, he simply stood and observed the sky as she did. When she didn't say anything, he placed a hand on her shoulder, nodding eagerly. "Marvellous."

She continued to dig and in doing so, freed her shoulder from his clutch. "Yes, I Suppose it is."

Best not to make the conversation easy for him. Looking at his agitated manner, she knew he was worried about Charlotte. He had spent nearly three years worrying about Charlotte. He kicked the dirt around his feet, and his white shoes turned yellow. "I wonder if I should see her."

"I expect she'll be busy."

"Karen. What happened to you? You used to love Charlotte. I'm sure she'd welcome a friendly face right now."

As always, she didn't answer. Because of course she couldn't answer truthfully. She couldn't say, 'I changed because I realised why you didn't want me to come' or I've needed a friendly face all my life and never got one.' Instead, she simply said, "I think she's needed a friendly face for the past three years, not now. She's about to wake him and all she will care about is that." She threw the spade down, more from exasperation than exhaustion. "Go and see her, if you must. Or is it just that together, they are a threat to us now?"

Daniel continued to regard Star Four's invasive gaze. "Oh, I don't think they will threaten us again. We nearly broke her on the ship, Karen. Giving her this little piece of joy back,

175

broken and damaged as he is, is the smartest thing we could have done."

She managed a tired grin. "Well, at least we agree on that."

He placed his hands in his pockets and rocked back and forth using his heels. Karen wondered how she had never noticed how *animated* he was before; perhaps the emptiness of the planet magnified everything he did. He made her feel tired. He avoided her gaze. "It's just that – darling – putting him to sleep, waking him. It's so…" He waved his hands in a manner that reminded Karen of his father – "It's so *untidy.*"

She smiled. "Daniel, do not worry. They will not pose a threat to us. I guarantee it."

"Yes but how-"

"I guarantee it."

Daniel started to turn away, but on doing so, seemed to remember why he had initially ventured outside, taking the plunge to leave his beloved office. "Oh, darling. Can you please give Christian some attention this afternoon? He's been spending too much time with those Sup children and it really isn't good for him."

Martin

Martin's first sensation was one of extreme heaviness, as if his limbs were filled with liquid metal. For what could have been a matter of several minutes, he lay still, terrified to open his eyes, determined to savour the delicious heat and stiffness of sleep. As the black behind his eyelids turned hot pink, he noted the absence of a glass dome surrounding him, and he instinctively searched his body for the gentle hum of Eve One. In many ways, Eve One had been connected to Martin like a soul mate, a fellow loner in a massive universe; he would later swear that he had felt its smooth movement even when in deep sleep. Perhaps that was why he now woke, because after thirty-four months of interstellar travel, he felt no smooth movement, no gentle hum. He was stationary, and, realising that there was now no glass dome to shield him from the evils of this world, the nausea and ice cold feeling of expectation took over. With a start, he took in his surroundings. The beige carpets and magnolia walls of Eve One remained, but beyond the window he saw luscious green vegetation and an amber sky. Tentatively, he approached the window, a thick dome above him, reminiscent of the ovoid curves of Eve One. He was in one of the ship's landing pods, serving its purpose as a makeshift habitat on Oscar 70. He was in one of the smaller rooms, but it was clean and comfortable and warm. He realised that he was in fact very warm, and his clothes stuck to him like melted plastic. He had been put into Suspended Sleep naked, but now he was wearing, yet again, the regulation Eve One white suit, thick and unnatural in this environment.

Strapped to his wrist was a red rubber device with a flashing green light, which he assumed was some kind of tracker. He made a mental note to ask about it later.

To walk to the window was torture, as Martin dragged his limbs from months of stillness, but to reach his destination only brought him further pain. He knew that Charlotte had cherished the ambition of arriving on Oscar 70, of seeing its beautiful colours and assessing the landscape. She had fantasised about orbiting the new world and savouring the arrival before taking a landing egg down. It was true to say that such a moment was to be the defining point of her entire life. And yet here he was, delivered to the planet in a state of unconsciousness, robbed of sharing the longed-for moment with her. For all he knew she wasn't even with him. He could have been dropped off somewhere else entirely. Memories of her impending labour and ignorance of what Karen had done to him crawled and bit him like attacking snakes. A frantic and disorientated panic seized his heart.

But he knew without a doubt that this was Oscar 70. Ever since the success of the first interstellar probes, humankind had been treated to a vast array of data and images regarding a whole host of habitable planets. They were digitally and artistically remastered, naturally, but looking at it now, Martin realised how close to reality those images were. Martin already knew, like everyone else on Earth, what the Paradise Strip's mountains and jungles looked like, as well as how pure and breathable the air was, despite the thick orange clouds that covered them. Experiencing the planet first hand, though, was another matter entirely. The brilliant richness of colour before his eyes seemed wrong; perhaps it was simply that he had seen nothing but blackness or artificial light for almost three years. Nevertheless, Martin could have sworn that he had never seen colours as rich as the ones on the other side of the glass. He was faced with dense green foliage, the leaves of the plants bulging forward as if in attack, pregnant with heavy water. Those leaves unnerved him, for they seemed to be brimming with a life form that he couldn't understand. Every shade of green and blue almost expunged itself with intensity, like a child had been rubbing a highlighter pen on a white sheet over and over, until the colour saturates and dulls the paper. Martin found his eyes aching at the sight, and had to turn away. Everything around him was at once familiar and alien, coated with a new shade of being which for some reason abhorred him. Walking backwards, he caught sight of an emaciated and haggard man, long of beard, and it took him a little too long to realise that he was looking at himself in the glass.

Yes, it could be no other planet. Charlotte had spoken of a spacious paradise covered in life and vegetation, and here it was. He could open the window and touch it, and breathe that air. For a man who had lived his life in dusty bedsits, Panel-funded buildings and science labs, this encounter with a world so new and untainted should have been an epiphany, even if it were through glass. As it was, he felt nothing. He was looking in on a paradise that could never exist for him, because all he wanted was her. When he did finally see her, he froze.

The landscape through the window had captured his attention so strongly that he hadn't looked at the room's interior since waking. She was sitting on the edge of a leather chair, arms wrapped around her small frame, frozen like an effigy. A few feet to her right was a small dining table and six chairs, and the table was piled high with food – a combination of the dried meals they had eaten on the ship and some of the exotic and colourful fruits that Martin had seen through the window. Charlotte ignored the food and stared levelly at him. He was sure, for some reason, that she had been in this position for hours. He was certain that he had only been in Suspended Sleep for just under three years, and yet she looked haggard and frail like she had aged twenty. This wasn't a trick of time dilation: something had aged her. He took in the lack of a swollen stomach and her hungry eyes, locked to his, and thought he understood. Charlotte gave him a weak smile. "We are here. We made it. Martin - this planet is the most beautiful thing I've ever seen. It's so," she searched for a suitable word and almost choked on it, "open."

That was all she could manage. She was suddenly in his arms, her sobs shaking her small body. Despite having so many questions, Martin simply held her closely and waited until she was ready to speak. She clutched his face with a ferocity that was on the brink of viciousness. "I've missed you so badly! Please tell me you feel well." Her words were shrill and panicked; he found that he simply couldn't reconcile this woman before him with the brave and intelligent lover he had left behind. Curling onto his knee, it was remarkable how little space she consumed. It was as if her ambitions had buoyed her physical presence on Earth and now, having found paradise, she was quite lost.

When she did speak, he felt lost also. "We've been here for a month. I wasn't allowed to wake you until the ship's pods were properly habitable," she attempted to gesture grandly with her shaking hand, "So here we are."

He still felt like he had been badly beaten; even his strong arms were struggling to hold onto Charlotte's feather weight. Making every possible effort to appear composed and strong, he asked, "You weren't *allowed* to wake me. Who stopped you?"

Charlotte's face fell. He knew that she had been living this life for years now, and her familiarity with the current regime, whatever it was, outweighed the handful of weeks they had shared together. She sighed. "You've missed a lot, of course. They said you were put into Suspended Sleep for threatening a mutiny. Is that true?"

"Of course not."

"No, I didn't think so." She lowered her eyes. "I'm sorry. I had to ask. Anyway, you and Olivia were in Suspended Sleep as examples of what can happen if you threaten the authority of the Panel. The Supplementary rights went back to what they had been on Earth, but it was zero tolerance. You break the rules – Suspended Sleep. It didn't ever happen, though. Nobody argued so nobody else has been punished."

Martin felt weary. "So is that where we are now? On the planet but Sups have the same rights as before?"

She avoided his look for a second time. "Well, yes, but – there's more."

"What happened?"

Her edginess unnerved him more than any news could have. She spoke in a voice higher than he remembered, and seemed to be putting emphasis on the wrong words. She threw her arms round him, in the manner of an intoxicated family member at a wedding. "Don't worry about that right now! Rest! Rest! Rest in my arms." It seemed that all she could do was touch him, perhaps to check if he was real. Her hands moved almost continuously to his face, his torso, his hands.

He held her wrists tightly. "I'm fine. Tell me." A tightness clutched his chest as he gripped her, but he attempted to remain still. Still and strong.

Charlotte sighed, and continued to hold her arms limply in his wrists. "Ten months into our mission, Olivia died." Charlotte inspected his face, and Martin fancied that she was assessing his reaction to this news out of girlish jealousy. He resented her immensely for it, but lacked the energy to say so. She continued, "I found her when – visiting you. I sat by you every day, for hours. I knew something was wrong because of the smell -" She paused, and Martin was reminded of her naivety to the horrors he had seen in his life. "Anyway, she may have been like that for a while before she was found."

"You visited me?" Martin thought for a moment. "You visited me *every day* but you didn't check on her? Her corpse was rotting before you found her?"

Charlotte looked ashamed. "I didn't really feel the *need* to check on her. That quiet room, those capsules...Unless you look into the glass, it's easy to pretend there is nobody there. I preferred that."

"I'll bet you did." Martin was unable to hide his disgust. After everything that had happened, she was still a Better – still willing to close her eyes to uncomfortable horrors.

"Please, Martin. These last three years have been the worst years of my life. I've been so lonely and unable to think clearly." She began to lose control of her voice again and her words were punctuated with gasps, "I've been so lonely. I needed you. And you weren't here!" She buried her head into his shoulder and sobbed again. Every so often, he heard her say, "Don't be angry" or "I need you" or some other barely audible plea. He tried to remind himself that she was young - she was four years younger than he, but really she was so much younger. Even so, he found himself pulling away from her.

"I wonder if you'd let me rest a while, Charlotte. I feel quite faint."

She clasped her hands to her mouth as if she had sworn, and sobbed louder. "I'm so sorry! You feel ill, don't you? Suspended Sleep is so dangerous – we must get you looked at! I've missed you so badly! I've needed to tell you things! Forgive me."

Martin decided that he didn't like this hysterical girl in front of him, but he was certain that the Charlotte he knew – the Charlotte he had unearthed - was in there somewhere. Clearly, much had occurred in the years he had been sleeping and she deserved the chance to explain herself properly. She continued, "After Olivia died, the Sups were harder to convince. Many refused to work, many mothers rejected their children," she paused and, seemingly, waited for Martin to ask about her child. He didn't, so she continued, "And now we are here, the alliance is very uneasy. Eve One's pods are landed close together so we can settle together before exploring the planet's less habitable areas. I don't think that Daniel and Karen are safe now that they are no longer needed to steer a ship. Come to think of it, I'm not sure how safe I am."

Martin knew that he needed time to assess the situation more carefully. He wanted to offer her words of comfort, words of love, but they turned to cold air in his mouth, and he realised, with a start, that he resented her presence. Karen had made it very clear that to be near her was to put them both in danger, and he felt a real anger that Charlotte had spent three years simply pining for him, and believing that she could be rescued.

The leaves at the window seemed to push inwards, fit to crack the glass. Staring at them with an intense fascination, she added, "And my boy is out there somewhere. He's nearly three now and, Martin, he's beautiful." She continued to gaze at the window, as if she imagined him to burst through it at any given moment. "I made a terrible mistake, you see. I didn't want him. All I could think of was how he was *his*, and how he had destroyed my body and made me weak when I needed strength the most.

"So I let the Dawns take him. Karen and Daniel, I mean. They're on Pod One now, with my baby boy. When I knew I'd see you again, I started to feel alive," She smiled as if reliving the excitement, and Martin couldn't help but wonder if he'd been a disappointment. "Things became so clear so quickly, and I knew I needed him back. He's a part of me. He's got my mother and father's blood in him. I'll never see them again. I need my precious Christian."

The fact that she could so easily converse with him almost took his breath away, but it was likely she had been speaking to his unconscious body on a daily basis for the last three years. He suddenly felt very weak. Despite being inactive for so long, he ached for sleep – real, voluntary sleep. He didn't want to go outside onto this alien world – he wanted to curl up and forget his existence there. His voice was a little over a whisper. "I will try to help you if I can, Charlotte, but the situation is…I don't know what it is."

She was disenchanted, of course she was. He could see that she had eagerly awaited their reunion; she had needed his reassurance and the fire in his belly. He didn't know how to tell her that it wasn't there anymore. He didn't want to fight and he didn't want to talk. He wanted to sleep, and sleep alone. His body and soul were poisoned and he needed her to leave – for her own good as much as his. For the second time in his life, someone who loved him inspected him like he was a complex puzzle. Charlotte whispered now, all hints of mania gone, "Martin, how are you feeling? Really?"

He looked at her wide eyes and could see the calculations taking place. *She's working out how much damage has been done*, he thought. *She's working out how long I have left to live.* He started to answer "fine" but then it was his turn to indulge in selfish fears. "Do I look terribly ill?"

She didn't answer, but stroked his face and beard like the mother she wanted to be. He decided not to send her away. Instead, they would get the rest that they both so badly needed, together, and tomorrow, they would face this new world of theirs. When she clung to him, though, the once-delicious smell of her now seemed cloying, and he would have felt more comfortable in his capsule.

185

Aaron

Walking onto the surface of Oscar 70 for the first time, clutching Aru's hand in the anonymity of a dense crowd, Aaron had felt joy and horror in equal measure. He wasn't as clever as anyone else he cared about, so quite naturally he knew very little about time dilation, but feeling his feet on the sandy earth, breathing in the air that felt so much thicker than any he had breathed before (but perhaps that was simply the heat), doing all of those things made the loss of his previous life far more real. A before and after line had been drawn in the sand.

The orange clouds gave everything, even the face of the beautiful woman by his side, a golden, almost iridescent sheen which he actually rather liked. Casting a shy glance to his left, Aru glittered in the atmosphere of the new world. Star Four was huge, or was it simply that he had not seen a sun for such a long time? The air was so warm, or was it that the climate on Eve One had been artificially conditioned? To spend so many years on a ship and return to Earth would have been disorientating enough, but to land on an alien planet...Looking round, it was clear that he was not the only one to feel out of sorts. Sups and Betters alike rubbed their eyes, blinked, and sat on the dusty ground.

As was custom, Daniel Dawns did a speech, his wife nodding proudly behind him at each word, but Aaron could not recall any of it afterwards. He was simply, like many others on the ship he supposed, taking in the marvel of this new world, this new barren world, this blank canvas. It was empty, it shimmered, and it was intoxicating. Aru had gripped his hand and whispered, "We're free. We did it!"

He smiled, and gripped her hand back, doubting both statements that his lover had whispered to him in such confidence.

Remembering this on his third week, Aaron was amazed at how quickly he had settled to life farming. Cultivating land and growing crops were, it seemed, real talents of his. He would rise from the comfort of Pod Twelve daily and water plants, dig soil, tend the virgin ground. Better still, farms needed animals – test tube animals to be precise – and they were the responsibility of Aru. Days on the Paradise Strip really were paradise, therefore, and they spent them together. He would watch her for hours and she squinted in intense concentration at her godless creations, asking her what she was doing and having very little idea what her answers meant. He never stopped to wonder why she was with him, why she loved him. It was enough that she was and that she did.

His only other activity during this time was communication. The pods were designed to communicate with one another whilst in Oscar 70's atmosphere. He was vaguely aware of a plan to sync the pods so they would be in contact with Eve One when she finally leaves the planet's atmosphere for Earth, but he had no idea how this worked; Aru told him that such a thing was possible but a long way off. Aaron would spend, religiously, one hour per day talking to his friends about plans to overthrow the Dawns. He and Roman had conversed for many hours on the subject, but timing was everything.

After a particularly intense conversation one evening, Aaron turned off the screen and sighed, rubbing his eyes. He had been working on the farm all day and his limbs and mind were exhausted in equal measure. He had taken to working shirtless and Star Four's closeness was beginning to leave a real mark on his skin. His athletic chest was beginning to sport patches of red.

Aru entered noiselessly and placed a slender hand on his heart. She said, "You're getting burned by that relentless sun. Remember your UV protector."

Aaron simply could not help leaning forwards and kissing her with an almost embarrassing passion. Her skin was like silk and she carried a gorgeous clinical smell with her. When the moment had passed, he looked beyond her to the window. "I know, but I always feel like I need to move down my to-do-list. You know? Sleep, farm, communicate. Repeat."

She smiled, stroking his hair, "Martin will be back soon. Soon, you won't be alone."

Aaron grinned. Despite their closeness, he knew and she knew that Martin was a fellow Sup – he was what Aaron needed more than anyone else. He breathed in Aru's scent again. It wasn't just clinical. Flowers. *Very clean* flowers. "Tell me again about your mother."

She smiled. This was a story that Aaron never tired of. He loved hearing about her happy past in general, her loving parents and three protective brothers. It didn't take a genius like her to realise that he craved such a history for himself. But Aaron's fascination in her mother was more elemental than this. She stroked his naked back as she spoke, feeling the harsh bumps of his spine against his young skin, "My

188

mother was a giant of a woman, six foot five and 127 kilograms of muscle. She could have beaten a skinny wimp like you any day in any given arena." She offered him a cheeky wink. Sometimes, such a jibe would lead to a playful wrestle, a silly tease in response, but Aaron was already somewhere else, so she continued. "She was a Superior Better, but not by choice. Her position as professor at the Institute of Science Bangalore made her an automatic Better." Of course Aaron knew all this. It didn't matter. "Anyway, she worked tirelessly to undermine the fabric of the intelligence test, to reveal that the questions didn't actually test the IQ. She wrote reams of material on this very topic, almost all of it utterly convincing, as you know." She clutched Aaron closer to her. "She never shared any of it. She also spent a large amount of time sharing her rations with the Supplementaries that lived nearby in the slums. The Panel Representatives caught her and I never saw her again."

Aaron kissed her cheek. "I love you, Aru. That story makes me happy, despite its ending. Your mother was the hope of humanity."

She leaned towards him, eyes closed, and held his naked skin to hers. He'd never know how much she loved his scent also: fresh earth and youthfulness. "No. We are."

A week later, Karen Dawns moved Aru to Pod Thirteen to work there as head midwife to the Supplementary babies. The news came as an email announcement on the screen, and Aru had left without a word. Aaron was informed of all of this via the forty word message left glaring on the screen, written by Karen Dawns and giving Aru her instructions. He was not surprised that she had gone without waking him.

After all, their relationship was not official, for who would have defended it?

But Aaron knew why she had been sent there. There were plenty of medics: why her? He cursed the stars, the ground, the air. He had hated Karen Dawns anyway, he realised, but he had never fully understood until this moment just how much she hated him.

Charlotte

The intensity of feeling in having Martin back was hard to handle; Charlotte had been empty for so long and now she felt full again. As he slept on, she allowed the soothing purr of his breathing to wash over her. Although she worried for his health, she felt the weaker one of the pair; he had survived what they had done to him and here he was. His waking brought her a fresh determination: she would see to it that they never hurt him again.

The clocks had signalled to her that it was midday, but she had no intention of leaving the pod; her only goal today was to get closer to the Martin they had put to sleep. She had so much to tell him, and she had so much she didn't want to say. Looking at his face, peaceful and content in her arms, she wanted to freeze the air around them so time would be frozen also. She was busy wishing this when the bell rang, announcing Roman's arrival, and putting an end to her wishing.

"Hi, Bright Eyes." Roman strutted to the bed and, for a panicked moment, Charlotte thought that he was going to wake Martin from his much-needed rest. She then realised he was speaking to her, and she relaxed. "How's the patient?"

She clutched her coffee cup to her chest. Although they had only been on the planet for 31 A-days, she was already starting to panic that Karen had found no vegetation to even vaguely resemble coffee. She had rather hoped that the planet's high altitudes, constant heat and regular precipitation would allow for such a bean to grow, but there had been no luck so far. Or perhaps Karen wasn't trying out of spite. Charlotte had precisely one hundred and seventy portions remaining, and it wasn't enough. She sighed. "He needs to rest, Roman."

"He's been asleep for three years! Isn't rest the last thing he needs?"

"His body is exhausted from fighting the Suspended Sleep drug. He has spent the last three years fending off death, quite literally. Not sleeping."

Roman had paced the room since entering and Charlotte thought, not for the first time, how restless he was. The small pod limited his furtive movements, and she was, looking at him, reminded of the rats in cages at Dawns'. On Earth, she remembered him as calm and collected, but now he seemed in a perpetual rush. Ever since Martin had been put into the capsule, Roman had been animated with a new purpose: to right the wrongs done by so many Betters before him. Now that Martin was awake, Roman was impatient to get going, she could see that, but he would have to wait a few days more. He rubbed the whiskers on his chin, hard hands on hard hair. "Have you spoken to him about our plans yet?"

She reminded herself not to get angry. It wasn't that Roman didn't *care* about Martin's welfare; he was just desperate to speak to him, tell him about all they had done in his absence. She supposed that it was like buying somebody a beautiful gift and waiting to watch them unwrap it. "I haven't, no. He's still weak and confused, Roman. You'll have to wait a couple of days more." Roman's silence brought on a smile. "Do you have what I asked for?"

Roman fumbled in his backpack a moment and retrieved an envelope. "They should all be there for you."

"Thank you." Charlotte put the envelope to one side on the bed.

"Did you tell him about Olivia?"

"He knows that she's dead."

"That's not what I asked."

She looked away. Of course she hadn't told him. His entire life had changed, his Sup status had been reinstated, and – she had to stifle a sob even thinking of this - he was possibly facing a massively reduced lifespan. She had spent so long missing him and praying that he would wake that she hadn't fully considered how he would feel waking up to such a life. Had she been truly honest with herself, there had perhaps been some expectation that, on his waking, their lives would be the same as they had been before. His waking had actually made her world different yet again, and she was so tired of change. Her behaviour towards him the night before had been simply appalling and she had spent hours calming herself, readying herself to apologise and convince him that she hadn't lost her mind entirely. And now Roman wanted to push him even further. No. She wouldn't allow it. She cleared her throat and placed the cup to the side of the bed. Martin slept on, but she felt him stirring, so dropped her voice to a whisper. "Look, Roman. You have no idea what he has suffered. He is more than just an instrument in our plan – he is the very reason for our plan." She smiled. "I owe you my life. I'd have never survived these past years without your support and I will support you in return - all the way.

But I've said it before and I'll say it again – a couple more days."

Smiling, Roman raised his hands in surrender. "I'm sorry, Sparky." A wistful sigh. " I forgot how much you love him." He seemed to examine every inch of her face until he was satisfied. "You know, I'll never understand spending three years pining for somebody you were with for a matter of weeks - "

"I loved him for far longer than that, Roman. I just didn't know it."

He held his hands up still. "All I'm saying is I'm glad to see the light back on inside of you. I hope he knows how lucky he is."

After Roman left, Charlotte lost track of the hours. It didn't take her long to tear open the envelope he had brought her. She often rationed her photographs of Christian, looking at each one in turn throughout a given day, but today had been a lonelier one than she had expected it to be, for Martin did not wake at all. She had therefore looked at all the shots that Roman could take, which was a grand total of eight. Christian playing in the sand. Christian eating. Christian clapping in a circle, surrounded by some smaller babies. Christian being held by Karen...

She knew that she could not simply rush back into his life. Too much interest on her side would have aroused the interest of the Dawns, anyway, who watched him like hawks. More than that, though, she knew it would have been unfair. He looked happy in these images, and it could be argued that he should stay with his adoptive parents. An outsider may have told her so, but she would not ask, because she needed him back. Just like she needed Martin, the need was physical. Inspecting the photographs now, she could tell that Christian looked like her, not Richard, and she was sorry for throwing him at the Dawns like a rejected toy. She wanted to shape him and make him like her, not his father. It had been an enormous error to reject him, but she had hardly been herself. It was not too late to right the wrong.

The artificial night kicked in at 9pm, as ever, but she sensed the light outside. Turning from it, despite the total protection of the pods, she felt Star Four watching her, the same colour as her blood.

If only she could erase what she knew. The papers were safely tucked away in her office: the boarding pass and documents belonging to Olivia Drake. With a shudder, she remembered reading the words. She could never unread them, never unknow them. That black ink on that white page, telling her the truth, the truth she knew might break him but that would be unforgivable to shield him from all the same:

Name: Olivia Drake

Supplementary number: 94587

Home town: Kolwick

Former name(s): Dinah Huthwaite

The light burned outside. Charlotte felt it burn her inside too. As Martin slept next to her, she basked in his ignorance, knowing that morning would bring with it a world he was not ready for.

Karen

The scientists leading on the Dawns Project had declared, with a grandeur not entirely deserved, that they were to colonise the stars. The problem had been that a ship that held a little over 200 people would not *colonise* anywhere. This is where the Population Project had come in, and it was something that made Karen Dawns' heart flutter with expectation.

Oscar 70's population was going to be a young one. Seventy-three Sup women had boarded Eve One after being artificially inseminated by the finest sperm available – all donors were athletic, intelligent and handsome. Only fifty-three pregnancies had led to healthy births in the first instance, followed by forty-five and then forty; Karen was certain that this was because Sup women, really, just didn't *deserve* children, and somebody greater than her was trying to say so. Whatsmore, to say that this was a drop in the ocean didn't come close. To colonise Oscar 70 properly, they'd need *thousands*. Like most others, Karen Dawns did not entertain the irony of vacating an overpopulated planet to force a population explosion on another – they were entirely separate issues. Others could follow in time, but for now, they needed people. A caretaker race, as she liked to call it. They were going to be caretakers of the planet as they waited for those on Earth to find them.

At the end of the day, like everything of value, it came down to Science. Karen observed the Population Chamber, the 100,000 frozen eggs that had come from Earth, and she touched the glass case like one in prayer. The eggs were already inseminated, and all it would take was a simple activation process in Eve One's Birthing Lab to nurture thousands of healthy babies. As many as she liked at a time. The Birthing Lab was so huge and so magnificent that it had to stay on the ship, but it required little staffing or upkeep, and in fact, even when the babies were born, Eve One boasted a thousand pairs of robotic hands that could feed, change, even caress . Karen regarded the capsule in front of her slowly, taking in its every feature. It was up to her when to start the birthing process, and she had decided. Now. The plan had originally been to wait until the Sup children were old enough to care for a child each, but Karen shuddered at the thought. There were enough Betters here to do a far Superior job. They could handle another forty children. It was still less, on average, than two children per adult. She grinned to think of Pods Thirteen and Fourteen: packed to the rafters with newborn sleeping chambers, and all Sup women running shifts to care for the babies. They could work harder, and she would see to it that they did. When the babies were to become children – when the nappy changing and bottles were over and done with – the Betters could then take over, and teach them how to live, and how to behave.

She knew that somewhere inside this capsule was a combination of her and Daniel. By her own request, she did not know which twenty eggs were hers, because she wanted to treat *all* the children on Oscar 70 as if they were hers – the ones that came from Betters, anyway. The Sup children would have to make do with being dragged up by their resentful parents. They were a stopgap measure, nothing more. At least Daniel had enforced stricter rations on these

197

children, so they didn't take away from her precious Christian.

That beautiful boy, with his brown eyes so rich they are almost black, and the dark hair in smooth ringlets, like melted chocolate. He deserved everything, and that stupid girl had given him nothing.

Karen was unsurprised that Charlotte's entrance immediately followed thoughts about her because she had been in her thoughts a lot in recent days. She had given up feeling sad about the change in Charlotte long ago, seeing her drawn and deflated features for what they were: the long-term effects of a spoiled child sulking. She had been given more than most and it still wasn't enough. She had also stopped demanding eye contact a long time ago, so was unmoved by Charlotte's avoidance of her gaze. Charlotte stood at the door of the laboratory, waiting to be invited in. When she was, she kept her glance cast downwards, clearly counting the seconds until she could leave again.

Karen couldn't help but enjoy herself. "Haven't seen you on Pod One for a while, Charlotte. Good to see you. How is he?"

As predicted, she didn't respond. Karen savoured the pause, feeling Charlotte squirm under the propriety that the situation demanded. Eventually, she muttered, "I'd rather not talk about it, if that's all right."

Karen beamed, "Of *course* that's all right, Sweetheart! I know that you have suffered so. I just hope the young man has learned his lesson and will be more careful from here on in."

Her gaze was still on the floor. "Yes, Mrs. Dawns."

"Don't do that, Charlotte. I'm still Karen. I still love you."

With a shock, Karen saw Charlotte's head snap up and she stared directly into her eyes. Karen thought she could detect a little of Charlotte's furious old glimmer in that gaze, and she didn't like it. "Why did you send for me, Mrs. Dawns?"

She sighed. At least the formality meant control. "I have decided now is the time for us to set off a tiny portion of the Population Chamber; I need you to accompany me back onto Eve One to start off the process. It should only take a few A-days. Of course you can take a small team with you." She paused. "All Betters, naturally."

"Now?"

"Now."

Karen had to Suppress a laugh as she saw Charlotte struggle with the thought of not seeing the boy for a few days more. Well, all the better. Karen felt that inward leap of power that she had become so accustomed to when conversing with Charlotte. "How is he finding you?"

Charlotte's eyes were cold, impassive. "What?"

Karen laughed, as if she had made a witty joke at a dinner party. "Don't be defensive, dear. I simply meant that, well –" she gestured up and down with her arm "– You've *changed* in three years, haven't you?"

Charlotte's voice shook a tiny amount, but it was noticeable enough, "I'm still the same."

Pretending to busy herself with the Population Chamber, Karen became the one to avoid eye contact, but only so that Charlotte could not see the joy in her eyes. "No, you're not.

Not in any way. You forget that Daniel and I have seen your unpredictable moods, the fact that you just don't sleep anymore. You used to have such drive and such passion and *now*. Well…" She let the comment hang in the air. She was going to mention something about how she had nothing left to strive for, nothing to live for, even, but she didn't want to give the girl a chance to deny it. Better to come to that realisation herself. Instead of completing her sentence, she said, "Christian's doing well. It's a while since you've seen him. You must visit Pod One soon. Or we could come to you?"

Charlotte was suddenly alarmed. "No. Don't do that. I'll visit you. Tomorrow. Before we go back to Eve One."

Artificial night was soon to kick in, and Karen was keen to get back for Christian's bedtime. "That will be all, Charlotte."

To her immense surprise, Charlotte did not leave. "Before I go, Karen. I wanted to ask you something," she was growing red and starting to stammer, "I was going to ask you about medical Supplies-"

So the boy was damaged. It was difficult to cover up her relief. "Is someone ill? Of course, if a Better on your pod is ill they would be entitled to whatever treatment we could afford, but I'd need to assess them myself."

"No. Nobody's ill. It's just – well – couldn't the medication be distributed more evenly between the pods? What if somebody grew ill and we didn't have time to consult you?"

The girl was growing rather jumpy, and a nasty red rash started to spread on her neck. Karen was disappointed, really. She'd have expected rather more composure from a

200

girl like Charlotte. "No, I'm afraid not. Perhaps we could discuss this when we have devised more means to create medication from the planet's resources, but for now, the rationing of medicines is vital to the order of life here. Only the Leaders on Pod One are authorised to access medicines, I'm afraid."

When she left, Karen felt satisfied but also concerned. So she wasn't welcome on Pod Eleven: no shock there. She was certain that there was a pathetic plot to overthrow them, but they could quash that without an issue. The fact that Charlotte had asked for help just showed how perilous the boy's situation was. No - what concerned her was the eye contact, the fire in that glare. Charlotte had not looked at her like that for three years, not since she had taken Christian away and temporarily disposed of that Sup. She and Daniel were fine as long as they maintained their image of absolute, unbending authority, and Charlotte's gaze had offered a glimmer of something that might question that.

No. She had not liked that look at all.

Martin

On waking, Charlotte had seemed calmer, more reasonable, and Martin regretted his former coldness towards her. He had held her in those sumptuous minutes between sleep and consciousness, and it was the first time since being on the ship that he had enjoyed human contact. He still worried that his feelings for her had altered irrevocably; on the ship they had loved one another with an unhealthy intensity and now, on this newly born world, he felt like a newly born man. When he finally did exit the pod and stand on the alien earth for the first time, he breathed in the warm air like it was the first air he had ever breathed. The orange clouds above seemed warm and full of promise. He had holidayed with his family as a young boy, before the Expansion, and this was a similar feeling. For the first time in his adult existence, anything could happen, and the certainty with which he had thrown himself into a love affair with Charlotte now shocked him.

For the briefest of moments, he considered ending it. It would solve so many problems and he would never be forced to fail her, because fail her he would. She loved and trusted him and that included laying herself bare at her lowest ebb; he wasn't sure he could drag her back to her former confidence. Idly, he supposed that he just didn't understand how any human being could trust another so intensely with their worst features. If she knew his, she couldn't love him, surely.

When she joined him, he was glad, but not excited. Any vestige of panic had left her now, and she was purposeful –

far more like his memory. Observing the landscape, she smiled and raised one eyebrow, "What do you think?" It was as if she had asked his opinion on a piece of art.

Martin considered. "It's so quiet. I don't think I've ever known a quiet like it." He closed his eyes and imagined himself back in the capsule. "And it's so *big*. There's so much *room*. It's what you wanted."

"It's what we all wanted."

Martin would have liked to wander the landscape for a little while alone, but he could find no way of indulging in such a luxury without hurting Charlotte's feelings, so he had to be content with a quick stroll around their section. Pods one to eighteen had landed within fifteen miles of each other on the Paradise Strip, enabling each group of settlers to research the land and start to farm, as well as begin to build, using their team of expert builders and architects and whatever resources they could muster. The tactile printers were a great help, forging complex structures such as planks, metals and tools using the most basic of codes. Eve One, in her orbit of the planet, had dropped satellites, which were used by the owners of the pods to communicate with one another, and, given the pods' abilities to drive across land and of course fly, they also had the added benefit of being a method of travel. The two remaining pods had been sent further afield, with a few tester Sups, to explore the habitability of the Twilight Strip, where Star Four's beams reached, but not as strongly. So far, they had heard nothing. Nothing? Martin had asked. Nothing official anyway, she had confirmed, with a promise to give him more details later on, when they "talked business." No pods had been sent to the Dark Lands on the side of the planet not facing the star, or to the Fires, the scorching centre closest to it. To do so would have been a waste of people and resources, after coming so far.

A quick stroll turned into a hike as Martin listened to Charlotte's constant chatter regarding Oscar 70. She told him about every plant and creature that had been found. Pod Six's team had discovered giant lizards that resided in the caves just north of where they were, while Pod Nine's team had found over 1,800 different insect species already. Karen and Daniel were doing very well on Pod One, she answered when questioned, but she had not mentioned her son since her outburst nor did she now. She told Martin about how they had sent their interstellar probes on a much shorter journey to the Dark Lands, the side of Oscar 70 that never saw Star Four, and she reported, with a chill, a barren and ice cold landscape, so different to this. Martin was reminded of how people on Earth had made a legend of the dark side of the moon, and smiled inwardly at her fear of the unknown, despite being one of the first humans in known history to traverse the universe. Have any probes looked at the Fires, he asked. She replied, yes. As expected, they transmitted nothing but angry, white heat; the Fires reached temperatures of 260 degrees due to their fixed close proximity to Star Four. She spoke and spoke about the planet's beauty, the orange clouds – they only appear orange because of Star Four's red hue, of course - the constant daylight – isn't it lovely, she had said – and the perpetual tropical heat, which he didn't have the heart to say was uncomfortable to him. Absent-mindedly, he held her hand, which felt cold and soft in his as always, and he was reminded of why he loved her. He had missed her passion and her knowledge, but he couldn't shake the feeling that there was something unsettling in her manner. Beneath her garrulous musings lay an unsettled heat. She reminded him of a kettle boiling, encased in an innocuous exterior but occasionally emitting steam. He took in the orange sun and thick clouds and felt enveloped by them, like he was being wrapped in a particularly dense blanket. It was both reassuring and suffocating.

They had been walking for around two hours when Martin realised that his chest was starting to hurt, and his breathing was unsteady. Sweat had started to surface on every inch of his skin and he realised he was hungry, and weak. He hadn't dared consider the state of his health, and, every time Charlotte asked if he wanted to sit down, he grew more and more stubborn. He shook and sweated, and needed sugar, and lots of it.

His feet felt heavy as he dragged them on the planet's sandy earth. When this earth was suddenly touching his face, he was confused and then relieved. He closed his eyes and allowed the blackness to take hold.

****

When he woke this time, Martin was surer of his surroundings, and he immediately sprang up, only to find Roman's strong arms gripping him. "Whoa, there! Take it steady, kid! Little Miss Rocket Mouth has already exhausted you. Just go slow."

He was in the same room, the same pod, and it occurred to him that he had taken so many things about his existence so far for granted. He was suddenly very keen to find out whether or not this was officially his room, where he could find food rather than have Charlotte bring it to him and, importantly, where he could have a shower. He hadn't showered in three years.

Sitting at the modest dining table, Aaron, Amy Terekhov and Charlotte sat expectantly. Their poise was businesslike, and he was suddenly nervous. Roman put his face in front of this view, smiling a warm smile, a smile that Martin expected he might use in an attempt to cheer someone just after delivering bad news. "I hope you're feeling fresher, Action Man. We need to talk to you about some important shit."

Amy laughed and sprang to her feet. "Leave him alone, Roman. We shall not do a thing until I have given him a thorough medical check up." Martin noted how her thick Russian accent had adopted an American tone, and he wondered how much time she and Roman had been spending together.

She smiled at him, as if reading his thoughts. "I am sorry, Martin. I realise this is all very confusing. I know I am not the best medic available, but I am, well, *available*. The other medics, such as Aru and Guy, they are with the Dawns." The anger in her eyes could have covered up the pain she was feeling, had she had a less astute and cynical audience than Martin. Charlotte, a Dawns herself, looked at Amy unsmilingly, and Martin jogged his memory for Charlotte ever telling him anything positive about Amy Tereckhov.

As she leaned in to touch him, he flinched. He was unsure why; of course he had been subject to countless experiments and medical interventions at the hands of Betters during his time on Earth. Perhaps Amy's touch was tinged with kindness, and that unnerved him. He was finding it hard to come to terms with how *kind* she and Roman were being towards him, anyway. It was like they knew him far better than he knew them.

He entered into a dreamlike state as Amy held a limb of his upright and then another, told him to blink, placed an icy stethoscope to his chest. Finally, she sighed. "I don't know what to say. I think in many ways, your health was poor *before* you were put into Suspended Sleep. You led such a crappy lifestyle, of course," Martin did his best, as Amy did, to avoid Charlotte's desperate eyes, "But your heart *does* seem to be beating irregularly. You have been feeling short of breath?" He nodded, stiffly. "It's only a guess; obviously I don't have the medical equipment here to inform you properly, but I think you may have an enlarged heart. It's been working too hard to keep you alive, and now it's..." She moved her bottom lip sideways and looked towards Roman for support, "Struggling."

Charlotte leaned forward, hands clenched, and Martin, for some reason, thought of a cat about to pounce on a bird or mouse. "What can we do to help him?"

Amy looked uncomfortable. "There are things, but I can't really do any of them. We don't have the equipment."

"We'll get it," Charlotte spat.

Amy's cheeks burned under the scrutiny. "I cannot very well go back to Earth to get everything we need to help him, can I? You know we have limited medical Supplies but they are on Pod One and you know who we need to speak to in order to get them!"

Charlotte was about to pounce, about to respond, when Martin interrupted. "I feel fine, honestly, and I would really rather talk about anything else, I think." He hoisted himself from the bed and walked to the table, ensuring with each step that the pain he was in did not show on his face. "Now, Roman, you were about to mention some 'important shit?'"

****

The five of them spoke for a long time. Martin would have loved to know how long, but he was not yet accustomed to judging the passage of time like the others. There was no sunset to speak past, no sunrise to reach, so the hours were automatons, trotted out one after the other, and they spoke, and spoke again. He was also tired to the point of believing he could never feel alert again. As he listened to Roman's animated update, he nodded, numbly, wondering if each nod would render his head immobile and send him into an eternal sleep.

Roman spoke of how years had been spent plotting, thinking. They knew everything about the positioning of the pods, the landscape of Oscar 70, and the resources available. Crucially, they knew the weak spots in Pod One, and which other Supplementaries could be trusted. Roman beamed as he declared how these four alone had formed a group to challenge the authority of the Leaders on Pod One and now, upon Martin's waking, they were ready. Martin stifled a groan out of politeness, but it was a disappointment to say the least. They had had three years, and the best they had done was *form a group*. Had they done anything? Martin's questioning had been hopeful, purposeful. *We have a lot of knowledge,* was their response.

It was clear they needed him. They had waited for him to rise from sleep like a Messiah and lead them to salvation. The problem was that he was tired, and unhealthy, and out of love with the entire idea. The planet was big, and he was starting to believe that he actually might quite like it. Perhaps they should just run away to a different part of it.

Leaning forward now and ignoring his exhaustion, Martin became the interrogator; it didn't occur to him how massively the balance of power had moved during the mission. "So what is the plan?"

Aaron didn't speak with the confidence of the others. Martin found this unsurprising and reassuring in equal measure. Being the only other Sup in the room, and therefore the only one with any real stake to lose, he clearly empathised with Martin's disappointment, his frustration at the lack of action. He spoke nevertheless. "We have been speaking to the scientists on Pods Nineteen and Twenty since their landing in the Twilight Strip; the Leaders seem uninterested in them, and have already written them off for dead. They are planning to support us in a revolt. They have many weapons." He paused, waiting for Martin's reaction. More blood. More fighting. Martin suddenly felt even more tired. It seemed that Aaron could sense his caution, as he continued, "But not yet. We're not ready for that, yet. We need the Leaders too much; they have all of the Supplies and keep the weapons in Pod One, which we are nowhere near able to access yet. So we need to leave, to place ourselves in a position where we can rally support but be far enough away from the Dawns to be safe. Roman, Amy and Charlotte can all operate the pods. Each pod is built to accommodate up to forty people, as you know, so using emergency provisions, we can find our own settlement and will be able to live comfortably out there for the whole year. We won't have medical Supplies, though – just Amy." Martin looked up at Amy, who offered a smile and a nod in acknowledgement. "She's a qualified medic but, well – we'll work with what we have." Aaron looked around the others, clearly considering what he had forgotten to say, "We can also take a Sup Baby Unit as security. The Dawns won't attack us if we have something so precious. I know a girl who looks after the babies on Pod Thirteen; I think I could persuade her to help us."

Martin couldn't help himself. "Drag a clan of babies across an alien planet to be there when we start a war? That's ridiculous. How could we possibly care for them?"

Aaron sighed. "Yes, I thought that, but we have to think long term. Children are leverage, and future supporters. Taking care of babies would be the least of our problems. And, like I said, I could get us help."

"What about Charlotte's child?"

"I want him too," Charlotte interjected before anyone else had the chance.

Martin blew out slowly and loudly. "So this is the best you have, after three years of plotting. Run away to a part of the same planet that is a little further away?"

Roman seemed hurt, despite his gruff exterior. "10,000 miles away, Moody Boy. It's hardly a simple stroll."

"But they could use their pods to reach us in exactly the same way."

Amy smiled. "But they won't. Fuel is too scarce, and they can track us using these anyway." She indicated the rubber, blinking band on her wrist that Martin had forgotten to enquire about. Her look to Roman was dreamy. "I think they'll just count their blessings and leave us alone, that is if Charlotte can be persuaded to leave Christian where he is. The other babies, they will let us have those. We could even start a civilisation of our own with them. If we kidnap the most important child on the planet, I think we'd be screwed."

The glow in Charlotte's eyes struck Martin as new. Roman cut the air between them, "I think the larger problem we have is persuading other Sups to leave with us. You know firsthand, Moody Boy -" he gestured to Martin roughly, "Sups don't like change."

Martin was starting to see why they needed him. Their plan really was the best option; they couldn't go back onto Eve One because they didn't have the fuel or expertise, in their small numbers, to make a journey back to Earth, and what good would that be, anyway? A full-scale revolt was likely to fail, again because they were so few; running away really was best. Establish a strong group and revolt...later. Aaron was charming and intelligent, but he was so handsome and so *young*. People might take him more seriously. He spoke clearly and loudly, for the first time in three years, "I can recruit people to come, but we should establish ourselves first. Take the pods, find a settlement and then use the televisions on the pods to communicate with Sups that we can trust. Is there enough fuel for one more trip? Possibly using the pod's ability to drive on land where possible? That would use less fuel?" Amy nodded. "Good. When we have enough followers to outnumber the Leaders, we go back for them, and deal with the Leaders at the same time. That is my proposal."

Roman immediately relaxed. Exhaling slowly, he returned to his seat. "Thank you, Martin. We can work with that. With your help, we have a future here. Since what they did to you and Olivia, I've not been able to sleep. It's like someone is shining a bright torch straight into my face and I need to turn it off, or at least find the dimmer switch."

Aaron sighed. "I think the light you are talking about is the truth." He stared at the table as he spoke. "Speaking of which, I think we need to fill you in on what happened with Olivia."

Rotting and smelling for months next to him. He didn't want to listen to that tale again. When he said so, Aaron was quiet, sullen, as were all of them. Only Charlotte was not quiet or sullen. The restlessness of the day before seemed to return. She immediately jumped towards him and tried to drag him out of the room, chirping, "I'll speak to him about it, Aaron. Just not now!"

He froze. So she was hiding something from him. Despite all of her self-indulgent confessions, her soliloquising about her love of the planet, she had lied. Just like so many others. He just wasn't sure what about yet. He removed his arm from her grasp and looked only at Aaron. Martin's voice was gentle but ice cold, "I think now, actually."

****

In the end it had been Aaron who told him. Aaron was the only one capable of knowing exactly what this cover-up, albeit only a twenty-four hour one, meant; their whole campaign for equality had been based on the need for transparency and to be kept out of the dark, and the very people who claimed to support him had denied him that. Charlotte had slept in his bed, held him close to her, told him her private nightmares, but denied him the truth about his own life. His knowledge was, yet again, second best to hers. And this was about him. A secret she should not have owned.

Only Aaron could have told him with the measured disinterest the subject deserved. Roman and Charlotte became close friends on the ship after Martin had been put into Suspended Sleep. Roman had felt guilty about what the Sups had suffered and Charlotte had needed a friend. As their friendship grew, so did their plotting for revenge and, more importantly, salvation for the Sups. Aaron had watched all this on the sidelines at first, but his friendship with Roman had grown. Martin had little reason to question any of this. He could understand why one would befriend Roman so easily.

And so the trio had established an uneasy friendship. Charlotte grieved for Martin, unreservedly and inexorably. To comfort her, Roman had confided in how he had enjoyed a brief affair with Olivia before she had met the same fate as Martin. Again, Martin was unsurprised – Olivia had thrown herself at most men and a brief fling would have been a distraction on a long mission for Roman. Perhaps he had brought it up to demonstrate to Charlotte that a Sup and Better pairing was far from unusual, or perhaps he really was grieving in a smaller way too. Whatever the reason, Roman mentioned how Olivia had confided in him about her past;

her brother had been declared Supplementary and had fled with their parents. Of course he had been caught – they were always caught – and in order to demonstrate the Panel's control of the situation, her brother Joseph and she were declared Supplementary also, despite having passed the Intelligence Test. Olivia Drake wasn't even her real name, either.

Martin was very still. He didn't ask her real name. He didn't need to. He simply left the room and ignored Charlotte's wide eyes as he passed.

****

Martin hadn't been to a beach since he was captured, and Oscar 70 didn't have beaches. Judging by what Charlotte had told him earlier, the water on the planet came from a combination of freshwater lakes and geysers from the massive cave networks. The planet did have a lot of sand, though, or at least something that felt a lot like sand to sit on. He therefore sat as he imagined one might on a beach, hands wrapped around bent knees, staring into the horizon. He would have given anything to regard a sunset at that moment but instead he had the unyielding glow of Star Four, staring at him, unmoving, unrelenting. The eternal midday this planet offered did not suit his current emotions, whatever they were.

He had never considered what had happened to Dinah and Joseph. Branded as Betters, he imagined that they wouldn't have helped him, even if they could. His view of Betters had been a rather dim one, after all. He shuddered to remember how he had shunned his sister at first sight on the ship, yet she had gravitated towards him. Had she known who he was? Certainly, she has reached out to him, and he had read it as a cheap sexual advance. It was clearly all anybody thought she was capable of.

Martin hardly noticed Roman settling on the ground next to him, mimicking his pose exactly, drawing his muscular legs close to his chest. His thick American drawl soothed him a little from his sadness. "Don't blame her, Marty Baby. She was so happy to see you. How could she have dropped an atom bomb like that on you, just after you woke up?"

He thought for a moment. "I don't blame her, really. Right now, I don't want to think about her. I want to think about my sister."

Roman regarded Star Four also, and Martin fancied that they both felt that watchful eye casting judgement on their every word, but of course neither of them said so. To do so would be madness. As he did speak, though, Martin noted that all traces of joking had passed; there were no nicknames now, no all-American gusto. "I can tell you a little more, but not much. I'm sorry to say that I didn't take her seriously. She was a bit of fun to me." He stopped. Perhaps he was waiting for Martin to jump to her defence, battle for her honour. A little late for that. "She always rattled on about how she'd passed the test and how much *better* than the others she was. Your brother, Joseph is it? Well, he's still on Earth. Lives alone. Or lived. Christ knows how old he'll be if we ever get back to Earth." Martin continued to stare at the eye in the sky, but he felt Roman turn to face him. "She had a daughter, though. Eleanor. She was premature. Had her before she was sterilised. The authorities took her when she was declared Supplementary. I think that's what did it, really. After her daughter was taken, she just thought, 'Fuck it.' She became a good time girl, except she didn't really have a good time."

Martin absorbed all this, but it sounded like Roman was talking about someone else's life, not his. He had chastised Charlotte for leaving her family behind on Earth, and yet he had done exactly the same thing. He thought again of the time Olivia – no – Dinah - had walked into his room on Eve One and sat on his bed, like it was the most natural thing in the world to her. How had he not recognised her? And when he saw her in Suspended Sleep – how, then? He had known and loved her for eleven years. There had not been a trace of the sister he knew in her voice, her movements, her appearance. Dinah had been a plump teenager of sixteen when he saw her last, with thick brown hair and dark eyes. Becoming Olivia had made her gaunter, hollower, duller. Duller was the word. Dinah had positively *sparkled. Sparkled* with enthusiasm, light, intelligence. Olivia, however, had shone with chemicals and spat like a vicious camel.

But he should still have known her. With eyes even slightly more open, he would have done. With a surge of hatred, stronger than any he had felt before, he considered the capacity of the Panel and those who work for it to change an identity – corrupt a soul. Had there been no tenderness? Had she never experienced any understanding? He had to ask, "It sounds like she really confided in you. Did you ever think you might love her?"

Roman chuckled, "Nah, Marty Baby. I'm not capable of that. But I think she loved *me*. It was all a front: the make-up, the cattiness. She told me what happened to her family, and she cried from start to finish. She was smashed on black market beer at the time, mind. I didn't think that the brother was you, though. Why would I?"

Martin didn't reply. He wanted to hear as much about his sister as possible and he didn't want to interrupt Roman's train of thought again.

He continued, "She wanted to win at everything, you see, to prove that she wasn't a true Sup. I think she threw herself at men and gave them what she knew they really wanted, to see if she could make anyone love her."

"She depended upon the kindness of strangers."

"Something like that. More fool her." Roman lifted his fingers to his lips before realising the imaginary cigarette wasn't real. "Aww, crap. Anyways, that's it. I don't have anything else to tell you."

Martin squinted at the orange clouds covering most of the sky, and thought about how far away Dinah's child really was. He had been so quick to run away from Earth and now he knew that Joseph was there, alive and well, and so was Dinah's little girl. Of course, to go back would be to lose a generation of time, but they still might be there. No doubt, Eleanor had heard all sorts of lies about her mother, and he felt sick at how Dinah had been misrepresented time and time again, not least because of him. He wanted to call across the sky to Eleanor and let her know the truth about her mother. He wanted to claw through the miles and the years and tell her face to face, see her react, perhaps even hold her.

The guilt of having failed her was no worse than the knowledge of why. He would have recognised his sister, surely, had he not been so drawn in by Charlotte and her world. He had been entranced, ensnared. Care for her as he did, he couldn't shake the anger. He would help them escape the clutches of Pod One, but then he needed to go. The light inside of him was starting to glow again, but it wasn't fuelling an urge to fight, it was fuelling an urge to get back to the family who lost so much because of him.

Star Four seemed to mock his wish to leave, blocking his passage, furious and bright, but he nevertheless stared on, calling across the universe to an old man and a little girl who couldn't hear him.

Charlotte

Back on Earth, the Panel had excited the masses with talk of Oscar 70's greenery and silver seas. The greenery was true enough, although it did have a darker hue than any found on Earth. The silver seas, though, turned out to be a complex series of caves, stretching for over 300,000 square miles, spanning the Paradise and Twilight Strips. The scientists of Pods Four, Five and Six had made slow progress in their exploration of this cave network, largely because there seemed to be plenty of entrances but no exits. The explorers would go so far, into a mile, perhaps two, of blackness and then return to the reassuring light of Star Four. They said they had returned for more resources, to report their findings. Everyone knew, really, that they had returned out of fear. On a planet of constant light, the darkness crept into their very pores.

Charlotte loved the darkness. Part of her role as Associate Scientist was to monitor the workers at almost half of the pods on Oscar 70, and when she reached those close to the caves, she always lingered. It seemed like a betrayal to admit that the planet's perpetual daylight wore heavily on her, but the caves were cool; and silent, and the darkness caressed her like a thick coat. In the month without Martin she had frequented the caves almost daily, finding time to sit and absorb the space that was hers, leaning against the cold stone and imagining all the years they had stood there, uninhabited, untouched. She had thought that on his waking she would frequent them less, much less, but since the declaration about Olivia, he had hardly spoken to her. He had shared her bed, made love to her, done as she bid him, but there had been something missing, and they both knew it. His lovemaking had been tender – yes – but more robotic than before. He didn't look at her anymore. He didn't ask her questions. She shuddered at the idea that he may be making love to her out of duty.

Perhaps it was her love of the darkness that caused her to invite him to speak to her in the caves close to Pod Six; she had been trying to consider what he was sickening for, and she wondered if, like her, it might be the darkness.

She had spent a while telling him about the chemical composition of the water that came from the geysers in these caves, the supposed layout according to research so far, and the perplexing lack of life in this area. Martin had spent the conversation propped against the uneven wall, his hand limply placed in hers and his eyes closed. His breathing had been bad today, and he looked older. Perhaps it was the light in the caves, but his skin seemed grey, like he was still in Suspended Sleep. She stopped speaking several times to listen for his breathing. Intermittently, she wondered if he was listening, but felt the need to speak all the same. Doing her best to sound bright, she continued, "Compared to the Paradise Strip, the caves seem positively sterile. The workers on Pods Five and Six have found several species of insect, small and black and very hardy, but nothing else. It's odd, because we humans could live here quite happily."

His eyes were still closed as he spoke, "Happily?"

She didn't panic. Thinking about it logically, she knew they had to have this conversation if they had any future together at all. She gripped his hand tighter, willing him to not let go.

"Martin. Listen. I think we *can* be happy here. I know it seems a long way off, but we *can*. Remember Karen and Daniel will be leaving in eleven months. If we wait it out until then, the balance of power will shift again. I'll be in charge." She tried to offer a confident smile. He did not let go of her hand, but she detected a slight bridling, a slight turn in the opposite direction. She inhaled deeply. "I'm sorry, Martin. I'm so so sorry. Of course I would have told you about your sister. Of course I would. Please believe that. Aaron just told you too early – not *too* early. Just earlier than I was going to. I was worried about you. I wanted to know you would be all right to bear the news."

He almost spat, "I don't care about that right now. There's so much wrong with this situation, I don't know where to start. I mean – do you really think they will just *go?*"

Sitting very still, she decided that, no matter how long it took, she would not speak again until he was done. He had agreed to come and speak to her. He was not lost.

"I idolised you on the ship. Do you know that?" She nodded, noting with a panic his use of the past tense. "Karen Dawns threatened you and your child if I didn't, in her words, 'Remove myself from the situation,' so I gave myself up. I'd have thought you'd know that, and I would have expected you to do *something*. And yet when I wake up, I see a simpering victim. You throw yourself at me like a child. And you don't tell me what's important. You care about preserving my life but you don't care about the quality of it. And they took your child, Charlotte! And you *let* them! And you *work* for them! On the ship, we were on the brink of rebellion. What's *happened* to you?"

221

A question, before she was ready to answer it. It was a good question. What *had* happened to her? Why had she not fought better? She had just given in, at the first challenge. If he had risen to leave, there and then, she would have told him to go, declared herself not worth loving. A warm rush ran through her when he didn't. He simply sat there, as beautiful and miserable as ever, awaiting her response. When she did finally speak, it was carefully, and slowly, as if each word was being sold at the highest price, "You have to understand, Martin, that when you and I were together on the ship, I felt whole. I felt like we could take on this new world and that the whole future was before us. And then you went. I was whole before you, but not whole after you left." She had to fight back the tears. "I didn't know you'd sacrificed yourself. I thought they'd just taken you from me, and I felt weak. I felt so weak, and so empty, and so helpless. I'd never felt like that before. I failed you, and I'm sorry. I should have been stronger for you. Strength is what you love, isn't it?"

He gripped her hand more tightly, and drew her to him. Knowing that any hint of her previous mania at that stage would have been unwelcome, she stifled a yelp. He stroked her face, "No. I'm sorry. You don't understand what it is to be a Sup. You try and you are made to fail. You create something and it is destroyed. You offer love and you are heartbroken. In the end, it's just easier *not to*. So I didn't. Until I met you." He stopped stroking her face and brought it closer to his, not to kiss her, but to look her squarely in the eye, she supposed, "You have made me weaker but you have also made me stronger, and I don't know what to do with that. I would have *never* offered to sacrifice myself on Earth for a Better, but then again, I'd never been happy on Earth either. I said that I don't care about the Dinah issue, but I do really. You have to know what trust is to me. If you are, as you say, *whole*, with me, then I have to be able to trust you entirely. Your thoughts have to be mine. I've thought long and hard about this and it has to be one or the other: you either love me, completely and without reservation, or you don't. And that means trusting me with everything you know, and treating me as an equal in all things. Your choice."

It would have been unwise to in reality, but all Charlotte wanted to do was laugh. How could he have possibly ever thought that she didn't love him, entirely and completely? She could understand his pride being hurt over recent days, particularly since his health had been an ongoing concern, but for that to be a sign that she didn't love him or respect him was unbelievable to her. She could have told him so many things at that moment, like how she had only been so inactive because she *needed* him, she had only been so unhinged because he wasn't there to ground her, but in the end she settled for simplicity. "I choose love, completely and without reservation. I choose you."

Upon this conclusion, they seemed to become aware of their world again, and noticed Star Four's glare snaking its way into their lover's hideaway; they needed to leave. The darkness of the caves had served them well, but they could not live in darkness forever. Neither of them said so, but the Twilight Strip suddenly seemed like a place where they could, actually, live happily.

Martin

Eve One's pods were a marvel. As he and Amy approached Pod Sixteen, already exhausted from the eight mile walk this location had cost them, Martin started to realise their magnificence fully. On the ship they had been capsules, existing to transport them efficiently. They had done that job excellently and had become very habitable temporary living spaces. Now, looming above them, Pod Sixteen was a glittering white fortress; its smooth walls mocked them, holding the door with no handle so tightly that the smooth egg-like shape seemed unbreakable. The brushed silver keypad next to the door was their only way in, and only the Leaders in Pod One knew the code. Aaron had gone to Pod Thirteen, as arranged, but that had been made far easier by the girl he knew, who Martin suspected was Aru. He hoped, in passing, that Aaron was being careful. Charlotte and Roman were to take Pod Eleven, which was hers anyway. The only complication was that it was monitored by Karen Dawns, but Charlotte had intricate knowledge of Karen's shift patterns and when there was dead time to escape. It seemed to him, and no doubt to Amy, that they had therefore drawn the short straw. Amy had ordered him to remain quiet and follow her lead, which he had not liked one bit, but he had decided, possibly too casually, that anyone observing them would deem the Better to be in charge, and therefore responsible for whatever came to pass.

When he realised what she had done, he hadn't really known what he had expected. Perhaps he had thought that she'd be able to charm Guy Roberts into giving her the code, perhaps she was plotting a forced entry using one of the few weapons they had access to. He hadn't expected her to produce an orange wrist device, owned only by the ten inhabitants of Pod Sixteen. Holding the telling bracelet in both hands, Amy made eye contact for the first time since they had left their pod. Her eyes told him her guilt. The bracelet was unbroken, so the only way she could be holding that device now was that the owner of it had lost a hand, at the very least. He didn't ask who, or how. For the time being, it hardly mattered.

She held the device next to the keypad and the red light instantly switched to green, with an inoffensive and light beep. The door seal came loose, and they entered. It was as simple as that.

A shining symbol of the supposed equality that was to prosper on Oscar 70 had been the fact that each pod was identical. The pair were therefore accustomed to the round entrance hall in front of them, with ten corridors leading onto different doors. Many had commented that this layout looked like a sunshine drawn by a child, when observed from above.

Martin hoped that the inhabitants of Pod Sixteen were out. Pod Sixteen was occupied by three Betters, all working as architects on building new structures on the planet. During planning, Martin had pointed out the dangers of taking this pod, for although they may leave the pod often to observe the building work taking place, they were equally likely to be at the base, planning, drawing, doing whatever architects did. Roman had met this resistance with the point that the remaining seven in this pod were tester Sups, so they were likely to be elsewhere. Feeling that familiar bubble of rage,

225

Martin didn't have to think for very long to work out who the wrist device would belong to.

It was very quiet. They had waited until precisely 10am in the hope that shifts for the day would have started for all inhabitants of Oscar 70, and it seemed, so far, that they were right. Feeling the tightening of his chest take hold for a second time that day, Martin leant against the wall as Amy sprang from room to room, checking for people.

On the seventh door, he saw her freeze. The only reason she would do that would be someone in the room, so he readied himself for combat. At least he mentally readied himself; physically, he was helpless. Amy was lucky enough – was lucky the right word? – to have a stolen gun in her pocket, taken from Guy's quarters a long time ago. Martin, however, was useless – a child under her protection.

For several seconds, nothing happened. Amy stood looking into the room, and he stood on looking at her. She didn't raise her hands in supplication, and she didn't speak, so what she was looking at in the room became more of a mystery. He moved slowly, more from physical weakness than fear, to see a room much like all the others; dining table, work desk, bed...So that was it. On the bed, despite it being 10am and well past the start of shifts, a young girl lay sleeping.

Becoming aware of every noise he was making, he slow-stepped closer to take a look at her. He didn't know her, but he knew what she was. Her hair, the colour of a strong tea, was bedraggled and spread messily over her pillow, and her face was young, so young...She couldn't have been more than fifteen. What earmarked her as a tester Sup, though, was the evil rash covering half of her body, like she had been sliced in two vertically. She was clearly sleeping off some bad reaction, possibly to a poisonous substance she had been forced to test on the planet, and the two of them started to breathe a little more easily, sensing how deep her sleep was.

Martin had had several silent conversations in his life, so he was able to communicate his feelings very easily as Amy reached for her gun. His eyes, his poise, told her clearly that if she brought any harm to this innocent Sup, he would harm her. What was their mission for, after all? Hadn't they waited for him, specifically, to recruit Sups to support them? Clearly, someone had already died for them and someone was one person too many.

Roughly, he gripped Amy's arm, reminding himself of the cruel Betters who would discipline him in his youth, and he dragged her from the room. His voice was little more than a whisper, "Lock the door. She is coming with us. Do not argue."

Amy didn't argue, but checked the remaining three rooms. All empty. Something like relief rushed over him as he realised he had saved a life. He watched from the corridor as Amy operated the glowing controls in the cockpit, and he tried to ignore the shaking of her hands.

Charlotte

It was only when she soared above Oscar 70 in Pod Eleven that Charlotte recognised a problem. Seeing the ground blur below her made her stomach feel empty. She felt the blood pump around her body. She wanted to laugh for no reason whatsoever. Being in the air, moving, finding new things: this was what she needed. Why, then, had she chosen a planet that, beautiful as it was, never changed? Why had she chosen a land of continuous day and hellish heat? Because she had never believed she'd get there, of course. But now she had. She had been settled but a month and was running away again.

Obtaining entrance to the pod's cockpit had been easy. Smiling, Charlotte had informed Lily, the pod's leading mathematician, that she wanted to perform a safety check of all transport equipment. Why was Roman with her? Training, of course. Absorbed in her impending expedition for the day – it seemed that it was a rest day for Lily and she was looking forward to exploring west of the pod – she had simply smiled and let the pair of them in. Lily hadn't known that they would steal her home, though, and Charlotte wondered how angry she would be. She imagined her returning from exploring and finding the pod gone. She pictured her pointed thin face scowling at the sky. Perhaps she would even shake a fist. Charlotte didn't really care. Plenty of new buildings were popping up, although creating a new civilisation was a slow business. She was sure they would be fine. And besides, they'd be in touch.

Remembering her training, Charlotte slowed Pod Eleven onto the grey earth of the Twilight Strip. Her first thought, looking at the cool and violet sky, was how she had missed sunsets. The sun was not setting of course – just differently positioned on the horizon – but the light was smooth and as cool as the air. Yes, she had missed sunsets. She had missed the colour grey. She missed Martin at that moment. She loved him so much that being apart from him even for this brief amount of time was like physical discomfort, and she shocked herself to be making connections between sunsets and romance. She wondered where the detached scientist that was Charlotte Dobson had gone.

They had planned to land one mile apart from one another, for safety and to spread their living space, so there was no initial meeting, no firm embraces. Charlotte and Roman were met with silence, and worry.

They had spoken a great deal in the past years, these two, but now there was nothing to say. There was also everything to say, but they couldn't bear that yet, so they settled for nothing, and they walked in silence to the agreed coordinates to meet the others. Every so often, Roman would glance at Charlotte and smile. As a man of many words, his smile meant much to her, and she found herself linking arms with him: two comrades discovering a new world together. At one point, she thought she heard another pod land - that beautiful technological hum before it hits the ground was unmistakeable - but her mind was swimming with so many thoughts and hopes and cares, it could have been an idle fancy.

She and Roman were the last to arrive, and a quick head count answered most of her questions. Amy, Martin and

Aaron were present and correct, and her heart leapt to see a young boy clutching Aaron's hand. Christian. He was silent and chewing his free hand, looking at each adult in turn. There was no other woman. It seemed that Aaron had travelled alone.

Charlotte ran to Martin and threw herself into his chest. The first words she spoke since landing the pod were to him, and she almost panted, "That's it. We don't leave each other again. Never."

Martin smiled, and she thought that she could detect a small twinkle in his eyes, despite his pallor. "Fine by me."

It took all of her self-restraint to not embrace him there and then, in front of the others, and it took a while for her euphoria to give way and for her to note the solemn expressions around her. It must have been instinct that caused the boy to move towards her and cling to her leg. Feeling a rush of something like pride, she drew him towards her and stroked his hair. It was thick and dark, like hers. She looked enquiringly at Aaron, realising that his face did not show boredom, but something like terror. He met her gaze, "They aren't here, Charlotte, the people on Pods Nineteen and Twenty. The pods are there, but not them. Weren't they supposed to meet us here?" His voice rose an octave. "At this exact time?"

The horror of them not being here would have been too much to bear, so she decided, standing there on that barren landscape, that they *were* there, somewhere. They must have gone deeper into the caves than originally planned; perhaps they had found shelter there that outclassed the pods. She managed a smile, "I'm sure it's fine, Aaron. They are archaeologists, after all. That's why they were sent here. They'll be assessing the landscape."

"Without leaving anyone to man their stations?"

"There are only ten of them. Perhaps they needed everyone. Have many resources been taken?"

"Quite a few, yes."

"Well, then." She felt herself becoming a leader, forcing herself to be composed when, inside, a riot was taking place. She smiled again. "It will all be fine. There are many reasons they might not be here at this moment."

Aaron's expression did not change. "We've travelled 10,000 miles to meet them. We've risked our lives. I just thought that they might have left a note." He kicked the dirt and sat down on the barren ground.

****
***

The next two weeks were full of frenzied planning, so much so that Charlotte was reminded of Dawns' Laboratories just before they left Earth. The knot in her stomach now, though, was more terror than excitement. Aaron spent all of his waking hours looking for their lost allies. Sometimes, he was gone for twelve hour stretches, but each time he returned, bringing no news and looking ever so slightly more deflated than the time before. Martin had sent a statement out to all of the pods back at the Paradise Strip, declaring their intentions to establish a fair and just society and entreating others to get in contact with them, by any means they could, if they wished to support them. They had received no responses yet, but every one of them was sure that this was because of fear rather than a lack of willing. Roman became especially loquacious, but his concerns were less practical, and he began lecturing the others at length at how they should establish an elected leader to start ensuring that, on this part of the planet at least, justice would prevail and they could deliver what Martin had promised to the others.

Charlotte was amused. "There are seven of us, Roman, and that includes a nameless girl who we are yet to see awake."

"It doesn't matter, Sparky. Get justice wrong, and you get everything wrong."

She found Roman difficult to speak to when he was so pensive, so serious. She knew that he was a world away from her in his thoughts, and to speak would be a waste of time, so she waited.

Eventually, he sighed and continued, "Did you know, in America, the Sups are executed as soon as they fail the test?"

"Yes, I did know that."

"Seems so much better in a way. Quick, simple, no pain. The strongest genes survive and everyone's happy."

"Apart from the eleven year-old children being executed and their parents being left behind."

He smiled. "Exactly. It isn't quick and simple, is it? Over there, we had glittering towers, wealth," his voice rose to a near shout, "We had enough for everyone, in my opinion, but they were *greedy!*" To her amusement again, he gestured at the sky, pointing to a remote country on a remote planet that didn't mean anything to them anymore. "They were greedy and they created the wrong kind of justice! You can get your

232

resources from the caves, you can seek out sustenance, but without justice...We are lost already." She was sure that Roman would light a cigarette after such a speech if he could, but instead he simply stood there, flexing his fingers at his sides.

And so it was decided that Roman would create a system of government on behalf of his comrades who trusted him so. Every decision would be based on a vote until their numbers were enough to elect a group of representatives, who would be re-elected on a yearly basis or stand down. They would *not* be called a Panel.

Yes, yes, Charlotte had told him. But first thing really is first. We need to find the inhabitants of Pods Nineteen and Twenty. We need places to live, we need to harvest the materials available to us. We need to be explorers.

And so, on A-day three of their wait, they went into the caves.

* *
* *

It became clear, standing on that hard grey dust, the swirling orange clouds above them, arms embracing their chests to fight off the chill of the Twilight Strip, that they would remember this moment for the rest of their lives. They had to go into the caves – it was the only logical solution – but for the first time in her scientific career, Charlotte Dawns felt like she didn't know enough. The interstellar probes had told the group very little about the cave systems, being aerial cameras, so the caves remained yet another of Oscar 70's enticing mysteries. For all they knew, the caves went down to the centre of the planet, although Charlotte had scoffed that that was rather unlikely. They could go all the way to the Dark Lands, though, and she had offered an involuntary shiver as she said so. The series of caves they had chosen sprang from the dust like knuckles, whereas others along the horizon sank into the floor like the knuckles had punched the earth and left a heavy dent. There were several openings, each as gaping and black as the last, and for a moment they all stood there awaiting her instruction. Nobody had been this far out yet, so each opening was equally mysterious. How could she know? In the end, she simply selected the largest opening, believing, idly, that it may lead to the largest cave. Her stomach lurched at the idea of pinning their hopes on a lucky guess.

There were so few of them, particularly in the absence of the inhabitants of Pods Nineteen and Twenty, so it was decided that only one person could be risked. True to Roman's system, everyone was given the chance to volunteer and then the group voted who should go first and report back. In the end, all had volunteered. She had promised to be his equal, but even so, Charlotte would have used force to stop Martin from going in there. His health had become increasingly concerning over the past fortnight, and she was unsure even about him standing there with the others in this chill, but she didn't say so.

In the end, she didn't have to say a thing, because of what Amy said.

It would be fair to say that Charlotte had overlooked Amy for the last month; she was very much Roman's friend, and the two women had little regard for one another, really. But she was their medic, she was strong and intelligent, and they needed her. She disregarded Amy going into the caves nearly as quickly as she did Martin.

But Amy shook her head, slowly and carefully, speaking in her beautiful Russian-English-American hybrid, "Aaron will not go, because then you would only have two Sups to represent you, and that includes a girl on the edge of death. Roman will not go, because I would not allow it." She paused and allowed her statement to hang in the air a moment. Charlotte had seen that look before. She didn't let it hang too long, though, before continuing, "And besides, he is needed for this 'new society' that you propose. Charlotte cannot go – she leads, and she is a mother." Charlotte felt a pang to remember the last three days, playing with her beautiful innocent boy, exploring and living. Living a life. Amy continued, "Martin wouldn't last half an hour in there, in the damp and the darkness." Amy shivered, and Charlotte started to wonder whether or not *anyone* should go in. She cast a glance at Martin, barely keeping his bloodshot eyes open. Had he lost even more weight since yesterday? Perhaps they should just go back – forget everything. Would living under the leadership of the Dawns be so bad, really? After all, they hadn't killed Martin, they had given him back... Amy continued. "In Russia, I was an only child – thank the stars. My parents pushed me hard. I think they wanted me to become a Superior Better to escape the squalor of our town. So I came here, and I helped discover a new world." Listening to her, Charlotte was sure that, in another time and place, perhaps they could have been friends. "And I did not get here by standing on the – do you say sidelines? - and letting others do things for me. I am strong. I am athletic. I go."

Roman opened his mouth to protest but she stopped it with one look. He clearly knew when he was beaten. Charlotte knew what Amy had done to get onto Pod Sixteen– Martin had told her the moment they were alone together, and she fancied that Roman knew it too. They all knew, probably, that Amy *needed* to do this to cleanse her soul, to be a hero once more, but that conversation remained silent, thickening the air but never to be given a voice.

So, Amy went.

She was unprepared, really. These pioneering scientists had traversed light years, and yet, when Amy Tereckhov stepped daintily into the mouth of that cave, she was armed with a torch, a blinking wrist band, a stolen gun, and a rope tied to her waist. Communication devices were unlikely to work when she was so far down, but she took her radio with her anyway; it would probably work for a while. Perhaps it also felt like taking company down there with her: a shred of civilization in the bowels of the most alien place they had yet been.

For over an hour, Amy sent reports via her radio. Their tense waiting was punctuated with phrases such as "it's so dark" and "it's getting colder. " Charlotte resisted the urge to roll her eyes at such banal and unscientific updates. An hour of reporting dampness and darkness, and then nothing. Perhaps Amy had grown tired of saying the same thing, and so they waited.

They had waited too long. They knew it, but didn't know how to say so. They had agreed, unequivocally, that nobody else would enter until she came back, but as the hours stretched into a half day, they started to wonder how long that would take. As they reached the ten hour point, they thought they heard a muffled bang come from the radio – a series of six muffled bangs in fact – so it seemed the radio had malfunctioned.

They had all been holding the rope, perhaps because in some sense it felt like they were holding her, so she was not alone down there. When Charlotte mustered up the nerve to tug it, there was no tension at the end of that rope. There was no resistance. No answering tug. There was only a weight, unrelenting and unresisting.

It was Aaron who had eventually risen to declare they had waited long enough. The end of Amy's rope was held taut by the cave entrance, and he held onto it tightly and started to walk, following the trail she had left.

Impotent and cold, the others waited. They had not argued with Aaron about going in; to do so would be to admit to the very real danger that they would never see him or Amy again.

When he finally dragged her corpse out of the cave, sweating and silent, Amy's rosy complexion was pockmarked and a vicious red, similar in colour to Star Four itself. Her face was covered in blood, as if someone had stabbed her with a thousand tiny spikes and upturned her flesh like it was fresh soil. Now the body was fully free from the caves, Charlotte gasped to see a black ghost, like a child's drawing, rise from Amy and fly back into the cave. It happened so quickly she might have dreamed it, and she blinked like a madwoman.

But of course it was not a ghost. She knew what it was. The entomologists on Pod Nine had warned them all of black insects the size of golf balls, with armour-like skin and razor-sharp teeth. Charlotte had not known that they lived in the caves. Amy had been the first casualty of these monsters, Charlotte believed, but she was unlikely to be the last. It seemed that they hunted in packs. It seemed that they resided in the caves as well as around Pod Nine.

What was more terrifying than Amy's mutilated body - and there was little doubt that this was a terrifying sight - was the idea that the caves were not habitable. Without the caves, without the water and shelter they provided, they were just six, now five, adults and some advanced huts. Added to this, their one qualified medic lay dead before them.

Roman's shoulders shook as he beheld this sight, and his eyes, levelled at Aaron, seemed to spit hatred, "Why are you still alive? What did you do?"

Aaron's face was open, honest, confused, "She was covered in those – those black things. I don't know why they didn't come for me. Not one of them landed on my skin. Before I knew what I was doing, I was carrying her." His arms flopped at his sides as he panted, avoiding Roman's gaze. "They kept biting her until I dragged her into the light."

****

Roman took Amy's body away. Nobody asked where he was taking her, and nobody offered to accompany him. He had declared, "I am taking Amy away," and it was only then that Charlotte noted how Roman did not – had not ever - used a nickname for Amy. That said something, although she wasn't sure what. For the hours following her death, Charlotte felt numb, and responsible and, worst of all, foolish. Looking into Roman's eyes, she knew that he blamed her, and there was little she could say to change that. They were here because of her, abandoned and lost on the other side of an alien world. She didn't know how much he had loved Amy because she had never asked, and as Charlotte sat and thought now, in the comfort of Pod Eleven, she told herself ardently that this had not been due to selfishness on her part, but pride and a sense of privacy on his.

Five A-days after Amy's death, Roman still had not returned, and the downpours came, regular as menses. Rain hammered the sides of the pods with a force so angry Charlotte could have sworn that Oscar 70 was saying to them, "Go away. Go away. You are wrong here." She recalled how, back on Earth, she had prayed for space and freedom. Now, she had that in abundance, and she felt sick, and small. At least there was Christian, who bore the rain with a restless interest, pressing his face to the windows and counting the rain drops in a manner that reminded Charlotte of herself.

Martin had been sitting with her all the while, and she had stoked his hair absent-mindedly as he slept. He had slept a lot in recent days, and it seemed that they all tried desperately to speak of anything but his health. As he stirred beneath her hand, she leant into him and closed her eyes also.

When he spoke to her, it was a murmur, "I want to go home, Charlotte."

She knew this, naturally. He had a family there now, and nothing she could say about the ravages of time dilation would deter him. Dinah's daughter may still be a relatively young woman, and he *owed* her, didn't he? She cursed his decency, yet it filled her with pride also.

239

He continued to mumble, sleepily and gently, "This planet isn't what you thought it would be, is it? It's hostile. It doesn't want us here. And Earth might be...better, when we return."

She attempted to sound dreamy, casual also, but failed. "It could be a lot worse." She gripped him closely to her, but not so tightly that she would hurt his chest, "Stay here with me, Martin. Stay here. Here is just me and you."

"And Christian."

She smiled. "Exactly. We can become something." She had spent her time over the last three days spreading herself between her son and her lover. Both of them had said little about the matter. Martin treated Christian like all the other people present did – with kindness and a gentle affection. Christian treated them all with an excited interest. Charlotte had been right: he was young enough for wrongs to be put right. She was exhausted, but full of joy.

He simply smiled. She could see that he was sinking back into the heavy sleep that he had risen from. She even wondered if he might not remember what he had just said. She could hope, couldn't she? She wondered how long she might create an artificial world that was just the three of them, free from the interventions and the selfishness of others.

Sinking back, his voice became even thicker. "Come back to Earth with me, Charlotte. That's where the real fight is. Let the Dawns take Oscar 70. Let's take the world."

She had expected to never go home. Karen and Daniel would go home, bask in the glory of a mission well done, and take her glory. But she would have her Oscar 70. That had always been the plan. Oscar 70 was her world, but, she realised with a grief that felt solid in her chest, it wasn't Martin's. She didn't answer him, but felt that, finally, after everything she had been through, upon this one drowsy speech, she knew what despair felt like.

Karen

Daniel had delighted in telling her that she had been wrong to wake the boy. She still didn't think so. Yes, she had seen the video, she had listened, as had the others, to the boy declaring how the Supplementaries were now free to choose a "new path" and would be able to enjoy a "beautiful and blossoming spring" or some such metaphor and, yes, it had filled her with rage, but her husband was a fool to think that this was not bound to happen. With a smile, she had told the others, by all means, listen to the speech, make contact if you like. Nobody had. They knew that the best way to survive would be to remain here, where order prevailed and where resources were plenty. Better to quash a rebellion than no rebellion take place at all. They would win the battle, and the war, not to be threatened again.

When she thought of how they had taken Pod Thirteen, though, and the seventy babies in it, her skin tingled with heat. The rage that had slept in Karen Dawns for years, disguised as petty bitterness and a lust for control, had become a waking dragon that would slay anyone who crossed its path. The loss of the Sup babies she could live with, they could make plenty more, but they had taken Christian. They had taken her, *her*, beautiful child, who bore the eyes of his father and who promised to carry on the Dawns name when they were dead. She saw a lot of Daniel in that boy, and if she tried really hard, and concentrated on the idea, he even seemed like her child...

At least Pod Thirteen had not had the Population Chamber and now, sitting in the crèche she did not dare leave, Karen clutched the glass case, noting for the first time how thin and papery her hands had become, violet veins rising from the back of them, soft and spongy, like worms. When had she gotten so old? Perhaps that was why Daniel never touched her anymore, never spoke of anything but Charlotte...

It was clear to her now. She should not have pushed Charlotte away. Vainly, she had planned to return to Earth with Christian and leave Charlotte here to rule in their absence. She and Daniel would never see this cursed place again but, oh! What stories they would tell back on Earth! And nobody on Earth would know. They wouldn't know how far Charlotte had fallen. They wouldn't know that the child simply *had* to be taken away from her, for his own good. Doctor Richard Dawns had wanted him to stay on the planet as some kind of leader, but Richard Dawns would be dead when they returned...

So, then. The solution was simple. She needed to get the child back. Get him back and take him away from her and let the others rot here together if that is what they wanted.

But, no. That wasn't enough. They had hurt her, and she wanted to hurt them.

The white door swept aside as Aru Hayer entered. In another life, this girl could have been an Indian princess; even Karen had to admit that she was an absolute beauty. The meaning of her name – Bright Eyes - was apt: the girl really did have the most captivating eyes. That beauty brought Karen no joy, however: only anger. She wanted to make her so utterly miserable that those eyes would never shine brightly again.

Three weeks ago had been a start, when she had seen Aru bid farewell to Sup Aaron 926501 for the last time. It

243

amused her to think that the girl had been unaware of how obvious their blossoming – romance was the word but Karen almost choked on it – blossoming romance had been. There must be something about Sup boys that she was missing. She scoffed at the very idea that the two had hoped to run away together. After a few weeks of recollection, she was no longer angry at this girl's ingratitude at being given the lofty position of head medic and daring to betray her. She was past that, now. At this stage, she found it amusing, and enjoyed watching the lovers' futile plans unravel before her very eyes. Then, though, she had been furious.

So she had done what she did best. Karen Dawns had destroyed their happiness, little by little. She had threatened and manipulated until there was no way out for the girl other than the path she so desperately did not want to take. She had watched those striking eyes fill with hot water as he left, for what they knew was the final time. When Karen had approached her, Aru's stance did not alter at all. She simply spoke in her usual perfect English, eyes fixed on Aaron's form dwindling, forsaking her. "You promise he will be unharmed?"

"Completely. That is, if you said exactly what I told you to."

She sighed and nodded, breathing deeply in what could have been viewed as relief, but perhaps it was grief. "Yes. I told him. I told him that I shan't be going with him. I told him that I do not love him." Her eyes remained fixed on the dot in the distance. "I even made up a lover back on Earth that I still care for. I wanted him to believe me, you see. I don't want him to die."

"Good. Good. And don't be sad. You've saved his life. He may never forgive you for lying, or he might try to get back to Earth - who knows? But you saved his life."

She had known of their plans to run away but not the plan to steal the pod, and since it disappeared, Aru had lived a life of misery. Karen had enjoyed placing extra shifts on her, giving her more babies than she could cope with, and had halved her rations. None of this was really necessary, of course, because she had lost that Sup lover of hers, and those black, enchanting eyes were once again empty.

This was the first time they had spoken since that day. Entering now, Aru might have been a Supplementary; the way she carried herself and the way she spoke displayed a person who had lost everything, and not really even fought for it. She didn't speak, but waited to listen. Good. Very good.

Karen smiled, imagining as she did so that this might be how a magnanimous Panel member might smile. Surely, after all of her services to the Cause, she would be given a place on the Panel when they return to Earth? She spoke with an authority like that had already happened. "Aru. I have one last favour to ask of you. I trust that I will meet no objection."

She didn't.

Charlotte

They didn't go into the caves again; Charlotte had expressly forbidden it. It was horribly clear to all of them, now, where the inhabitants of Pods Nineteen and Twenty were, but despite all this they remained optimistic. Daily, Martin plugged at the pods where they thought support might be best mustered, and he even spoke to a few old friends from Eve One, but they always got the same response. We agree with you, we admire you, but we won't fight. There aren't enough like us. We won't win.

And so her dream came true, in a fashion: she and Martin were left alone to enjoy one another's love. They even had Christian, and what could have been a tale of despondency became a tale of joy. The rains stopped, as they always did, and the calmer air brought with it the milky hue of twilight that she was coming to associate with her own happiness. Every A-day they would walk with Christian, avoiding the caves of course, and breathe in the fresh air around them, savouring the quiet that was like none they had experienced before. Martin seemed to grow stronger by the day, and she started to hope that he might make a full recovery. Roman had returned and seemed lighter, as if a great burden had gone. The tester Sup that they had brought with them – Lavinia, she was called - had woken and was blossoming. Her hair, once dry and pale, had become a glowing chestnut. She cared for many of the babies in Pod Thirteen and, crucially, she cared for Aaron. She seemed to fill an emptiness in that boy that none of them had even known was there. They saw them often, matching chestnut hair and beautiful bodies,

246

talking, smiling, laughing, and they would smile to think of the future in this place. A future existed, and it was good. They hardly looked up to see the interstellar probes checking on their location. So the Leaders knew where they were. They still wouldn't care enough to get to them. Regularly, Martin reminded her of the plan to overthrow the Dawns, and pleaded with her to go back to Earth with him, somehow, when the time came, but her response was always the same. *Later, later…* For the first time in her short life, she had found a kind of peace.

Just as the ever-fixed sun did not alert them to the passing of the hours, they had no seasons to warn them of the changing months, and it seemed that she had only had a day or so like this when the calendar read that they had been there six months. One artificial morning, she woke from sleep but seemed to be waking from another kind of sleep also. Time, that beast that controlled so much of what she did, was running out.

She had stretched next to him in bed, as always, and allowed her small frame to be wrapped in his larger arms, as always. What she said next, though, was new, "Martin. It's time. Let's fight them."

And so the planning began in earnest. This time, the plan was simple. Get to Pod One by using Pod Eleven's driving capabilities on land, enter it in the same manner Amy had entered Pod Sixteen, take the weapons, take the supplies, and fight them. They were few, but they were determined and, more importantly, they would take the Dawns by surprise. Why had they been so determined to increase their numbers first? Take the power base first: that was the way to do it. Authority would follow.

Six A-days before the attack was scheduled, Charlotte decided to take a walk alone. She did this rarely, loving Martin and Christian's company so, but they were getting close to their final mission, or what felt like their final mission anyway, and she wanted some time in the company of the planet that had defined her very being for so long. She trod on its ground, as if in worship, and told herself, as she had done all those months ago when she first arrived, *I am really here. This is really Oscar 70 and I really got here. I can do anything. I can defeat them.*

It turned out that they had been waiting to find her alone for a long time. As she basked in the arms of the planet, she thought she saw some white forms, blurred and ethereal in the distance. It was just fancy, of course; she knew that everyone was back at the pods. But no, she saw them, really saw them; this wasn't like her nightmares from before. Three men, burly and serious, men who she vaguely recognised but couldn't place, wearing Eve One uniforms, were running towards her. She smiled, and even began to wave, frantically with both hands. Perhaps they were the inhabitants of Pods Nineteen and Twenty? Her smile faded and her hands fell when she saw the guns they carried.

* *

Piercing pain welcomed her on waking, as if her head had been sliced by a thousand internal knives. Pathetically, she clutched her head, and thought this headache alone would kill her, if whatever came next did not. She was in a pod that was not their own, on a bed that was not hers; she realised this quickly, taking in the walls that were familiar and unfamiliar at once, the furniture that had a different coat thrown upon it, the walls that held different paintings...

248

When she turned sideways, her breath caught in her mouth. Had she the strength or the courage, she would have screamed, but all she could do was whimper like a captured animal. At her bedside, serenely stroking the blanket smooth, was Karen Dawns, and that smile.

Her voice was like a lullaby. "Don't worry, Sweetheart. I'm not angry. I know you're simply confused. I've given you a little something to take the confusion away, that's all. The plant life on this planet really does yield the most wonderful medicine. Just relax and let it take hold fully."

Charlotte felt the cold stab of what was yet another needle, and this time she did scream. Or at least she thought she did. Disorientated and weakened as she was, it could have simply been another whimper.

Karen continued, in the same soothing but not soothing voice as before, "Now you need to listen carefully to me, Charlotte. I have drained the fuel from every pod that you left behind to get to you, but now we need Christian. To get Christian, I need you. When you feel better, you will go, with me of course, and we will collect him. Then we will go back to Earth. Together."

There had been times, in recent months, when Charlotte Dawns had thought she was losing her mind. She saw now, though, that she was perfectly sane, and it had simply been her priorities that were hazy. She wondered how she had missed Karen's insanity, though, as she sat there like a benevolent saint, planning kidnap, and possibly worse. Charlotte opened her mouth to speak but found that she could not.

Karen mimicked a concerned nurse, or something very much like that. "What was that? Pardon?" She widened her eyes in mock surprise. "Oh! You don't *want* to! Oh, well then! Fine." She paused, one heartbeat. "But of course I will have to kill the boy. That Sup boy, I mean. I can't imagine that he'd be hard to kill, not with the friends that I have."

At that moment, a beautiful Indian girl walked into the room. Charlotte had seen her before, not since being aboard Eve One, but she knew who she was. Martin had sat with Aaron many an evening, lamenting the heartbreak that this girl had caused. Had she been able to move, or speak, she was sure that she would have done or said something spiteful. Karen continued her pantomime of surprise, "Ah! Aru. Thank you for joining us. I'm afraid I have given Mrs. Dawns a chance to cooperate and she will not, therefore we need to move to Plan B."

Aru didn't react. A beautiful robot, she walked to the television screen, 150 inches high as was the regulation for all communication screens, and asked for Pod Eleven. Charlotte could see this all from the corner of her eye, but the screen itself was just out of view. She did, though, hear Martin's voice when he answered. The worry in his voice dulled every other sense and she tried to shout, tried to move. Of course it was hopeless, so she lay there, as he had done for those years on Eve One in Suspended Sleep, and she allowed the events to wash over her.

At every panicked word, her heart broke a little more. "Aru?" Martin had said, "Why are you contacting me? Of all people?"

But Aru would speak to nobody but Aaron. That was the way of Karen Dawns, in the end: kill them with love. She lay, useless and inactive, as Aru told Aaron the whole sorry tale. She told him how Charlotte had been apprehended by the Dawns, how, foolishly, she had fought against them. But then she had realised the error of her ways. No, she did not wish to speak to Martin, or anyone. She never wanted to speak to them again. But she wanted Christian back, and could Aaron please see to it that this happened? They were waiting less than twenty miles away, and could be with them soon. If he did all this then, perhaps, he and Aru could be together again.

And Charlotte could do nothing. The drugs that Karen had given her were powerful, and they were sucking her under quickly. She struggled against the tide of unconsciousness that was sweeping over her, and she remained long enough to hear Aru say, "Please come back to me, Aaron, and bring the child with you. We're all dead if you don't."

Martin

Since leaving Earth, be it due to exhaustion or distraction, Martin hadn't had quite so many nightmares, but, ever since Amy's death, his nightmare had been a nightly visitor again. It would come, clothed in the delectable guise of sleep, and bleed into the cracks of his unconsciousness. He knew that he looked peaceful as he slept, because Charlotte had told him so, but he suspected that his tranquil exterior was a side-effect of how weak his body was. Of course he did not tell her that; he would much rather she believed that he slept peacefully and with a contented soul because of all that she had done to make him content and peaceful. He did not consider this dishonest in the way that she had been. It was his private torment, and her knowing it would do no good whatsoever. He was adept at hiding his private terrors, so he was sure that the calm exterior remained when he woke also.

It was always the same. He was back at Sup Unit 81. The days there reminded him a little of A-days on Oscar 70 (he recalled with more than a touch of irony) because they seemed to never end. From putting his bare feet on the ice cold floor before sunrise, to passing out from fatigue at the end of the day, it was all one.

Enough of that. His dream did not recall the days, but the nights. They focused on a Unit Master who went by the name of Mr. Hope; Martin could hardly conceive a less befitting name and he was sure it was a pseudonym, possibly created to torment the Supplementaries in his care. Funnily enough, he never dreamed of Mr. Hope's nightly visits to the boys' room, and how he had placed his freezing hands under the covers, nor did he dream of the beatings the boys received if they did not satisfy the man, or his guests...No, he didn't dream of these things.

He dreamt of the light on the landing outside his room in that godforsaken place. The boys would sleep at least twelve to a room, stacked atop one another like crates, two to a bed. Mr. Hope would leave that light on, blazing through the crack in the door, a physical reminder that he was there, watching, waiting, even as they slept...

After these dreams, Martin did not like to open his eyes for fear of seeing Star Four. He knew it was foolish, but the glare of this sun, always following him, watching his every move, made him feel as naked and as vulnerable as when he had been a young boy, clutching the covers up to his nose, watching the door, waiting for it to open and for light to fill the room...

This morning when his eyes filled with light, he reached his arm out to her, as always. He needed her embrace to take the horror away. Instead, he was met with a soft blanket, a cold pillow.

But Aaron was there. He had been there since the news, if one could call it news, for he was sure there was not one shred of truth in it. Of course Martin didn't believe it, and he had persuaded the others that it wasn't true also. What was true, though, was that Charlotte was with them, and she was in serious danger. Christian was sitting on Aaron's knee, absorbed in a book and muttering under his breath. Since the news (if one could call it news) Christian had never been left alone, and Martin could see that he needed some time alone. He was accustomed to it, after all, and he was certain

253

that the child who had so enjoyed solitude for so many years, solitude punctuated by the overbearing affections of Karen Dawns, when she had time, was suddenly confused by this great fuss surrounding him.

For many months now, he had been feeling sprightlier, and Charlotte's kidnap and the threat that brought had only served to fill him with renewed energy. He was surprised he had slept at all, actually, but, seeing the child, a tormented frown shadowing his usually wide eyes, he felt angry, and more awake than ever. He wanted her, so badly, he wanted her back with him, to hold her, be with her, to grow with her. But, equally, he wanted to reunite her with her son. God knows, he had been offered a confused version of childhood thus far, and she had offered him some form of normality. More important than that, she loved the child with an intensity that rendered him lost for words.

He knew that they were coming. Aaron had refused to hand over the boy, and in doing so invited the full force of their wrath to their quarters.

The wrath came at noon. Oscar 70 didn't, it seemed, have the climate for an attack at dawn. After all, each hour was the same. Their noon was the purple haze that had filled their eyes for the past six months. He was convinced that if he ever saw the brightness of the Paradise Strip again, he would go blind. He preferred the dusk, settled over them and calming before the storm comes.

It was Pod One itself, humming – did it hum louder than the others? It dropped into place two hundred yards in front of them. Three of them - Martin, Aaron and Roman– stood waiting, a perfect line. They knew that, when the door

254

opened, a hundred slaves could pour out and murder them. Carnage could ensue. But the child made that unlikely. The Dawns did not know that Christian was safely tucked away in Pod Sixteen with Lavinia. It would take hours to find him, and Martin suspected that they'd try the caves first.

It really is true, Martin thought, that time slows when you are waiting for something. Forget time dilation, the idea that suspense bends time is *real*. Charlotte would find that funny; she'd roll her eyes at the silly romantic that loves literature and explain to him why, actually, it isn't real. He made a mental note to discuss it with her when he had her back.

So. The waiting. They waited, with nothing but their worries and their hopes to keep them company. And a stolen gun.

The door whispered open, and, as he had suspected, it wasn't a rush of attackers, but one man, fuzzy black hair and white suit, standing in the centre of the white pod. He was so white that only his hair defined him. Martin craned his neck to look beyond Dr. Dawns, but the space behind him was empty.

Daniel Dawns clearly wanted to appear authoritative and calm, but, as he spoke, he realised his voice would not carry, so he had to shout. He therefore sounded agitated and nervous. Had they not held the woman he loved in their clutches, Martin might have found it amusing.

There was nothing amusing about what he said. "Traitors, your little mutiny has gone on for long enough. Give up the child, and you shall live. We will leave you here and we will even allow you to keep what you have stolen from us, as an expression of our benevolence."

Nobody moved. Martin found that his breath was rather noisier than the others, and he made every effort to steady it. Stony silence was their only answer to such an insult.

Another voice. A female voice that sent a chill through his soul. "I think we need to bargain a bit more heavily than that, Darling." A thin frame, tanned skin, a shock of red hair. Martin could recognise Karen Dawns from any distance. He could also recognise the woman she held at arm's length, and the gun held against her temple. If he was breathing loudly before, he was sure that now his breathing had stopped altogether.

"If I do not get my boy back, she dies. Try and ignore *that*!" She had a way of shouting that meant she never once had to inhale. It was like shouting was her natural way of speaking. She could have been sitting at a coffee table and saying these things. Her natural composure made the loudness of her voice seem almost normal. It was also as if every sound was amplified but muted at the same time, like loud music in a carpeted room.

Even from the distance they stood, he could see that Charlotte was not herself. Her movements were slower. He was sure that, staring down the barrel of a gun, she would stiffen; she was no fool. But he could see her, clear as if he had binoculars, a looseness of limb and lack of reaction that told him she had been drugged.

It all happened quite quickly after that. All that Martin remembers is seeing Daniel Dawns run towards his wife, and the sound of a gunshot. The white that was Daniel's suit began to turn red and he slumped to the ground. Later on, when Martin had time to think about this scene, he realised that the gunshot and the blood had seemed to happen at the same time, probably because light travels faster than sound but it would have taken a few seconds for the blood to come. Those little details gave the scene a dreamlike quality, like it was happening in a cartoon. He remembered cartoons; they made death seem funny. A character might have suffered from a gunshot like that and jumped up a moment later, with a few twittering bluebirds circling their head. Martin felt the gun in his pocket, checking that he hadn't pulled it out and shot the man without knowing it. The metal in his hand was cold. Karen screamed now. She could scream, after all, "You've chosen her over me for the last time!"

So that was it. Daniel had loved Charlotte also. Martin could see her sobbing now, lamenting the life she used to have, the regard she used to have for the very people who now threatened her. She seemed to be getting more alert, though it was hard to tell from this distance. It was possible that the shock of what had happened had brought her back to reality.

In the end, the three of them ran at her. For his part, Martin had decided that he *needed* to be closer; he needed to look Charlotte in the eye and tell her, silently, that all would be well. He also could not negotiate from this ridiculous distance. Aaron and Roman simply followed, and, thinking back afterwards, Martin was forced to admit that it would have looked like an attack. It was possibly not the wisest choice, then – to approach a screaming woman with a gun who had just shot her husband.

Luckily for them, Karen was a terrible shot, and she fired five remaining shots, one after the other, into the air, and the bullet cases plummeted back to the ground like intermittent rain. Out of bullets and out of ideas, she started to retreat to the ship, dragging Charlotte with her.

He shouldn't have been there, the little boy. He should have been safely hidden with Lavinia in Pod Sixteen, as agreed. Seeing her march towards the ground between them – the No Man's Land – with Christian holding her hand, trotting along like it was the most natural thing in the world, made everyone freeze.

It didn't take him long to realise. Clearly, Martin had underestimated Karen Dawns' capacity to exploit a person's weakness. Aaron did not look at him, but muttered, staring into the distance, "I'm sorry. I really am. I'm sure Aru was lying. Nearly sure. I couldn't risk it. I know what she did to me but, the thought of her in danger..." He shook his head, but Martin hoped he could not quite shake the guilt so easily. So he had persuaded Lavinia to betray them. Poor girl. He was surprised to feel his old bitterness return as he thought to himself, wryly, yes: this is what love does. He saw that, but he saw it too late. Disappointment, confusion and rage whipped at him all at once, but he didn't have time to think. They were approaching the pod at a startling rate, with Karen standing by the door, Charlotte discarded now, beckoning to them, "Come on, Christian, that's it. Come to Aunty Karen." Her smile was wide and she might have been at a children's party. He remembered parties.

Thinking about his actions afterwards, Martin had no reason to think he'd have ever done anything else. He knew how much she loved Christian, but his desire to keep Charlotte with him was stronger. So he ran towards the door, gun poised, and intercepted the boy. He tried to ignore the fact that the child squirmed and screamed in his arms, confused

258

as to why he could not play with his beloved aunt. It was his turn to deliver ultimatums. His was simple. Take the boy but give me her.

He wanted to gesture to Charlotte that all would be well, get across to her that he would be able to save them both and that Karen simply needed to be distracted for a moment. But it was no good. Charlotte looked at him like she had never really known him at all. Her eyes were wide like a doe staring at a hunter, and she actually backed further into the ship.

Ignoring his racing heart and the familiar cold sweat starting to take hold, he ran, squirming child and all, up the ramp to the door. In horror, he supposed, at Christian's trauma, Karen had placed the gun on the floor, and Martin kicked it aside. Roman and Aaron swarmed at her and held her down.

He was close enough to grab Charlotte's hand, and he felt how cold it was, as always. She clutched onto Martin so hard that he was sure he would bruise, not that he minded. He only hoped that her other hand, clasped onto Christian's shoulder, was not applying the same force.

They made their rushed and clumsy descent, the three of them, and, for that moment, Martin thought that they would make it. The door was wide open, and they were making steady progress. He saw Karen fighting fruitlessly against the clutches of Aaron and Roman, and he knew they would not let go. He saw the ramp rising, and the keypad next to the door blinking amber, signalling a countdown to closing. He did not have time to consider who activated it. He just carried on. It was only when he was a foot away from the door that he saw him – Guy Roberts, the third technician – bespectacled and with too much gel adorning his hair –

exactly as he remembered him. He snaked between the others and grabbed her. He took her with such force that her feet actually left the floor, like he was a child snatching a rag doll that he wanted. The last thing that he saw as the door closed was Karen's smile.

Martin saw the closed door and knew that she was on the other side. His vision blurred and he could have sworn that he felt his heart rattle against his ribs. Christian, confused and frightened, mewed pathetically in his arms.

Charlotte

They had lost. She knew that now. But she had lost the most.

She could hardly see the screen in front of her for tears. Those tears had fallen, persistently and shamelessly, as she felt the pod rising out of the planet's atmosphere, taking her away from everything she held dear. She didn't know what would happen to her now, and she didn't much care. Karen was inconsolable, and the last she had seen of her had been Roman and Aaron, stony-faced, dragging her away as she raved and pulled at her red hair like a lunatic.

Because it was too late. Eve One's exit programme had been activated and it was automatic from now on. Only Daniel Dawns knew the override code and Daniel Dawns was dead. Seven of the pods – the ones they had been able to activate and the ones with enough fuel- rose into the air, destined to click into the waiting cavities of Eve One. God knows who they contained; the ascent was hardly planned. Her world was receding below her and she was rising, like a helpless gas molecule in the air. Bound for Earth. Bound in technological chains.

As she had done all those years ago, she pressed herself hard against the window pane, not to touch the stars, but to touch him. She clutched the glass like it was the only thing in the world and she told herself that she could never touch him again.

He's down there and I'm here. He's down there and I'm here and we're being torn apart and I'm helpless and he's helpless and we're lost and I love him and it's hopeless and I'll never touch him again and my heart is broken and everything is broken because he isn't here...

She barely noticed when the screen clicked on, and there he was, his face 150 inches high, lighting up the room, just like he had lit up her soul. He looked ill again, and she realised – she couldn't believe she had only just realised – that he was ill when *she* wasn't there. She made him better, just like he had made her better. The heart-wrenching grief washed over her anew. Forgetting her former pride, she flew herself at the screen just like the glass was his arms and she pressed both hands against it. It was cold, so cold, and she thought about how warm he would be, only a few hundred miles below. "You're so close. If I could just fly down, I could get to you in ten minutes." She pressed herself close to the television screen, willing the space between them to close. "You're so close to me," her voice began to break and tears sprang without warning, "You're so close but so so far away!" Had she been able to, she was sure she would have broken the glass and let herself fall. She would fall and she would die, but she would be there, with him and with her child, not transported across the stars to a future she did not care to see.

Remembering, almost too late, the mania of recent months, she forced herself to be calm. They were defeated, she knew it, and she wanted him to be proud of her as they said goodbye. She tried to say something profound, something befitting of her genius IQ, but all she could manage was, "I love you. Love Christian as much as you love me." Despite herself, her voice cracked, "I don't want you to be far away from me."

Martin looked at her with those ice blue eyes - those sad sad eyes that told of a thousand miseries. She could see that he had surrendered also, and she was reminded of the lowly Sup who had worked with her at Dawns' all those years ago. It made her angry, but not at him. He sighed and never looked away. "Darling girl," he said, his voice composed and even, "I will always love you, but you have always been far away from me." With a metallic clunk, the pod attached itself to Eve One and the screen went black.

Part Four: The Empty Years

"All your letters in the sand cannot heal me like your hand,
For my life
Still ahead
Pity me."
Brian May, '39,' Night at the Opera.

Prologue

In the end, it was Doctor Charlotte Dawns who steered Eve One home. The crew was a haphazard smattering of who had been in the pods when the automatic exit had been activated, and this resulted in, naturally, mass discontent. Charlotte was not the only one to be torn away from someone she loved. It had been unplanned, chaotic, and Charlotte Dawns became famous, not for her work with Speedlight, not for her findings on Oscar 70, but for her ability to create order from the chaos.

Everyone on board was forced to work harder on their way home, partly due to the ironic lack of people but also due to the lack of Daniel Dawns' knowledge, and Charlotte worked at least fourteen hour days, being a constant presence on the ship and offering help to all the Sup crew members who were suddenly burdened with flattering but overwhelming responsibility. She never mentioned him, and she was admired amongst the crew of 78 for her steeliness in the face of obvious heartbreak. Occasionally, when she and her friends (she called them friends, now) were laughing together – how rare these moments were – Aaron or Roman would mention him and she would smile. She never went as far as to deny his existence, but she never said his name. It was only in her sleep, unshadowed by her reputation, that she allowed herself to remember him, and then the tears flowed as naturally as the pumping of her blood. She would clutch the pillowcase, the duvet, anything, and it would be him, it would be her son, it would be her lover, it would be the life she had been torn away from. And that was how it

266

was. She was torn. It was only after the event that she realised how apt that careless metaphor was. Martin and Christian had become an extension of her, and when they were taken away, she was broken, ragged, damaged. Torn.

But nobody saw this. Instead, they saw the strongest captain to ever steer a near light speed ship across the stars. They saw drive, fortitude and reliability. Nobody asked and nobody knew, but she had decided, early on, that she would not give way to heartbreak. She would not let it take her because there was no reason to be heartbroken; Martin and Christian were alive; they slept and they woke and they breathed just as she did. Martin would be 89 if she returned to Oscar 70 the way she had arrived, and it was unlikely he would live anywhere near that, with his damaged heart – damaged in more ways than one. But, she had not gone back yet, and he was therefore still alive, still waiting for her. And besides, she had enabled the human race to visit a planet 25 light years away, and she had survived the machinations of the Dawns family. She was not defeated, and she had therefore decided to not be heartbroken.

But Karen Dawns was. On Eve One's outward journey, it could be argued that she had carried 125 Sup prisoners, although such a word was never used, but now the ship had its first official prisoner. They did not count Guy Roberts as a prisoner. In a less admirable moment, Roman had beaten the man bloody, and he hadn't spoken since. He simply lived on the ship, subdued and planning. His door was locked also, but he was no prisoner; he locked it from the inside. When Roman created a lock for Karen's room, Guy had asked for one also. Roman hadn't said a word but simply nodded: it was the best truce they could hope for.

It wasn't spite, it really wasn't, but they did not know what else to do with her. Execution would have been unbecoming of them, and not indicative of the kind of world they were fighting for, but Karen Dawns was dangerous, to herself as well as others. So she was kept in the locked quarters that had been hers when they set sail all those years ago, except that anything dangerous had been removed, including access to any of Eve One's controls. They checked on her officially three times a day, when a servant delivered her meals, but Charlotte watched her often on the cameras. In many ways, her pacing, tearing her hair, banging her fists against the glass, were physical representations of how Charlotte felt, and it was a kind of therapy to watch her. Her grief was improper, embarrassing, but it was also raw and honest and Charlotte admired that.

In the days before they had imprisoned her, she had spent over two days at the controls of Eve One, trying to guess her husband's code. She had worn her fingers bloody trying to get back to the child, to undo her terrible mistake, and Charlotte was reminded of the lab rats back at Dawns', who had been given a treat at random when pressing a button in a maze. Crucially, they weren't given the treat every time, so the odd disappointment was to be expected. Eventually, the scientist controlling them would stop the supply of treats but the rats would keep pressing that button, day and night, until starvation or exhaustion would render them too weak.

Hope is a terrible thing when there is no hope to be had, so they locked her away. It didn't seem important. Far more critical was the fact that they didn't know what they were sailing towards; she was a small problem in an ocean of possible dangers.

The calculations were flawless, if difficult to comprehend. When the pods landed on Earth's soil, the travellers had been gone for seven years, but they were welcomed by a world that was fifty one and a half years older. At the time of leaving, they had discussed so many what ifs – what if we are unwelcome when we return – what if Earth is destroyed in our absence – what if they no longer *need* Oscar 70? It had been decided and it had been done: no risk without gain.

The time had come to see if the risk had been a wise one.

Charlotte

She didn't think she had ever felt so tired, and so in need of caffeine. Back on Oscar 70, it had escaped her notice that the coffee was gone, because she had Martin, and her life there had mostly been a dreamy unreality. Now she was back to working shifts, doing regular checks, being called upon for advice daily, and she was tired. She was lacking in sleep, but mostly she was tired of routine, of the same faces, the same artificial light. Her hands shook as she operated the ship's gleaming controls, but nobody noticed because she had perfected a face that said nothing. She had applied this face like make-up each morning, for the past three years, and she tried her best not to remove it at night, lest emotion undo her.

It had taken her a while to realise that Roman had always worn such a face. Since Amy was lost, though, she had started to see the cracks, and she loved him for it. She also loved the fact that he clearly knew her artifice, and he never said a word about it. His presence each morning to accompany her on the Fuel Point checks was almost as refreshing as coffee, or at least she told herself this. His smile this morning – the morning of the final check - was not blank – it told of a journey nearly over, of very real hope but also very real fear. They had been slowing down for 362 days and now, 2,504 days since leaving, they were going to return to Earth. An Earth that was 18,280 days older. Despite their early departure, Roman had decided to keep the arrival time the same; this was the way to avoid suspicion with whoever welcomed them back on Earth. This had been easy enough to manipulate; as soon as the ship started to slow, he was able to manage its speed but not its course. Charlotte smiled to herself as she remembered his promotion from technician to pilot; it had been one of her wiser moves.

He usually welcomed her with a joke, tired and clichéd as it often was, but this morning he said nothing, so Charlotte was the first to speak. She felt her cheeks burning, but to mention anything other than their impending return would have been socially ridiculous, "I don't know what I'll say when we make contact. I had a whole speech prepared, Roman, but I don't think I can say it. How can I be ready when I don't know who will welcome me?" She stared at the stars outside her window, a familiar sight that she was sorry to say goodbye to. Even now, she liked being enveloped in the vastness, despite the fact that her love had made the vastness unbearable.

He smiled, warmly, and she considered, yet again, how lucky she was that he was on her side of the doors when they closed that day, "You'll think of something, Sparky. I've seen you think on your feet before."

She managed an appeasing smirk, but they both knew that she was right. She couldn't possibly be ready. When they had left, arrangements had been made for a Panel welcome; all thirteen Panel members – whoever they may be - would make the trip to London to welcome the Eve One crew home. The date was set: 15th May 2065, at precisely 3.36pm. The ship would make contact via its radio link before the pods made their final descent.

All very well, if the status quo remained intact. But what if they were no longer welcome? There may be nobody to take

271

over Richard Dawns, so Project Eden could be under new management, and the Panel members were old when they left. Surely they were now all dead? What if a rebellion had taken place and the Panel was no longer in control? How odd to wish for something so ardently yet fear it at the same time.

She had to give her worries a voice. Her initial training had involved a working knowledge of Psychology; she supposed this was because she needed to be able to cope, as well as help others, under very strange and demanding conditions. She knew, therefore, that her way of surviving for the past three years was self-destructive. She needed to vent. She needed to trust someone a little. "One thing is for certain: I won't allow them to manipulate us, Roman. We've come so far in seven years, and seen things that most of them never will. Whatever has happened, they need to listen to *us*."

"Okay, Sparky, but tread carefully." She expected Roman to applaud such a sentiment. After all, it had been he who had pushed her in this direction recently. *Don't bend to their will,* he had said. *Don't let them make you forget what you know now*. Clearly, her face had shown him this, because he held up his hands in defence as he had done so often before. "All I'm saying is, don't give them a battle before we're ready. We need to know our enemy," he breathed out, deliberately, "That's if they are still the enemy. We need to assess the field properly before battle."

A thought that had burrowed into her heart for months was threatening to surface, like vomit. She didn't look at him; she couldn't. "It shouldn't be me, Roman."

She felt the sharpness in his voice, even though she wasn't looking at him. "What do you mean?"

"It shouldn't be me who leads the fight, if a fight is needed."

He positioned himself in front of her face, and she could see at once that he wasn't angry, but frightened. "You're the only person. You were a key supporter of the Cause and now you are converted. People admire you. People *love* you. It has to be you."

Those stars again, outside her window. He was behind one of them, waiting for her. He'd be looking at an angry red sun, she knew, but behind that angry red sun were these stars, and her, looking right back at him. She tried to avoid her voice shaking, and was subsequently furious at the beast inside her that refused such control, "I need to get back to them, Roman. Nothing matters apart from that."

He gripped her hand, and she felt at once how unlike Martin's his hands were. She remembered his hands even after three years – warm and rough like cotton. Roman's hands were sweaty, and his fingers felt too long draping over hers. He spoke slowly and deliberately, "He'd want you to fight." He loosened his grip a fraction, "And besides, you need the resources back on Earth. What happened to Merge Theory?"

Charlotte sniffed, "But Merge Theory is just that - a theory."

"Your theory. It will work. I trust you. To the moon and back, Kid. Except we've been further. You know what I mean."

As the day drew onwards, she felt like she was about to be bereaved. She had been readying herself for this for three years, convincing herself that she'd find a way to defeat the regime and get back to Oscar 70. Despite all that, at 3.20pm local time, as she addressed her devoted crew for the final time, she could not suppress the pounding in her chest. She looked at the expectant faces before her and was reminded of herself, looking up at Richard Dawns on the day she received her position at the Labs and he delivered some sanctimonious speech or other to many awed onlookers. She tried her best to shake the memory away.

Her voice was once again bold and steady, as it was on the ship when she challenged Daniel Dawns, all those years ago. She thanked them for their unbending support, and wished them well. She even managed a joke about preparing a second ship, if any of them were keen to attempt another epic mission. Her real message, though, was what she finished with, and she stood as straight as she possibly could as she delivered her final words, "We only exist now to defend the rights of every human born to be treated equally, and given equal opportunities. The days of division are over. This is the real Cause of all we do." She was met with rapturous applause. Aaron and Roman, motionless and loyal behind her, smiled as she became embarrassed by the whooping and cheering that reverberated around the ship.

The celebration was cut short by nothing more than the blinking of a green light: Earth was making contact. With hands now balanced, Charlotte turned on the television.

She had heard the phrase "my blood ran cold" several times in her life, but it had never really meant much to her. Now, though, looking at what seemed to be a distorted waxwork of Doctor Richard Dawns staring back at her, ancient and smiling, 150 inches high, she knew.

Her blood ran cold.

****

It was no waxwork. Of all the things she had expected, she had not ever imagined the horror of seeing that face again. She had expected time, in almost all ways her great nemesis, to be benevolent in this instance, and rid her of this man. Yet there he was. 115 years old. Alive. And speaking to them. His fresh and confident voice was incongruous with his polished, plastic appearance. "Welcome, Travellers!" She was sure he was surprised, although the capacity to demonstrate this in his face was long gone. "And I see I have the unexpected honour of welcoming my wife home." A pause, only a fraction, but certainly there, "Darling! Welcome." He spread his arms wide so that they filled the screen, and she ached to imagine how she had spread her arms on this very screen to hold an image of a different man, worlds away from her now.

His speech continued, and with each word, she felt undone. "I see the confusion in your faces. Do not despair, Travellers, we are not an ancient population; I am the lucky exception. I am, in every way, proof of what Science can achieve." He laughed, and she saw that familiar wave of the hand. Selfish, I know, but I had to be here for this moment." He leant back in his chair, white and plastic in a busy control room, and smiled. Charlotte was sure that the skin around his lips would crack at the effort. "Travellers, descend. Your journey is over. Welcome home."

****

They were unprepared. Having been in the company of roughly 200 adults over the past seven years, spread across an entire planet, they were now faced with an immeasurable crowd. Thousands of faces, beaming and expectant, stretched into the distance, like a wallpaper of emotion. Charlotte's impassive façade found itself challenged by fanfare music, waving flags, cheering, colour, noise and people. So many of them, synthetic, blank. Why were none of them him?

The pods clicked onto the metallic structures that they had left all those years ago. As they purred into place, Charlotte laboured on the notion that, despite everything else, the pods had been dependable to the last. It made her sad to think of them sitting empty on those structures. The grey bars seemed to dig into the beautiful white veneer. A strange thought, but she clung to it all the same. Better to think of that than consider the strangeness of the world she was about to enter. They exited the pods silently and tentatively, as if traversing alien ground once more. The only crew member who was not silent was Karen Dawns, still in chains, held firmly by two stony-faced guards, entirely in black. She had seen, as had everyone, that her father-In-law was still alive, and this seemed to renew her energy. She desired a private audience with him, it seemed, and repeatedly requested this, loudly and with a rising shrillness in her voice. She could only be heard by those on stage, though, and, as planned, she was kept at the back. Charlotte hated every note of it, but the music helped in this respect.

The stage they stepped onto was elevated above the crowd, and she had to suppress her desire to fall into them and disappear. After coming so far and losing so much, she had to face the people waiting for her on the stage. The Panel — she supposed it was still called that — awaited her, wearing their custom business wear. They were all old, many of them unnaturally so, and she found it difficult to smile back, observing the taut skin stretching around their aged lips. They stood in a line facing the crowd, waiting for their special guests from the stars. Richard Dawns stood proudly in the centre, clutching an ivory headed cane and sporting a tailored suit, just like the others. Was it the same suit he had worn, all those years ago? No, surely not; this man was far thinner than the one she had left behind. His face, though, was swollen, pink and flaccid. She felt sick to look at him. Smiling all the while, she tried to remember every inch of Martin's face: his smooth marble skin; his defined cheekbones; his ice blue eyes; the strawberry hair spurting from his chin, soft and warm...

The crowds expected an embrace: that was the worst thing. As he stood there, barely vertical, tottering on emaciated legs, arms outstretched, Charlotte steeled herself. Of course she would embrace him. She would beam to the crowds and exclaim, "My darling!" in joyful surprise. She would do this because to do otherwise would be foolish, and pointless. The crowds would cheer and whoop and stamp their feet and then, then, only then, would her heart really break. She wanted to keep Martin's touch like a tattoo on her skin. He had been the last man to hold her and she never wanted to be held by anyone else. Dr. Dawns, unbelievably, carried the same scent as he had fifty years ago, sweet and fresh and heavy, like death. She saw the beads of sweat on his fleshy skin, too rosy and too healthy; aged and wrinkled, of course, but with an unnatural sheen of youth that could only be a result of advanced technologies. He was not wearing the black spectacles of his younger years, and it changed his face entirely; his eyes looked baggy and sore, like a basset hound. She smiled and embraced him and she knew she would win. All that mattered to her, behind that smile, was that she would destroy the man in front of her. She would tear his world apart, and then find a way of getting back to her own.

Martin

He had no idea how he had been so calm when speaking to her. When the image of her finally died on that huge screen, he finally lost control. Anything that could be picked up was thrown, and he punched the black screen until it was cracked and his fist bloody. He ran outside, stumbling and staggering through his tears, into that huge expanse of land, and screamed at the sky. He felt like Romeo defying the stars. He remembered his selfishness and his cruelty. He lamented that he could never make amends to the woman who had saved his soul.

He stopped when he saw them: the two people he had left. The two living ones, anyway; Daniel Dawns lay a hundred feet or so ahead of him, soaking the ground with his blood. The two living ones had been watching him all the while, and neither had said a word. Lavinia, thin and pale, stood awkwardly clutching the hand of Charlotte's son, who regarded him calmly. She was grieving too, he realised, although her subdued tears, apologetic and awkward, spoke of her recent servitude. Christian showed no emotion, save perhaps a little confusion. The third person to gaze at Martin like he was a puzzle.

Except now, he was a puzzle to himself. What to do with a lifetime of isolation? With a sharp intake of breath, he remembered the seventy babies to care for in Pod Thirteen, and only he and Lavinia to do it. They were 10,000 miles away from anyone else, with no fuel and no means of communication. The only thing to do, really, was to explore the area properly, and regard it as home. That meant going into the caves. They had a few spacesuits, relics of earlier missions, perhaps intended for some kind of eventual museum, with them. Perhaps he could use those to protect him from the insects. Lavinia would care for the boy.

But no. Charlotte would not want anyone else to care for him. Love him, she would say. Love him as I do. Observing this quiet and distant boy, it was a tall order, but there was nothing else to be done.

Nothing else to be done but settle in for the long wait. Nothing else to be done but wait for her and love her from afar. She'd be back. It was the first time he had given way to hope in his life, and he did it because there was nothing else to be done.

Charlotte

When the music died, the embrace ended. The grip of Richard Dawns had dug into the fabric of her suit, and the creases in the material had made creases in her skin; she could feel it like a hundred cuts. The crowd instantly dropped to silence, and she suddenly felt, despite her entire crew standing behind her, vulnerable and exposed. The onlookers must have mistaken her look of confusion for joy at her husband being found alive, and she saw several nods of approval in the front rows. Her crew were silent also, even their prisoner. Time enough for personal interviews.

A woman with bleached hair and a bright pink suit tottered to the podium that was centre stage. Numbly, Charlotte thought that she recognised her. Could it be Penelope Salt? The leader of the Panel? If Charlotte was right, she must be even older than Dr. Dawns. She saw the woman grip the brass podium and clear her breath to speak. "Welcome home, brave explorers."

Yes, it was her. Charlotte would recognise that voice anywhere. As Penelope Salt spoke, she barely moved. A solid woman, tall and wide, she simply pivoted from the waist upwards to regard Charlotte, standing behind her. Her gold chains and bracelets kept catching the sun and spiking the observers with light. It was a light that seemed too bright and too yellow after a year of looking at Star Four's amber hue. This only added to the effect of her seeming inhuman, like she had been crafted deliberately for the event and would be put into storage again soon afterwards. "I can only imagine the mixed emotions and you must be feeling. Joy, I am sure, and wonderment also. In many ways, the people before you may seem like strangers," she cast a sweeping hand over the crowd, "as many of them were not even born when you left us." She turned fully now, but curled her head to speak into the microphone, "But we remember you, brave travellers, and to those who do not remember you, you are the stuff of legend. We welcome you. You will have many questions, I am sure, but for now, we must celebrate." The crowd echoed with a thunderous applause.

On this noise the music started again, and Charlotte could feel several people behind her jump at the explosion of noise. The cheers continued, and reached such a crescendo that her ears hurt. The other Panel members began to exit the stage, so Charlotte beckoned to the others to follow them. On doing so, Penelope Salt spoke again. "Mrs. Dawns, you seem to have returned with a mixed gathering. I'm sure we will hear the reasons for that later. If the Betters could please follow us, we'd like the Supplementaries in your party to remain on stage."

Glancing at Roman and Aaron behind her, looking equally panicked, she knew that this could not happen. She had no idea why they would want the Supplementaries to remain on stage, but it was unlikely to be a good thing. Equally, she did not want to confront the woman before her, in front of a huge and supportive crowd. They didn't know enough. They needed time to appease others.

As it was, freezing had been enough. Penelope Salt suddenly wore the look of a harassed teacher; it was clear that she was accustomed to being obeyed without hesitation. "Mrs. Dawns, the Betters need to exit the stage, please."

She thought quickly, and then smiled. "Of course, Madam Salt. It's just – we are *all* Betters here. Every single Supplementary remained on Oscar 70." Really, it wasn't a complete lie; the Supplementary label had been removed, at least it had at some point, and she regarded everyone standing behind her as Betters. It had also been the plan for only the Betters to return, so she felt safer, and breathed a little easier, as they all exited the stage following the Panel.

They were led through a series of grey corridors to a large auditorium, possibly used for lectures, and they were asked to be seated. It was empty, apart from twenty or so young men, dressed in khaki, stony faced, gripping enormous guns, flanking the room. The crew were robotic in their movements but every single pair of eyes moved quickly, dotting around the room, at the Panel members, and then back to Charlotte. She felt the weight of 154 eyes on her back. Sitting herself on the front row, in the centre, she saw Richard Dawns approach the podium on shaky, ancient legs and a screen blinked to life behind him. A presentation. Quite a dry welcome, then. She had positioned herself so she could see the apple symbol on his lapel; she could see the red stitching, the stains from his dinner on the front of his shirt, the whites of his eyes. For some reason, being able to see him so clearly, and his many physical flaws, made her feel calmer and more in control.

The beaming smile had gone, along with all the theatrics of the stage. Charlotte readied herself for anything, and she could feel Roman and Aaron, one at each side of her, tense. She wanted, more than anything, to hold their hands, but this would have been inappropriate. They all held their guns beneath their clothes. Dr. Dawns coughed, and it wasn't just to clear his breath; it was the cracked and spluttering cough of an ancient and dying man. That made her feel better, also. His words did not. "I'm afraid we have a problem. You disappoint, Project Eden, you really do. In your absence, we have not found a way to transport mass numbers of people to Oscar 70, so it seems your mission was wasted. We cannot get back except by the means initially used. Time dilation makes this a significant obstacle."

Had they not even *tried* in the preceding years? She felt disappointed, certainly, but she knew that there was more to come: something worse. He spluttered again and, from this distance, she could almost feel the dryness of those coughs. He desperately gulped at the glass of water in front of him as the words "THE SUPPLEMENTARY ISSUE" flashed, ten feet high and red, on the white screen. He looked directly at her, or was he looking a little to her left, at Aaron? Aaron shuffled, ever so slightly, and this time, she did squeeze his hand. "You see, after you left, Travellers, the Expansion worsened. Supplementaries continued to use valuable resources and the population problem did not right itself through sterilisation alone. We therefore introduced Handing In." As he said this, the phrase "HANDING IN" flashed huge and red also. He smirked, and Charlotte shivered to see those black eyes twinkling, as they had on the night he had fucked her. "Handing in was *my* idea, but it is something that the Panel, and therefore the entire world, has embraced. You see, what we did before was so *half-hearted*, and therefore not effective, so Handing In solved that. We worked closely with our American friends on this. The solution was simple. Now, should a child fail the test,

284

they are Handed In, immediately, to one of our centres, and dealt with."

Dealt with. Everyone in the room knew what that meant. Charlotte's mind raced at the horror of what had just been said. All those people. All those *children*. And what about the existing Sups? Had they been "dealt with," too? She wanted to cry out and ask. What about Martin's brother? His niece? For the first time in three years, she was glad that Martin was not with her.

He continued, and the energy with which he spoke, in that used-up human frame, would have been almost comic, had the subject matter been different. "Travellers, we welcome you to a new age. When you leave us today, you will see clean streets, new buildings, there is enough for everyone. The world can be enjoyed again. We have colonised Oscar 70, with your help, but we have also, in your absence, taken control of our own planet once more."

Silence. Did he expect applause? Nobody moved, Charlotte included, so the monster in front of her – she had decided that he *was* a monster – spoke again. "And as I mentioned earlier, that leaves us with a problem. We know, you see, that several people in this room are not people, but Supplementary Humans. We have been embarrassed enough in the past by escapees and silly attempts at rebellion. I know it has been a long time, but we *know*. You are the most famous faces in the world. Now we do not wish to create a scene. Let us handle this matter properly, behind closed doors."

At his word, the khaki-clad machine-like men at the sides of the room spilled into the rows, and took a Supplementary each. Their precision was staggering; each man had clearly decided on a target as soon as the party had entered the room. Charlotte heard intermittent and muffled gun shots, followed by screams, and within a matter of seconds, everyone in the room was spilling over the chairs, creating an auditory patchwork of screams and pleas. A youth, who couldn't have been more than sixteen, grabbed Aaron by the corner of his shirt. He would have used the gun he clutched, also, had he been given the chance, but Aaron's gun met his chest, and the explosion was so close that Charlotte found herself screaming. Looking to her right, Roman was gone, and she was sure that he had immersed himself in the crowd somewhere, fighting, as always.

She had seen Daniel Dawns shot, but that had been from a distance, and she had been able to imagine a neat red hole, a small trickle of blood. In this room, people were exploding around her, and the whiteness of their suits became angry red within seconds. The red apples were pinpricks compared to the chasms of gore emerging on the white suits everywhere she looked.

The composure of the past years had broken, and she was afraid – not for her life – that had been rendered worthless long ago – but for her reputation and her legacy. Merge Theory had to work, but she needed the people in this room. She would also not be known as the woman who led the crew of Eve One to certain death, like a blind puppy. Not after everything. She gripped Aaron's hand and ran full-pelt at the door, shooting anything khaki that she could see.

****

286

Six of them waited at the agreed spot. It had taken them two days to get there, under cover, seeking refuge and free transport wherever they could. Despite what Richard Dawns had described as their famous faces, they found getting help quite easy. Aaron knew where to look for escapee Sups, and there were many. His famous face was helpful, because everyone knew, of course, what they needed. It also helped that he was disgustingly handsome, and Charlotte found herself turning away again and again as he charmed men and women alike on the road to their destination. A free ride for a smile. A bag of food for a hopeful glance. He was prostituting himself for them both and she hated every second of it. Despite this, Charlotte found, somewhere within herself, the capacity to be glad. She was glad that the utopia Richard Dawns had described in the auditorium was not a reality. She was glad that people were surviving it, and that they wanted to help them.

Before landing, she had told all of her crew to meet on the outskirts of a town called Rundleford, ten miles south of Kolwick, should there be a need to do so. She had shared the coordinates of a forgotten and neglected valley in the centre of some heath land, hoping, like a woman in the dark, that it would be as forgotten and neglected on their return. She had chosen the area almost at random; anything with too much meaning attached would mean that they would be found. This place was perfect, or it had been fifty one years ago. It was unimportant, invisible and did not register in the memory.

Better still, it hadn't changed. Aaron had managed to salvage three tents from some Sups they had met on the outskirts of Manchester, living in one of the many landfill sites around there, and so they waited. They camped in the clement weather and they enjoyed the sunrises and sunsets. They drank in the changes in the atmosphere. She thought of Martin often, and Christian also. To have them next to her was impossible, and yet it was the only thing she really wanted.

After five days of waiting, they were a party of twenty one. Charlotte remained hopeful, all the same. Perhaps many of them had found sanctuary elsewhere; they weren't necessarily dead.

Nevertheless, when she saw Roman making his way down the steep decline of the valley, she could have wept for joy. He was hurt – even from this distance she could see him limping – but he was alive, and a quick head count told her that sixteen people followed him.

Thirty eight people, then. That would be enough, she thought.

Karen

Those years in that luxurious room clung to her like an unwanted stench. Waking, sleeping, screaming, sleeping, waking, screaming, crying, pacing. The days had all been the same and the years had been invisible – a blur of misery. It had taken her a while to come to her senses.

When the bloodshed had broken out in the auditorium, Karen Dawns had waited patiently. The men would not hurt her, she knew it; if everyone in the room bore a famous face, hers was one of the most famous of all. Richard had heard her pleas – of that she was certain. She just hoped that he wasn't killed in the crossfire. That would have been ridiculous, after all she had endured.

Her two guards, sitting next to her like pillars, thick and stupid, were shot in unison, and she almost cackled as the force of the bullets drove them backwards, loosening their grip on her and on life. How foolish of Charlotte to allow Supplementaries the honour of guarding her. She was sure it had been a deliberate insult. It was amusing that it had served her so well in the end.

Most of them ran out of the doors. She remembers thinking, what cowards. She had no idea where Guy had gone – if only she had been able to speak to him on the ship – and she scoured the floor for his body. Not there. After a few minutes, and it couldn't have been more than five minutes in total, the only people in the room were the guards (a few alive, but not many), Richard Dawns, and her. They looked at one another across the groans and the demands for attention, and both of them managed a smile.

The sobs came naturally. She didn't need to pretend. She felt her shoulders shake as the force of her emotions overcame her. In almost equal amounts, she felt relief, anger, hatred, and fear. Yes, fear. She wanted to throw herself under the protection of the Panel, but what if they somehow knew what she had done?

It took him a while to reach her, and his ascent to her seat, right at the back of the room, was laboured to the point of becoming awkward. By the time he reached her, she had controlled her weeping, and managed a watery smile. "Father. You have *no idea* how glad I am to see you."

****

He took her back to her old house. The main thing she noticed was how the street smelled so much cleaner than she remembered. Despite his age, he led her, she gripping to his forearm like an invalid. The walk was slow, so she had plenty of time to take in the street she had once known so well. It was cleaner, certainly, but there was still that unmistakeable air of decay, of a world standing still. She remembered why she had wanted to leave for Oscar 70 so badly, and she thought, inertly, about her plants growing there right now.

When she saw her garden, she felt bereaved once more. Clearly, her father-in-law did not share her passion for horticulture, and in what had been her modest but loved garden were eight square concrete slabs. They weren't even neat; the floor below them was bumpy and it looked as if an earthquake had taken place. A variety of weeds, strong and sinewy, meandered around the corners. She didn't want to seem foolish, so she didn't say a word, but she couldn't help looking at those slabs and feeling that everything she had ever achieved on this planet had been erased forever. The beautiful flowers she had nurtured were long dead, and weeds of every description had taken their place. It reminded her of the Sups; they, too, were an unwanted infestation taking the beauty away from those more deserving. Why could Charlotte not see that?

The interior of the house was similar, but cleaner. The trinkets of her married life were gone, as had what must have been seen as unnecessary furniture, although the photographs still adorned the walls. She couldn't work out if Richard had decided to leave them there out of sentiment or if he simply didn't care enough to remove them. Looking at the photograph of their wedding day, from the days photographs were still printed, she felt nothing. She was in front of Daniel brandishing a large knife (she remembered it, and its polished marble handle that shone next to the silver blade) and her new husband stood behind her, holding her hands as she sunk the knife into the flesh of the cake. The cake was adorned with fresh flowers. They both smiled widely, displaying pearly teeth, and she started to consider how everything in that photograph was now gone. The cake had been eaten shortly after the wedding, and the flowers would be long rotten. They would have collapsed into the Earth, just like Daniel was mouldering on the ground on Oscar 70. She doubted they'd had the good humour to bury him. The decorative knife had probably been melted for its metal, as had the rings they wore. The pearly white smile remained, but she no longer felt it; all happiness was artifice – that was simply the way of things now. It told a story of its own, that picture. It had not been her favourite, but it had been one of the few that didn't feature Charlotte, so it had been preserved in the frame. A standard wedding picture; everyone had done the same pose. Why preserve that moment? She could have saved herself the bother of being there at all. Just copy and paste a face.

She started when he spoke, and it was almost like he was listening to her thoughts. "So where is he?" An inevitable question, delivered casually, but she detected the worry underneath.

She could have lied, but she didn't. The truth, or some degree of it, served her purpose better. "He's dead." It had been a long journey, and she would have loved him to ask her how *she* felt, how being a prisoner to one's inferiors had eaten at her soul, how it felt to lose a child…Had he asked her a thing, she would have given him anything. Her desperation was so thick it felt visible, like the need for love was flying out of her pores. She drew it in – managed a respectful sniff.

There was no answer from behind her, but she assumed that he had stopped whatever he had been doing, for the clattering from the kitchen stopped. Carry on, she told herself. She kept her voice as steady and neutral as possible. "You have another son, you see. Christian, we called him. He's wonderful." She was going too quickly, and she knew it. Better let him take in the headlines.

"A son? And you named him?"

Ah, how perfect. "Yes. Charlotte didn't want him; she was too busy… *making love* to Sup Martin 81873. It was disgusting, how she carried on. She neglected her duties, ignored her son..." She felt her nails dig into the flesh of her hands at the memory. "They even stole a pod and ran away together, wasting valuable resources and fuel. She changed almost instantly after leaving Earth. People are dead because of her." She was enjoying herself now; she felt like a child telling tales at school, but she loved every ounce of power it was giving her. Finally, she was wakening from her stasis.

He was quiet for a while, and she turned round to see him actually crying. His face was not designed for this, clearly, and his expression barely changed as the water leaked from his eyes. It was like he was being showered involuntarily, and the water was freezing his face. "And they killed Daniel?"

She didn't falter. "Yes. A scuffle took place when we tried to defend the boy. Martin shot him in cold blood."

"And the boy?"

"He's alive, but I'm afraid Martin has him."

Doctor Dawns sighed, and hovered down to a sitting position. Karen was close to believing that he would never get up again, "On Oscar 70. Years and years away from us."

She shivered with emotion as the sobs threatened to surface again. "I'm afraid so. And I've been a prisoner for nearly three years. You're the first person I've spoken to in three years who wants to listen." She could have gone on, naturally; there was a whole sorry story to tell. What was truth and untruth barely seemed to matter now. But the tears spoke for her in the end. She stood next to the picture, looking at the old man before her, knowing that he was her only hope. He didn't move to comfort her, but closed his eyes and kept saying something like "we will put this right," or "we will right this wrong."

She couldn't have sworn to what he said because she had stopped listening. She would eat, rest and speak for today, but then she must return to her own personal mission. Her closed eyes filled her mind with a furious red, and she allowed the dragon to take hold of her once more.

Roman

Splashing his face with the hard, cold water of Kolwick's spring, Roman breathed in Earth's air in sharp gasps, hungry for that beautiful oxygen. The artificial environment on Eve One was meant to prepare the crew for the subtle changes in atmosphere between the two planets, but he realised now, gulping the sweet coldness around him, that this had not worked as well as they believed. It should have been like stepping off a standard aircraft, but landing on Earth had felt physically harder than landing on Oscar 70. His limbs were dead weights on a weak body.

The landing base at Kolwick was alien territory to Roman, and it had taken him a while to find somewhere safe to hide. He did not know how many people he had killed on exiting that auditorium; that had been the easy part. He had imagined those khaki suits as black beetles flying at him, threatening to devour his skin. He had ran, and shot, and then ran.

His first thought had been returning to Charlotte, and the coordinates she had given him were, of course, imprinted on his mind. His wristband would find the coordinates easily. He was thirty miles away – he could run and be there in far less than a day – a marathon and then a little more. The only issue was he was tired, in spirit and in body. Worse still, he was hunted, and famous.

He would never tell Charlotte that his first twenty-four hours of freedom were spent hiding in an abandoned storage container one mile from the landing base. He assumed it had been used as a hiding place before, boasting its own hand-dug crevice in the corner, where the corrugated metal wall had long rusted at the bottom. He had seen the Panel authorities and their torches, sweeping over the open door of his refuge. Luckily for him, their search of the area had been lazy, almost as if no enemy worth their salt would hide so ridiculously close.

When morning came, he cursed his foolishness and lack of care. He would not be so lucky twice, he knew, and so he ran. He thought of Aaron, and how he would certainly have found someone he knew who could help him. Roman, a Better, unbeknown to Kolwick really, apart from a few select workers at Dawns', had nobody.

He therefore moved as if he was nobody, keeping to the dark corners, walking in the hours when he knew the world slept. If he saw anyone else, he hid. Like a rat. He shuddered at his lack of bravery and was glad that his friends were not there to see. He remembered Amy flying out of that cave, her marble skin bitten and torn. She would be disgusted to see him skulking like a thief, guilty, ashamed, in a world that one believed he owned. That thought alone shook him to his senses.

On the second day – or the third – he was not so sure – he met a middle-aged woman, walking as he did, wearing a battered Eve One suit. They smiled and did not speak, but continued together. On the third day – or the fourth – they were not so sure – they met others.

And thus they continued, until he saw Charlotte's face, and felt proud again. They had waited for him, and they were ready.

That evening, he and Charlotte spoke in the seclusion of the beige, moulding tent that she had somehow found. He knew there would be a story behind it, but he did not care to hear it. He wanted to know her plans. He therefore sat in silence, breathing in the musty air with an inexplicable fervour, ready to hang on her every word.

Without Martin, he had become increasingly uncomfortable about the nature of their friendship. Before he knew her, Charlotte was quite literally a poster girl in his workplace - an object of lust and admiration. On Oscar 70, she was unavailable. Now, she was desperate and isolated; she needed him and Aaron and that made her vulnerable to men like him. Or what he used to be like, anyway.

 She wanted to kill Doctor Dawns, that much he knew before she even spoke, and Roman was afraid. He wanted the man dead, of course, but he also wanted safety for himself and his friends. He wanted the Panel destroyed – not just one man – and he worried that Charlotte had lost perspective. All she could say, in between frantic tears, was that she wanted him dead. He would have told her how wrong he thought this was, but as he turned to speak, she gripped his thigh with her fragile hand and kissed him roughly on the lips. Everything about it was rushed and clumsy. It felt wrong and insulting.

His lack of response made her stop, and she sighed and apologised, flatly. Everything about her deflated manner bothered him; to the crew she was strength personified but here, in a secluded tent, in some respects ideal for love-making, she was utterly broken. He didn't know what to say, but he had to respond to her apology. He wanted her to leave, he felt violated, but he forgave her, and tried to tell her why.

297

He placed a friendly hand on her shoulder. "Don't worry, Smarty, you're just lonely - that's all." He even rubbed her arm playfully, as one might a friend who had made a silly error. He thought that she would smile, perhaps even laugh - at least do something to assuage the awkwardness. Instead, she froze in her sitting position, knees drawn to her chin, her eyes burning onto the floor. The entire space smelled of stale plastic. She breathed steadily and calmly, and spoke in a mere whisper, but he soon realised that he had never made a woman more furious. He thought it was hurt pride, and was about to tell her so. He almost made a second joke - something about her tough luck at catching him on the one day in his life when he didn't feel like it, but she spoke before he made such an error.

"You take that back, Roman Smith."

"I'm sorry?" He was genuinely confused. After all, his refusal of her had been chivalrous, surely?

"You said that I was *just* lonely." She looked at him, then, her eyes deep pools. "There is no such thing as *just* being lonely. Loneliness eats away at a person like a concealed cancer, a hidden shame. It breaks you beyond repair and you have *nobody* to tell. Not that anybody would listen or help or *care* anyway. To say that I am *just* lonely besmirches the memory of what I have lost. I am not *just* lonely, Roman." Her voice rose to a cracked wail. "I am *lonely*. I'm lonely and it's all a terrible terrible mistake." He could see that her eyes, staring at him expectantly, were saturated with uncried tears. What she didn't know was that he felt it all, too; he felt the vulnerability, the anger, the regret, the *loneliness*: he was just less honest about it than Charlotte. He knew what it was to carry heartbreak like a wound, to look at other people who aren't suffering your pain and long to tell them how much it hurts. He knew what it was to decide never to tell anyone, because nobody would understand and his complaints would probably bore them anyway. He couldn't say, *I know*, because he didn't, not really, but she didn't know his suffering either.

He felt sick as he said what he knew he must, "You can't get back to him, you know. It's scientifically impossible."

He was glad of the small space; it meant that she could not throw things, stand up, march around. Instead, she continued to sit, knees drawn to her chest, like a child in a particularly uncomfortable assembly. "I didn't ask for any of this, Roman. I just wanted to give Mankind something new."

Roman smiled, genuinely, for the first time in many years, "You did, Smarty, but not in the way you expected. You gave them hope."

Then was the time to cry, for Charlotte to shake her small frame to pieces under the power of the sobs. She did, but, to her eternal credit, she stopped as quickly as she started. Gathering her shaking voice, Roman strained to hear her say, "I didn't know that hope was so costly."

"Neither did I, Smarty. I suppose we didn't know anything about hope before."

Charlotte

Richard Dawns had been right about one thing: the streets of Kolwick were spotless. The stacked rubbish was gone, and flowers grew in beds at the side of the pavements. Lights gleamed in houses that were not allowed electricity before. There was even the odd car on the road, trundling along proudly like a risen corpse. It was, she had to admit, a small paradise compared to the Kolwick she had left behind – a small paradise to *other* people anyway. She had promised Roman that she would stick to the plan, and she would not give way to sentiment, but she could not help herself. She knew where they would be buried, and she was good at hiding. It would only take a moment.

They had bought a burial plot when the Expansion first started, in the days when people thought that there wouldn't be space to bury any more people and when any method of body disposal but cremation was going to be outlawed. She had known they were there but it was a shock all the same, to see their names etched, permanently, officially, into the dull grey stone: Kevin James Dobson and Amelia Rose Dobson. The dates were a shock: 2025 and 2015 respectively. So her mother had died while she was still travelling to Oscar 70 and her poor father had lingered on for another eleven years, alone. She had always feared him dying first, and leaving her mother to worry, not cope, fade away; she had never, she realised with some surprise, even considered it happening any other way. Her heart ached at the thought of her father, sitting next to that grandmother clock, watching the minutes pass him by, until his time came. Alone.

The plan had been for her to go straight to Dawns' Laboratories, but, it seemed, coming here was the best thing she could have done. She did not cry; it seemed that she had no tears left, and she was glad of that when she saw them approaching her. Doctor Dawns had three of those same khaki-wearing men behind him, or at least they looked like the same men. They marched towards her as if in attack but Doctor Dawns was smiling, as was she.

He stood behind the graves and smiled. She imagined him in such a grave soon, and smiled yet more widely. He opened his mouth to speak but this time, she spoke first. "Ah, Doctor Dawns. I was about to come and find you."

****

His office still had the same chair, the same desk. The dried foods in the corner were gone, and Charlotte supposed that this was a sign that food production had started again under his glorious new regime. Really, that was the only difference that the room had seen in half a century, apart from the red-haired woman now sitting behind the desk, smiling.

Charlotte sipped the first hot coffee she had drunk in three years, and she had to suppress a groan of joy. Karen was watching her every move, so the façade was again required. Charlotte fitted her face accordingly.

Richard was pacing the room, each step accompanied by a heavy thunk as his cane hit the walnut floor. "There is no need for lies, Charlotte. Karen has told me everything."

Charlotte shook her head a fraction. "I wasn't going to lie."

301

He continued as if she had not spoken at all, "The public know nothing, which is a relief. Your silly little escapade occurred behind closed doors, so the world believes that you are simply enjoying a well-deserved break."

She couldn't help herself, "They won't believe that for long."

The cane hit the floor with a clatter and suddenly, Richard Dawn's face was an inch from hers, those ancient eyes spitting with hatred, "Don't you *dare* threaten me! I made you, you little whore! And you will *not* destroy everything that this family worked for!" He gestured to Karen, who continued her serene smile. "And to think I *touched* you, after what you've done!"

Charlotte did not move, even when his spit flew in her face. "I'm sorry, Richard. I think you misunderstood me, but it's good to know how you feel. I meant that the public won't think I am having a break because I will be working. Here."

"Is that so?"

"I have an exciting new theory I'd like to share with you." Karen's smile had fallen, which renewed her energy a little, "And I know you care so much about this family's reputation. I will work for you, as long as I can use the resources here. As much as you believe that you *made me*, as you so modestly put it, you know that my knowledge far surpasses yours, and the only other person who could offer such knowledge is now dead on another planet-"

She saw Karen rise out of her chair. Stop now. Enjoy the moment.

Doctor Dawns moved back a little, and leaned against the desk; clearly, his little outburst had cost him, physically.

Karen was leaning forward to speak but he raised a hand to stop her."If, *if* I were to allow such a thing, you would have no freedoms whatsoever.   We would be watching you, always."

Again she didn't move, and managed to smile back at Karen. "I'm sure it wouldn't work any other way."

****

Before her voluntary imprisonment, Richard had agreed to take Charlotte on a walk looking at the past. Karen had protested profusely, but her protestations were cut short. Do not worry, dear, he had said. She is one woman. She cannot hurt us.

He must have assumed she had been hiding for a week in a closed room, because he took it upon himself to describe everything that she saw.   He took on the role of a knowledgeable tour guide, proudly pointing out the Intelligence Testing Centre's new Handing In rooms, gesturing to the cleanness of the streets, the neatly trimmed gardens.

It was the strangest thing, finding her childhood home so perfectly preserved. She had expected a lot of things, like barren space after the house had been torn down, or for the Georgian semi-detached home of her childhood to have been made into a block of flats. Neither of those assaults on her memory had taken place. Instead, she was faced with a perfect vision of seven years ago, down to the perfectly pruned rose bushes fronting the small lawn.

The surrounding houses were equally unchanged, save a few hints: a broken window repaired here, a new driveway there.

It was a marvel that they still had driveways- surplus space like this was being sold fifty years ago. She wondered if this intense preservation was something to do with her; she was, as Richard reminded her frequently, incredibly famous.

But only one house was perfectly preserved, with the tell-tale blue plaque boasting its connection to the Associate Scientist on Eve One: a true campaigner for the Cause. Richard had told her that this home was a museum now. He'd said it as if she would be pleased, like turning her parents' well-loved and private home into a public spectacle, for droves of Cause enthusiasts to gawk at, was something to be envious of. She wondered if the bed spreads were still on, if the toilet was still used. She felt that familiar heat and wetness as tears fell down her cheeks yet again, and she didn't question them. Had she been asked - and there was nobody who would ask - she wouldn't have been able to explain the tears.

He had insisted on walking with her, so it had been painful: physically for him and emotionally for her, but he had already swanned into the museum itself, excited and hasty on his aged legs. His legs had far too much space in between them, and he wobbled as they formed a near-perfect diamond of beige corduroy descending into the open door.

Perhaps his presence was why she was crying, but she didn't think so. Granted, her current misery could always, in no small part, be attributed to the presence of the man himself, but being in front of this house, without Martin, and without her child, she finally realised the magnitude of her loss. The last time she had seen her parents, they had bid her a frosty farewell, and they all had known that she was abandoning them for bigger and better things. Her father's eyes had said it all; if only what she was running to had been better...

Her dear dad and poor mother were in the past, and the other part of her- it hurt her to imagine them both - were adrift in time. He had no way of reaching her and, should she travel to him, she would meet him fifty years older, or worse...Back on Oscar 70, she had worried that his health was poor and that he didn't have many years left. She had started to count those years before they had happened, coveting them in advance like a miser. And now they were lost. Something within her that felt like rocks in her stomach informed her that Martin would not enjoy the same extended life that her husband had. Time was not on their side.

So, utterly alone. That house, different and yet the same, mocked her isolation. She was that house also, different and yet the same, a piece of flotsam on a tumultuous and uncaring sea. And she couldn't tell him. Standing there in front of that house, she knew what Martin had meant about how terrible it would be to never see someone again, to not be able to share your private thoughts and fears.

She followed her husband in, leaving the guards outside. He must have asked them for some privacy with her.

Perfectly preserved was an understatement; every detail was identical. The floors shone warmly and the grandmother clock ticked, inoffensively and reliably, in the corner, as always. She gasped to see her father's chair empty, and his glasses on the arm of the chair. Several plastic signs adorned the room, no doubt offering facts about her life that she would rather not read. The smells had gone, though. Her home had always smelt of luxurious food and excessive cleaning. Now, there was nothing. Standing there, observing this as an outsider, felt like the ultimate betrayal. She looked at the red leather sofa behind her and she knew that she would never sit on it again. It was not part of her home anymore.

This was why he had brought her here. He must have known that such an experience would disarm her. Realisation of this made her not angry, but simply all the more determined to carry out her plan.

She turned the familiar corner to see him clattering in the kitchen. How odd: all the cutlery was still there. Or some of it at least. Perhaps the rest had been harvested, or sold to the highest bidder. He was opening the cupboard doors and running the water as if he lived there. She suppressed her growing rage as he talked, "Of course the public aren't allowed to help themselves, but we're not the public now, are we?" He poured the boiling hot water into two mugs. At least he knew how she liked her coffee. Strong. Black.

The only thought playing in her mind as he re-entered the living room was how he was committing sacrilege by being there. *Don't sit in my father's chair don't sit in my father's chair* reverberated in her skull, and of course he did, raising his mug to her in a silent toast. After taking a cursory sip, he stood up once more, and staggered towards her like one drunk. Everything about his manner appalled her, and she realised, far too late, the security camera in the corner of the room, blinking at her like a familiar enemy. He smiled a waxy smile, whispering, "I want the world to catch us being reunited as a couple. It is not enough for you to work for me. You must embrace me for a final time." She would not have thought him capable of such strength, but she almost fell sideways as he lunged for her and clumsily grabbed her lower back. His face was inches from hers, and she felt his dry lips on her neck.

She remained standing as she watched the poison take hold, inches from him still. She watched every second with increasing relish. He started with the vicious dry coughing that he was so used to, only this time it did not stop; the coughs started to push forth a furious red liquid that dribbled rather pathetically down his chin, like he had been struggling eating dinner. Then the gasps started, dry and desperate. His small, watery eyes fixed on hers with hatred, or realisation, or perhaps both. She felt a rush of something like joy.

"You see, my darling husband, there are various plants on Oscar 70 that your talented daughter in-law harvested. One such plant is called the Succubus plant, so called because of its intense beauty but deadly poisonous qualities." She laughed quietly into his ear, ever aware of the cameras, "But of course, you can feel the latter for yourself! It's ever so striking, you know. It's intensely black, so it soaks up the power of Star Four better than some other plant life there." She didn't hear how like Karen Dawns she sounded; her hatred of him had gone too far for that. "Three Tester Sups lost their lives because of this little beauty. I never got the chance to ask them how it feels. How does it feel?"

But Doctor Richard Dawns would never speak again. His eyes were wide as he struggled with some internal agony she could hardly imagine; she remembered all the heartache he had caused, the immeasurable horror. She would never, even if she lived as long as him, be sorry for this. She was glad to make something happen in a house of dead memories.

She would have liked to leave it longer, to make sure, but she hadn't bargained for the cameras. She ran to the door and screamed to the guards, "Come quickly! It's Richard! I think he's had a heart attack!"

He was announced dead at the scene. The medics seemed satisfied enough: it had been the drama of the last few days, seeing his beautiful wife home, those drugs couldn't sustain him forever...One woman even commented that she thought he had been "keeping himself alive" until she returned, and now, well, now was "his time." Charlotte nodded sagely to all of these suggestions, carefully sniffing into a tissue. Occasionally, she commented like a bereaved wife doubtlessly would, using phrases such as, "but he was so full of life this morning" and "I could have done more. I blame myself."

Returning to Dawns' Laboratories, she knew that someone from the Panel would not be far behind her. She also thought of Karen, and how best to deal with her. She didn't feel like she could kill someone else, and not Karen. Perhaps she had some vestige of respect left for her, somewhere. Dawns' Laboratories was a family business, so a fight was between her and Karen was likely. Karen would not entertain her story for a second. All she had to do, though, was delay, delay, until support came. Without Richard Dawns, the Panel was undoubtedly weaker and possibly, one day, more open to listen. At least the dotted line had been signed: she was the Associate Scientist at Dawns' Laboratories once more. Upon the death of the Head Scientist, her role was negotiable, and she felt a rush of excitement at the thought.

As the car slowed, she saw a familiar man walking next to it, cigarette in hand. Did she ever, really, imagine that he would have abandoned her? A gun poked through the window and she was soothed with a gruff American voice, "Good to see you, Sparky. Run like hell."

****

Aaron had said very little as they made their way there. He'd spent weeks researching and digging, exploring every underground Sup settlement he could find. She could see in his manner how nervous he was. Roman had been delighted to get his hands on some contraband cigarettes – a real sign of the times. The fact that such items were starting to make their way to England again said more about increased resources than any amount of rubbish collections ever could. It was Aaron's stolen car, but Roman had insisted on driving. Neither Aaron nor Charlotte complained as the battered Vauxhall Astra filled with cigarette smoke as he lit one straight after the other and steered the car with one hand.

It was rural; that was to be expected. They had heard of an Underground Movement, several in fact, and all had left the exposure of the city. Approaching what looked like an abandoned farm, Charlotte looked for signs of life. It was a beautiful Edwardian house, or it would have been beautiful one hundred years ago, standing proudly in the centre of several square fields. Now, it was dilapidated and tired; the white rendering was coming loose in chunks and many pieces had fallen to the ground and stayed there, like the house was weeping concrete. As the car slowed, Charlotte read a faded wooden sign next to the gate. It read, "Monkwick Farm." Aaron's sharp eyes stared ahead for a moment, taking in every detail. Charlotte knew better than to speak. "This is it," he said finally, "We walk from here."

She had seen places like this in films, but never in real life. Before flying to Oscar 70, she had been limited to Kolwick; travelling had been too much of a luxury to support the Cause and her parents weren't the holidaying type anyway. She'd never had a reason to leave town, so didn't. Now, she saw a solitary man sitting on a porch. He was thin and very old and stared into the distance. One hand clutched a glass of something black and the other twisted upwards, painfully arthritic, it seemed. Aaron was completely tense, and stood before the man as if ready to fight him. The man hardly seemed to see them. Finally, Aaron broke the silence, "I'm here to see the Blues."

The man continued to stare ahead as if he had not seen them. The hand holding the glass jerked behind him, indicating the door.

The room they entered was more like what Charlotte was used to before they left Earth. Dust covered almost every surface and the furniture, mismatched and much of it broken, cut into the path through the room at jagged and clumsy angles. They were in almost total darkness, save the odd chink of light fighting its way through the torn curtains. Framed pictures were scattered on every free surface, unmatched but each bearing a caption which Charlotte assumed was a name: *The Saviour, The True Leader, the Captain.* The people in the pictures were total strangers to her, except the last man. She had seen him wandering the streets of Kolwick in her youth. He would mutter oaths and blasphemies that had made her parents cross the road, her father drawing a young Charlotte close to his side. She had assumed he was insane. Looking at this man's face reminded her of the grey and dust of her youth. Was that worse than the dust and heat of Oscar 70? She was no longer so sure.

She and Roman waited, useless and confused. It seemed that Aaron knew exactly what to do, and he picked up a golden bell with a wooden handle, like the one they used to ring at the end of playtime at school. He shook it gently.

They continued to wait Charlotte had resigned herself to a few moments of silent waiting, at least, so she was surprised when Aaron gripped her arm, "This is to say I'm sorry, Charlotte. Martin gave me so much, and I betrayed him. He'd probably be here with us now if it wasn't for me. Or you'd still be there."

This was true, she decided, but she didn't blame him. Very few people on this planet understood what the last few years had been like, and she could not, in any way, cast the first stone. She didn't have a chance to respond, though, because at that moment a middle-aged woman swept into the room. Her dress, sky blue and long, tickled the floor as she walked, and Charlotte noted immediately why these people were called the Blues. She wondered why they had chosen this colour to represent them. The blue of the sky, she supposed. The blue of the sea. Travel. Hope. Perhaps they chose it simply because it was calming. "So you found us," she beamed, and Charlotte noted an ice blue twinkle in her eyes. She smiled and, for a moment, Charlotte had the sense that she had known this woman her entire life. "I am Eleanor. I believe you knew my mother."

****

The Blues had gone underground twenty-five years ago, just after the Panel had introduced Handing In. They had established farming communities across the country and, Eleanor proudly declared, they were at least 10,000 strong. She couldn't be sure of the exact number, as locations and names were kept confidential, to protect each unit. Her charming smile faded as she skirted over stories of capture and torture, and farms being uncovered, in the early days. The authorities had no issues whatsoever in murdering innocents and children, as they all well knew, and Charlotte sensed that this woman before them, this child of Dinah's, could have spoken of as many horrors as her uncle.

But they had emerged from the horrors, and they lived peacefully, Eleanor had declared proudly. But we do not forget. And we plan. "Your friend is very resourceful," she said, nodding to Aaron, "Few people from the outside ever find us. There is something people like about his face, clearly." Charlotte couldn't help but be amused. Another admirer.

Roman, who had been smiling, Charlotte noticed, far more than in recent days, suddenly asked, "How has the Panel not found you? They know everything, don't they?"

Eleanor laughed, and her eyes twinkled. "Oh, young man, who knows so little but has done so much! They know hardly anything, you know. Not really. They are all television screens and posters and words. They have no real power. Do you know, the Earth isn't even overpopulated? It never was. All lies! They just wanted more than everyone else and saying that there wasn't enough made that so easy."

The whole group were silent. A lie. The Expansion. The Cause – all lies. Eleanor could be lying, of course, but they knew she wasn't. As Charlotte's mother might have said, she could feel it in her bones.

A burly woman, slightly older than Eleanor, entered with something that smelled like herbal tea. "Thank you, Leanne," Eleanor smiled. "Leanne has been with us for a while now. She was tortured by the Panel for a period of several months, long ago, and she hasn't spoken since, but I like to think she is happy here. She spends a lot of time tending the garden."

Charlotte could not shake the revelation of the Expansion being a lie, "So why was everywhere so crowded?" She remembered the queues, the lack of food, the tokens.

Eleanor smiled, "How far have you travelled in your life? Only the places you went to were like that. You didn't *go* anywhere else. Even if you owned a car, you wouldn't have had the fuel to really *go* anywhere."

Aaron nodded. When I was fourteen, I tried to run away. I reached the end of this long motorway – I'd been walking for days – and there was this big, electronic gate and a tall wall that stretched for what looked like miles. I got picked up by the authorities as soon as I reached it, and returned to the home."

"Yes," Eleanor nodded, "Had you gotten further, you would have seen mansions, cars, every glittering luxury you can imagine, all being enjoyed by the Panel and their families." Eleanor jerked her head towards Charlotte, anticipating her next question, "Not Karen and Daniel Dawns, no. Not even your husband."

"Late husband."

Another serene smile. "Late husband. No. The Dawns family existed for the Cause. I'm sure that Doctor Dawns was all too willing to offer a 'noble sacrifice' for the others. I'm also sure he enjoyed certain perks."

Charlotte remembered the suits and the dried food. How much did he have, hidden away? She looked searchingly at Roman, "But you lived in America..."

He was already shaking his head, "Never went more than a mile out of New York." He closed his eyes, re-doing the calculations in his head. "Dang. What fools we are."

"Not really," Eleanor cut in, her voice syrupy. "You had no reason to believe otherwise."

She couldn't stop the calculations in her mind. She remembered flying away from Earth, waving goodbye to a planet she thought she knew so well. No other questions were necessary. She didn't need to ask why resources were so scarce, because she knew, at that moment, that the Panel had taken them. She didn't need to ask why they had pushed the Cause so fervently because she knew that the Expansion had been a lie to mask a lust for interstellar colonisation. And it had worked. With an IQ of 162, she had been duped by a set of old men and women in suits.

One question remained, though, and it grounded her, "But what about your other uncle? Joseph?"

Eleanor closed her eyes, like she was trying to recall the answer to a question in a very important examination, "Yes, Uncle Joseph. Well, as you know, he and my mother were declared Supplementary and became Jason and Olivia. You know what happened to my mother." Charlotte knew, yes. One day, when they had more time, she would tell her absolutely everything about her mother. "Joseph, or Jason, spent many years in and out of various Sup units. He had a very hard life."

She felt deflated. Martin had so wanted to speak to him. Make things right. She was planning to do so on his behalf. "When did he die?"

Eleanor looked confused. "Oh, no. Uncle Joseph isn't dead. The Blues rescued him. He leads a farming community 200 miles north of here. He's 87, though, and getting on a little nowadays. No advanced drugs for him." She winked. "Sorry. I know you probably won't want to be reminded of him."

Charlotte smiled, "No, it's fine. I need to be reminded. We have a real fight ahead of us."

Eleanor looked pleased, and, placing her delicate china cup on the table, gripped both of Charlotte's hands. "Well, young lady, I certainly agree with you there. They'll never leave us alone."

She squeezed Eleanor's hands in response, and she knew that, now, Aaron was entirely forgiven; he had given her a gift larger than he knew, for, holding this woman's hands, she felt Martin with her. They did have a fight ahead: they needed to fight the Panel and Karen Dawns, yes, but more than that they needed to fight the universe. There was a way, she knew it, to claw through the void that was the universe and reach him, intact. But time, the greatest enemy of all, was eroding everything around her. She held onto Eleanor's hands and felt like she was gripping the edge of an

315

enormous precipice, with this wonderful woman pulling her out. Merge Theory would work, she knew it, but she needed the resources at Dawns' to put the theory into practice. Well then, she'd have to get them. With an army of 10,000 behind her, and this woman, she had a chance.

Martin

As the days turned into weeks without her, Martin longed for Kolwick Library and for books. The lonely ache he felt was like a part of him, and he reflected with no gladness whatsoever that Charlotte would be bearing the loneliness far less well than him because for her, such abject loneliness would be new. But as familiar as this ache was, he used to be able to sooth it with books, books containing worlds and characters that were nestled safely in his mind, never to be taken away. Eve One had brought books with her, and deposited them on one pod or other, he was sure, but they were not the kind of books he needed. Quantum mechanics did not feed his soul.

He thought about *Great Expectations*- a novel he had spent many an hour poring over as a lonely youth. The idea of a mysterious benefactor coming to a lost boy's rescue had excited him so. In a sense, he had been rescued, but that was not what he thought of now. He remembered something that was said about a broken heart being exquisite - he remembered that word - and how it would make you think that you would die but you don't, and that was actually worse, because you had to live with the pain.

Day after terrible day, the book had said. And that memory was apt because each day was terrible. Each morning he surveyed the landscape and each morning it presented itself as a wasteland to him. Noon was the same, the evening was the same. He was quite lost. It was a graveyard where his hopes and Charlotte's dreams lay, rotting and mouldering before his very eyes. There were four hundred people left on the planet, with nearly 75% of the planet's population being less than a year old. Martin did not think of the future; he only thought of how he was the past, and how Charlotte was also. Soon, they would be in different time frames but they would still both be history. There was no more living now for either of them.

He remembered how he had criticized Charlotte for leaving her parents. He had said something about how she'd never be able to share major events with them again, and how she'd never be able to tell them a new idea, thought or joke. Missing her, though, was worse. Before her and after her, his life was a void, and all he could do was remember. He didn't want to share a comment on current events with her because there were no current events. He couldn't tell her about his day because there were no days. There was just Star Four, always, burning away at his spirit. And Christian. Charlotte and not Charlotte. A living reminder that she had been real. He had thoughts like this on a daily basis but they passed when he looked at the boy, handsome and cherubic as he slept, so close to Pod Eleven's window. The boy still unnerved him, true, but he was a living part of Charlotte. He had grown inside her and wore her touch on his young flesh. Every time he touched him, he imagined Charlotte's skin, how soft and cold her hands felt. Christian was not the same. His skin was smooth and warm; it smelled of milk.

Every morning, afternoon and evening, he looked at Star Four, caring very little about the potential destruction to his eyes. It never moved, of course, and its immobility made him nervous. It reminded him of his own paralysis.

His heart, though, was not paralysed, and it called across the distance between him and Charlotte. Trapped as he was, he had to believe that he could, one day, reach her. Every morning, afternoon and evening, Christian would spread his arms to the clouds, as if to welcome incoming ships.

22866097R00187

Printed in Great Britain
by Amazon